Even for a wid_____m,
Lady Beth_____
Earl of Trev_____ was outrageous behavior.
If she won, her prize would be Fairhaven, an island
her grandfather had forfeited to the previous earl.
But if she lost, the penalty was to become his
mistress! And most shocking of all was that a small
part of Lady Allerton secretly hoped she might lose....

"One throw of the dice. The winner takes all."

Marcus hesitated. It was clear from Elizabeth's words
that she would be his prize if he won, and it was very
sporting of her to offer her services free. The reckoning
would come later, of course, if they suited each other:
the villa, the carriage, the jewels. But if she won the
wager...

"I like your terms, but what do you want from me if I
lose?" he drawled. He waited for her to name her price.
A necklace of diamonds, perhaps.

She moved closer until he could smell her perfume. It
was a subtle mix of jasmine and rose petals, warm as the
sun on her skin, and it sent his senses into even more of
a spin. Damn it, whatever the price, it had to be worth it.

"I don't want a fortune, she said sweetly. "I want
Fairhaven Island."

* * *

Lady Allerton's Wager
Harlequin Historical #651—April 2003

Praise for Nicola Cornick's previous titles

LADY ALLERTON'S WAGER

Nicola Cornick

TORONTO • NEW YORK • LONDON
AMSTERDAM • PARIS • SYDNEY • HAMBURG
STOCKHOLM • ATHENS • TOKYO • MILAN • MADRID
PRAGUE • WARSAW • BUDAPEST • AUCKLAND

ISBN 0-373-29251-1

LADY ALLERTON'S WAGER

First North American Publication 2003

Copyright © 2001 by Nicola Cornick

Available from Harlequin Historicals and
NICOLA CORNICK

Lady Polly #574
The Love Match #599
"The Rake's Bride"
Miss Verey's Proposal #604
The Blanchland Secret #630
Lady Allerton's Wager #651

Please address questions and book requests to:
Harlequin Reader Service
U.S.: 3010 Walden Ave., P.O. Box 1325, Buffalo, NY 14269
Canadian: P.O. Box 609, Fort Erie, Ont. L2A 5X3

To the girls.
Thank you.
This one is for you.

Chapter One

The Cyprians' Ball was scarcely an event that featured on the social calendar of any of the debutantes of the *ton*, although more than one bitter chaperon had observed that it was the only place outside the clubs where all the eligible bachelors could be found. The most unobtainable of gentlemen, who would scorn to step inside the doors of Almack's Assembly Rooms for fear of ambush, showed far greater alacrity in striking up an intimate acquaintance of quite another sort, and a masquerade was ripe with all sorts of possibilities.

It was late in the evening when Marcus, sixth Earl of Trevithick, joined the crowds of revellers milling in the Argyle Rooms. Being neither a callow youth nor particularly requiring an *inamorata*, he had seen no need to hurry to be first through the door.

The room, with its elegant pillars and lavish decoration, seemed as gaudy as the birds of paradise that flocked there. Marcus knew that he was already drawing their attention. With his height, stature and wicked dark good looks it was inevitable, but he felt little pride in the fact. Once his name was whispered amongst the Cyprians he knew that some would lose interest and hunt for bigger game, for they were motivated by cupidity rather than lust. He had the looks and the title but he had little money, for he had inherited estates that had gone to rack and ruin.

'Been rusticating, Marcus? I had heard you were still in northern parts!'

It was his cousin, Justin Trevithick, who had clapped Marcus on the shoulder. Justin, the only child of a scandalous second marriage between Marcus's Uncle Freddie Trevithick and his housekeeper, was a couple of years younger than his cousin. The two had never met as children, for Marcus's father, Viscount Trevithick, had disapproved of his brother's morals and had steadfastly refused to acknowledge his nephew. When Marcus was twenty-two he had bumped into Justin at White's and they had hit it off at once, to the amusement of the *ton* and the despair of the strait-laced Viscount and his wife. Now, eleven years later, they were still firm friends.

Marcus and Justin shared the distinctive lean Trevithick features, but whilst Marcus's eyes and hair were the sloe-black of his pirate forebears, Justin's face was lightened by the fair hair and green eyes that in his mother had captured the attention of Lord Freddie. He turned and took two glasses of wine from a passing flunkey, handing one to his cousin. Marcus grinned, inclining his dark head.

'I have just returned from Cherwell,' he said, in answer to Justin's enquiry. 'I was there longer than I had intended. The tenant there has been fleecing the estate for some time, but—' he gave a sardonic smile '—it won't be happening again!'

Justin raised his eyebrows. 'I don't believe our

grandfather ever visited that house. Towards the end he never even left Trevithick. It led the unscrupulous to take advantage.'

Marcus nodded. He had inherited from his grandfather a bare fifteen months before and had swiftly discovered that people had indeed taken advantage of the late Earl's infirmity in his last years. It seemed ironic that his grandfather, whose soubriquet had been the Evil Earl, had himself been cheated in his old age. The Trevithick estates were huge and the subsequent confusion had taken until now to sort out. There were still places that Marcus had not had the time to visit, business that remained unfinished.

'Do you intend to stay in London for the little Season?' Justin asked.

Marcus pulled a face. 'I should do, as it's Nell's debut. I would like to, but—'

'Lady Trevithick?' Justin enquired.

Marcus took a mouthful of his wine. 'It is damnably difficult to share a house with one's mother after an absence of fifteen years!' He grimaced. 'I have already asked Gower to find me a set of rooms—preferably on the other side of town!'

Justin smothered a grin. 'I saw Eleanor at Almack's earlier this evening,' he said, tactfully changing the subject. 'Pershore and Harriman were dancing attendance, to name but two! She seems to have taken well, which is no surprise since she has all the Trevithick good looks!'

Marcus laughed. 'I do believe that Mama is uncertain which of us to make a push to marry off first, though I believe she will have more success with my sister! I don't look to take a wife just yet!'

'Well, you certainly won't find one here,' Justin

said, turning back to scan the crowds. 'Women of another sort, perhaps…'

'Perhaps.' Marcus allowed his gaze to skim over the ranks of painted faces. 'It is a complication I could do well without, however.'

Justin grinned. 'There's one that would be worth it!'

Marcus turned to follow his cousin's gaze. The ballroom was packed and the dancers were executing a waltz, which was the excuse for much intimate and provocative behaviour. Yet in the middle of the swirling crowds, one couple stood out, for they danced beautifully but with total decorum. The gentleman was tall and fair, but he did not have much of Marcus's attention. The lady in his arms was another matter, however.

She was taller than most of the women present and only a few inches short of his own six foot. She wore a silver mask and her silver domino swung wide as she danced, revealing beneath it a dress in matching silk that clung to a figure that Marcus could only describe as slender but voluptuous. Her face was pale with a hint of rose on the cheekbones and her ebony black hair was piled up on top of her head in a complicated mass of curls that was just asking to be released from its captivity. Marcus grinned. Her hair was not the only thing that looked as though it would benefit from being given its freedom—the silk dress hinted at all sorts of delightful possibilities and he was already entertaining the idea of peeling it off her like the skin of a ripe fruit. Glancing around, he realised that at least half the men in his vicinity were thinking along the same lines and his grin broadened. Perhaps they had tasted the fruit already, for the very fact that she was at the Cyprians' Ball marked her as no lady. Marcus shrugged. It mattered little to him who had been before him, but he had every intention of being next in succession.

'Setting your sights, Marcus?' Justin Trevithick enquired, a smile in his voice. Like the Earl, he was watching the dancing couple. 'From what I've just overheard, you are at least tenth in the queue!'

'I don't like waiting in line,' Marcus murmured, not taking his gaze from the girl's face.

'Who is she, Justin?'

'Damned if I know!' Justin said cheerfully. 'No one does! The guesses are inventive and range wide, but no one can put a name to the face!'

'What about the lady's escort?'

Justin was laughing at his cousin's persistence. 'Now, there I can help you! The fortunate gentleman is Kit Mostyn! A shame we are not on terms with the Mostyns and cannot beg an introduction!'

Marcus gave his cousin an incredulous look, then laughed in his turn. 'Mostyn! How piquant! Then it will be doubly enjoyable to take the lady away from him…'

Justin raised his eyebrows. 'Is this love or war, Marcus?'

'Both!' his cousin replied promptly. 'They say all is fair, do they not? Well, then…'

The dancers were circling closer to them now. Marcus thought that the lady looked very comfortable in Lord Mostyn's arms, for she was talking eagerly and smiling up at him. Marcus's eyes narrowed. He had nothing against Kit Mostyn personally, but there had been a feud between the Mostyn and Trevithick families for centuries. Marcus knew little of the detail of it, and just at the moment he had no interest in healing the breach. He waited until the couple were directly beside him, then made a slight movement that attracted the lady's attention. She looked up and their eyes met for a long moment before she deliberately broke the contact. Marcus had the impression of a wide, smoky gaze, a slightly deeper silver colour than her dress. A moment later, she looked back at him over her shoulder, with what he could only interpret as a gesture of invitation.

Justin laughed. 'A result, I think, Marcus!'

Marcus thought so too. He watched as the music ended and the lady and her partner strolled to the edge of the dance floor, then, without haste, he made his way towards them through the crowd.

'Your servant, Mostyn.' There was a mocking edge to Marcus's drawl and he saw the younger man stiffen slightly before he returned his bow with the very slightest one of his own. Marcus's attention had already moved to the lady, which was where his real interest lay. At close quarters she looked younger than he had imagined, but then he realised that it was not so much a youthful quality but an impression of innocence. Her eyes lacked the knowing look that characterised so many of her profession. Marcus reflected cynically that that air of innocence must be worth a great deal of money to this particular lady. Gentlemen would pay over the odds to possess so apparently unspoilt a beauty. It amused him, for in his youth he had become entangled with a Cyprian who had pretended to a naïveté she simply did not possess and had tried to sue him for breach of promise. Such candour was appealing but ultimately an illusion.

He held out his hand to her and after a moment she took it in her own.

'Marcus Trevithick, at your service, ma'am. Would you do me the honour of granting me a dance?'

Marcus felt rather than saw Kit Mostyn flash the girl a look of unmistakable warning. She ignored him, smiling at Marcus with charm but absolutely no hint of coquetry. Grudgingly, Marcus had to admit that she might have been at a Dowager's ball rather than a Cyprian's masquerade. She had an inherent dignity. As she smiled, a small, unexpected dimple appeared at the corner of her mouth.

'Thank you, my lord. I should be delighted.'

He bowed slightly and led her on to the floor, where a set was forming for a country dance.

She carried herself with a poise that contrasted starkly with the flirting and ogling that was going on all around them and Marcus found it oddly touching—until he thought that this was no doubt all part of the act. Innocence, dignity... It was a clever way to set herself up as out of the ordinary. Nevertheless, her artfulness mattered little to him and he was confident that they could come to an understanding. Sooner rather than later, he hoped. He was beginning to want her very much. He studied her bent head and the way that the ebony curls brushed the nape of her neck. He wanted to touch her. Her mouth was as sultry as her figure, promising sensuous delight. He felt a powerful impulse to kiss her where they stood.

'Will you give me a name for a name?' he asked softly. 'You already know who I am.'

Her smoky grey gaze brushed his face and made him feel suddenly heated. She smiled a little, the dimple flashing. 'My name is Elizabeth, my lord. In fact, I am known as Beth.'

'Yes? And…?'

She considered. 'That is all I wish to tell you. There are no names at a masquerade. You have already broken the rules once by telling me your own identity.'

Marcus laughed. He had no problem with breaking any of society's rules that he did not agree with.

'What is Mostyn to you?' he asked, as the music brought them together again. 'I would like to know— before I attempt a trespass.'

He felt her fingers tremble in his before she freed herself and stepped away from him. She danced most gracefully.

'Kit is very dear to me,' she said, when eventually they came back together.

'I see.'

'I doubt it.' Once again that silver gaze pierced him. 'He is a friend. Closer than a friend—but that is all.'

An old lover, Marcus thought, with a vicious rush of envy. That would explain why they looked so comfortable together, yet had none of the heat of sensuality between them. Old passions had burned themselves out, leaving only the flame of friendship. It made him jealous to think of their past relationship, yet it also implied that there might be a vacancy…

'And is there anyone else?' Foolish question, when she probably had a dozen admirers paying for her favours! Yet her cool gaze searched his face and she answered quietly.

'I do not care to discuss such matters here, my lord.'

Marcus allowed his gaze to hold hers for several

long seconds. 'Then may we discuss it in private? I confess that would suit me very well…'

He felt that he might reasonably have expected some encouragement at this point, even if it was only a smile, but Beth gave his suggestion thoughtful consideration, and then inclined her head.

'Very well. There is a study off the hallway—'

'I know it.'

She nodded again. The dance was finishing anyway, but no one paid any attention as she slipped from the line of dancers and went out into the entrance hall. Marcus waited a few moments before following her, pausing to see if he was observed. It seemed that everyone was too preoccupied with their own *amours* to be concerned about his.

He picked his way through the entwined couples and crossed the checkerboard black and white tiles of the hall. He vaguely remembered that the study was the third door on the left and he was just in time to catch the faintest swish of material as Beth whisked through the door, leaving it ajar for him.

Marcus smiled to himself. The situation was most promising and, despite his cynicism, he had to admit that there was something intriguing about the lady's air of aloof mystery. Perhaps it was all assumed simply to whet jaded appetites, but it was working on him and he was more world-weary than most. He quickened his step, went into the study and closed the door behind him.

It was a small room with a mahogany card table and chairs in the middle and matching mahogany bookcases about the walls. Long amber curtains shut out the night and the only light came from one lamp, standing on a side table.

Beth was standing beside the window. She had taken the dice from their box on the table and was tossing them lightly in one hand. She did not look up when Marcus came in and for a moment he thought he sensed something tense and wary in her stance, though the impression was fleeting.

He took a step forward. 'Would you care to indulge in a game of chance, sweetheart?' he asked.

She looked at him then, a stare as straight and protracted as the one she had first given him in the ballroom. Marcus was amused. He knew of few men and even fewer women who were so direct. Her eyes were a shadowed silver behind the mask, her gaze as deliberate and fearless as a cat.

'If you are sure that you wish to play, my lord.'

They were talking in *double entendres* now and Marcus appreciated her quick wit. It made the pursuit even more enjoyable. He wondered if she knew who he was, even though he had given only his name and not his title. It was entirely possible. She had focused on him from the first and he did not flatter himself that it was simply because she was attracted to him. She might well consider that his status and physical attributes outweighed a lack of fortune. And fortune was relative anyway. He could pay her well enough.

He kept his eyes on her face and smiled slowly. 'I'm sure. Which game do you prefer?'

The lady smiled too, the dimple quivering again at the corner of her deliciously curved mouth. Marcus suddenly wished he could cut to the chase and simply kiss her. It was a high-risk strategy and might backfire, but it was very tempting. He took a step closer. She took one back.

'Hazard might be appropriate,' she said coolly,

tossing the dice from one hand to the other. 'One throw of the dice. The winner takes all.'

Marcus hesitated. It was clear from her words that she would be his prize if he won and he considered it very sporting of her to offer her services for free. The reckoning would come later, of course, if they suited each other: the villa, the carriage, the jewels…

But if she won the wager…

'I like your terms, but first I need to know what you want from me if I lose,' he drawled. 'I do not have a fortune to offer. What would you settle for, sweetheart?'

He waited confidently for her to name her price. A necklace of diamonds, perhaps, to outclass the exquisite but tasteful grey pearls already around her neck.

She moved closer until he could smell her perfume. It was a subtle mix of jasmine and rose petals, warm as the sun on the skin, and it sent his senses into even more of a spin. Damn it, whatever the price, it had to be worth it.

'I don't want a fortune,' she said sweetly, 'just a small part of your patrimony. I want Fairhaven Island.'

Marcus stared. It comprehensively answered the question of whether or not she knew who he was, but it seemed an extraordinary suggestion. Fairhaven fell in the part of his estate that he had not yet had time to visit, but as far as he was concerned, it was a storm-swept isle in the middle of the Bristol Channel that supported a few people, a flock of sheep and nothing else. There was no earthly reason he could see why it should appeal to a courtesan. It was worth absolutely nothing at all.

Part of his mind prompted him to ask a few questions and get to the bottom of the mystery. The other part, tantalised by her perfume, suggested that there was no need to cavil and he was bound to win the bet anyway. Even if he lost he was fairly certain that he could persuade her to humour him. The time for a discussion on land and property was not now, when he wanted to sweep her into his arms, but later and best left to the lawyers.

'Very well,' he said, adding slowly, 'Do you always honour your bets?'

She looked away for the first time. 'I do not usually gamble, my lord. Do you honour yours?'

Marcus laughed. No man would have dared ask him that question but, after all, he had questioned her integrity first. And she still had not really answered him.

'I never renege,' he said. He took her hand in his and felt her tremble slightly. Her skin was very soft; he turned the hand over and pressed a kiss on the palm. 'But you did not answer my question.'

There was a flash of something in her eyes that almost looked like fear but it was gone as swiftly as it had come. She raised her chin.

'I will pay my debt, my lord—if I lose.'

Marcus nodded. He drew her closer until one of her palms was resting against his chest.

'And if I wish to take something on credit?' he asked, his voice a little rough.

'Then you might find yourself even further in debt since there is no guarantee that you would win.' She looked him straight in the eye. 'If you are willing to take the risk—'

It took Marcus only a split second to decide that

he was. He bent his head and brought his mouth down on hers.

He was experienced enough not to try to take too much too soon. Even a Cyprian liked to be courted and he was no naïve boy to pounce without finesse. He kissed her gently, exploratively, holding her like china until he felt the tension slide from her body and she started to respond to him. She tasted soft and sweet and very innocent. She even trembled in his arms. It had to be an illusion, but it was such a beguiling one that Marcus felt his self-control slipping dangerously. He deepened the kiss and, after a moment's hesitation, she kissed him back tentatively, pressing a little closer to him. Desire surged through his body, so powerful it pushed all other thoughts aside and he pulled her to him fiercely, careless now of gentleness. But it was too late—she was withdrawing from him, as elusive as she had ever been. Marcus stifled a groan of frustration.

'The game, my lord?' Her voice was husky.

The game. He had forgotten. Intent on a different game of his own devising, he had not been certain that she would persist in their wager. Still, he was quite willing to indulge her.

'If you wish.' Marcus shrugged. 'All on the one throw.' He gave her a slight bow. 'I will concede you the honour of calling the main, madam.'

Beth threw him one swift glance. 'Then I call a nine.'

She took the dice up and cast them on to the walnut table. Marcus watched them spin and settle on the polished wood. A five and a four. She really had the devil's own luck. He could not believe it. He smiled a little. 'Will you play for the best of three?'

'Certainly not.' She sounded breathless and as she turned into the light he saw the expression on her face. He had expected triumph or greed. What he saw was relief.

'Fairhaven,' she said, on a questioning note. 'You will honour your bet, my lord?'

Marcus did not reply. For the first time, doubt surfaced in his mind, faint but troubling. She had come close to him again; her skirt brushed against his thigh. Part of him responded to her proximity, but he clamped down hard on his desire and tried to concentrate.

'Why do you want it?' he asked.

She laughed then and he saw the triumph that had been missing a moment before. 'Your question comes a little late, my lord! Surely that is academic now.' She took a step back and her silken skirts rustled. 'My man of business will call on yours on the morrow. Goodnight, my lord!'

She turned to go, but Marcus caught her arm in a tight grip and spun her round to face him. He tore the mask from her face with impatient fingers. Without it she was even more striking than he had supposed. Her face was a pure oval, the smoky eyes set far apart beneath flyaway black brows, the nose small and straight, the sultry mouth that was not smiling now. She was breathing very quickly and he could tell that she was afraid. And that she was not the courtesan she pretended to be. For some reason that took all the anger out of him.

'One of us is in the wrong place, I believe,' he said slowly.

'It is I,' she said simply. 'Did you truly believe me a Cyprian, my lord?'

Marcus started to laugh. He could not help himself. 'Assuredly. Until I kissed you.'

That gave him the advantage. He saw the colour come up into her face and she tried to free herself from his grip. He stood back, letting her go with exaggerated courtesy. No, indeed, this was no courtesan, but even so he still wanted her. He had no idea whom she was, but he intended to find out.

'You will honour your bet?' she asked again.

Marcus grinned, folding his arms. 'I will not.'

He saw the fury come into her eyes and held her gaze steadfastly with his own.

'I will *make* you do so!' she said.

'How?' Marcus shifted slightly. 'Are you telling me that you would have honoured yours had I won? If so, I would press you to play me for the best of three!'

She blushed even harder at that but her mouth set in a stony line. 'What I would have done is immaterial, my lord, since you lost. You claimed never to renege!'

Marcus shrugged. 'I lied.'

'A liar and a cheat,' Beth said, in a tone that dripped contempt. 'I repeat, my man of business will call upon yours on the morrow, my lord, and will expect you to have ready the title to Fairhaven to hand over.'

The study door closed behind her with a decided snap and Marcus heard the quick, angry tap of her footsteps receding across the marble hall. He picked the dice up casually in one hand and sat down in one of the chairs. A whimsical smile touched his lips. He could not believe that his judgement had been so faulty. To mistake a lady for a Cyprian, even given the circumstances… He had been thoroughly misled by his desire, like a youth in his salad days. Led by the nose—or some other part of his anatomy, perhaps. It had never happened to him before.

He tossed the dice absent-mindedly in his hand. So he had been richly deceived and for an intriguing reason. He wanted to know more about that. He wanted to know more of the lady. Damn it, he still wanted *her*. Marcus shifted uncomfortably in his chair. And he needed a drink. Urgently.

Justin found him in the refreshment room after he had already downed a glass of brandy in one swallow. Justin watched him take a refill and despatch it the same way, and raised his eyebrows.

'Unlucky in love, Marcus?'

'Unlucky in games of chance,' Marcus said feelingly. He took Justin's arm and drew him into the shelter of one of the pillars, away from prying gossips. 'Justin, you know more of West Country genealogy than I! Tell me, does Kit Mostyn have a sister?'

Justin nodded. 'He has a widowed younger sister, Charlotte. Allegedly a blonde beauty, but she lives retired so it is difficult to say with certainty.'

Marcus frowned. Beth had never been a blonde and she could scarcely be described as retiring. Perhaps she was Mostyn's mistress after all. Yet something in him rebelled at such a thought.

'What is all this about, Marcus?' Justin was asking, looking puzzled. 'I thought you were about to make a new conquest, old fellow, not indulge in a mystery play!'

'So did I,' Marcus said thoughtfully. His face light-

ened and he held up the glass. 'Only find me the
bottle and I will tell you the whole story!'

'I cannot believe that you just did that, Beth.'

Christopher Mostyn sounded mild, but his cousin
knew full well that he was angry. She had known him
well enough and long enough to tell.

Beth sighed. 'It was your idea to escort me there,
Kit—'

'I may have escorted you to the Cyprians' Ball, but
I did not expect you to behave like one!'

Now Kit's voice sounded clipped, forbidding further discussion. Beth sighed again. Kit was head of
the family and as such she supposed he had the right
to censure her behaviour. The fact that he seldom did
owed more to his easygoing nature than her obedi-
ence.

Beth rested her head back against the carriage's
soft cushions and closed her eyes. Truth to tell, *she*
could not believe that she had behaved as she had.
And she had only told Kit half the story, the half
relating to the wager. She knew that if she had told
Kit that Marcus Trevithick had kissed her, very likely
he would have stormed back and challenged the Earl
to a duel and matters would be immeasurably worse.

Beth opened her eyes again and stared out of the
window. They were travelling through the streets of
London at a decorous pace and the light from the
lamps on the pavement skipped across the inside of
the carriage in bars of gold and black. It hid her
blushes and a very good thing too, for whenever she
thought of Marcus Trevithick, she felt the telltale colour come into her face and the heat suffuse her entire
body.

Not only had she overstepped the mark—by a long chalk—but she knew that she had been completely out of her depth with such a man. She had a lot of courage and, allied to her impulsive nature, she knew it could be her downfall. However, her nerve had almost deserted her in that secluded room. If he had won the bet... Beth shivered. Like as not he would have demanded his prize there and then on the card table or the floor... But he had not won. She took a deep, steadying breath.

Marcus Trevithick. Children of her family were taught to hate the Trevithicks from the moment they were born. There were tales told at the nursemaid's knee—stories of treachery and evil. The Earls of Trevithick were jumped-up nobodies, whereas the Mostyns could trace their ancestry back to the Conquest and beyond. The Trevithicks had stolen the Mostyn estates during the Civil War and had wrested the island of Fairhaven from them only two generations back, taking the family treasure and the Sword of Saintonge into the bargain. No good had come to the Mostyns ever since—their fortunes had fallen whilst the Trevithicks had flourished like an evil weed.

Marcus Trevithick. Beth shivered again. She could not believe that he was evil, but he was certainly dangerous. He was also the most attractive man that she had ever met. Having been a child bride, her experience was necessarily small, but even so she was certain that he could stand comparison in any company.

The carriage drew up outside the house in Upper Grosvenor Street that she had rented for the little Season. Kit descended and helped her out with cold, studied politeness. He did not say a word as he escorted her up the steps and into the entrance hall. Beth bit her lip. She knew she was well and truly in disgrace.

Charlotte Cavendish, Kit's sister, was sitting in the red drawing room, her netting resting on the cushion beside her. She was reading from Oliver Goldsmith's *The Vicar of Wakefield* but cast the book aside with a smile as they came in. Like her brother, she was very fair with sparkling blue eyes, slender and tall. A scrap of lace was perched on her blonde curls as a concession to a widow's cap.

'There you are! I had almost given you up and gone to bed…'

Her smile faded as she looked from her brother's stony face to Beth's flushed one.

'Oh, dear. What has happened?'

'Ask your cousin,' Kit said shortly, stripping off his white gloves. 'I will be in the book room, enjoying a peaceful glass of brandy!'

Charlotte's gaze moved round to Beth. 'Oh, dear,' she said again, but there was an irrepressible twinkle in her eyes. 'What have you done, Beth?'

Beth wandered over to the big red wing-chair opposite and curled up in it. She was beginning to feel annoyed as well as guilty.

'It is all very well for Kit to act the moralist, but it was his idea to go to the Cyprians' Ball in the first place—'

Charlotte gave a little squeak and clapped her hand to her mouth. 'Beth! You told me you were going to Lady Radley's rout!'

'Well, so we did, but then Kit had the idea of the Cyprians' Ball!' Beth wriggled uncomfortably under her cousin's horrified stare. 'We were masked, so I thought there would be no harm…' She looked defiant. 'Very well, Lottie, I admit it! I was curious!'

'Oh, Beth,' Charlotte said in a failing voice. 'I know I cannot accompany you about the town, but I thought you would come to no harm with Kit!'

'Well, you were wrong!' Beth said mutinously. It suddenly seemed much easier to blame the whole thing on her cousin. 'None of this would have happened if Kit had not decided to have some fun!'

'None of what?' Charlotte asked, in the tone of someone who was not entirely sure they wanted to know the answer.

Beth yawned. She was very tired and suddenly wanted her bed, but equally she wanted someone to confide in. Her cousin had been as close as a sister this year past, closer than they had ever been in childhood when Charlotte's five years' seniority had put Beth quite in awe of her.

Beth, Kit and Charlotte had grown up together, but time and differing fortunes had scattered them. Charlotte had married an officer and followed the drum, Kit had spent several years in India and Beth had been orphaned at seventeen and left penniless. Friends and relatives had murmured of schoolteaching or governessing, but two days after her bereavement, Sir Frank Allerton, a widower whose estate marched with that of the Mostyns, had called to offer her an alternative future. He had not been a friend of the late Lord Mostyn, but Beth knew that her father had esteemed him as an honest man, and so she had accepted.

She had never regretted her decision, but she did regret the lack of children of her marriage. Her home and parish affairs had given her plenty to do, but when Frank had died, leaving her a widow at nineteen, she had been lonely. Though Kit had inherited Mostyn Hall and the title he was seldom at home, and it was Beth who kept an eye on the estate. Then, a year into Beth's widowhood, Charlotte had lost her husband during the retreat from Almeira and had come back to Mostyn. Fortunately she and Beth had found that they got on extremely well. Charlotte was cool and considered where Beth was impetuous and tempered some of her cousin's more madcap ideas. Beth's liveliness prevented her cousin from falling into a decline.

'So what has happened?' Charlotte asked again, recalling Beth's attention to the lamp-lit room. 'You went to the Ball…'

'Yes. We only intended to stay for a little, although I think Kit might have lingered if he had been there alone!' Beth said, with a sudden, mischievous grin. 'At any rate, it was not as I had imagined, Lottie! There was the most licentious behaviour—'

Charlotte looked exasperated. 'Well, what did you expect, Beth? You were at the Cyprians' Ball, not a Court Reception!'

Beth sighed. 'Yes, I know! Everyone was staring at me—no doubt because they thought me a demirep!' she added, before her cousin could make the observation herself.

'Yes, well, it was a reasonable assumption—' Charlotte looked at her frankly '—and you do have a lovely figure, Beth! The gentlemen—'

'Spare me,' Beth said hastily, remembering the disturbing heat in Marcus Trevithick's eyes. 'I thought you wished to hear what had happened, Lottie?'

'Yes,' her cousin said obligingly, 'what did?'

'Well, Kit and I had a few dances and, as we were waltzing, the behaviour was becoming more and more uninhibited so I decided it would be wise to come home. Then a gentleman came up to us and asked me to dance.'

Beth looked away. When Marcus Trevithick had first approached her she had been amused and some dangerous imp of mischief had prompted her to play along. She had not known his identity then, but she had been tempted by the atmosphere, tempted by *him*...

She looked back at Charlotte, who was waiting in silence. 'We danced a country dance together and he introduced himself as Marcus Trevithick. I had had no notion—I have never met Trevithick before, and although he knew who Kit was he did not know me, though he made strenuous attempts to find out my name...'

'I'm sure he did,' Charlotte said drily. 'Did he proposition you, Beth?'

'Lottie!' Beth looked shocked, then smiled a little. 'Well...'

'Well, who could blame him?' Charlotte seemed torn between disapproval and laughter. 'The poor man, thinking you Haymarket-ware and no doubt getting a set-down for his trouble!'

'It was not quite like that,' Beth admitted slowly. 'Yes, he did...make his interest plain, but I did not discourage him exactly...' Suddenly, foolishly, it seemed difficult to explain. Or at least difficult to explain without giving some of her feelings away, Beth thought hopelessly. And Charlotte was no fool. She would read between the lines and see all the things that Beth had not admitted.

'It is just that I thought of Fairhaven,' she said, in a rush. 'You know that I had been intending to make Trevithick a financial offer for the island! Suddenly I thought how much more fun it would be to make a wager...' She risked a glance at her cousin from under her lashes and saw that Charlotte was frowning now, all hint of amusement forgotten.

'So I suggested that we step apart, and then I challenged him to a game of Hazard, with Fairhaven as the stake—'

'Beth!' Charlotte said on a note of entreaty. 'Tell me this is not true! What did you offer against his stake?'

Beth did not reply. Their eyes, grey and blue, met and held, before Charlotte gave a little groan and covered her face with her hands.

'Do you wish for your smelling salts, Lottie?' Beth asked, uncurling from her armchair and hurrying across to the armoire. 'You will feel much more the thing in a moment!'

'I feel very well, thank you!' Charlotte said, although she looked a little pale. 'I feel better, in fact, than you would have done if Trevithick had claimed his prize! I take it he did *not* win?'

'No, he did not!' Beth felt the heat come into her face. 'I won! And if I had lost I should not have honoured the bet! It was only a game—'

'No wonder Kit cut up rough!' Charlotte said faintly. 'Stepping aside with a gentleman who already thought you a Cyprian, challenging him to a game of chance, offering yourself as the stake...' She took the smelling salts and inhaled gratefully. The pale rose colour came back into her face.

'I have shocked you,' Beth said remorsefully.

'Yes, you have.' Charlotte's gaze searched Beth's face before she gave a slight shake of the head. 'Each time you do something outrageous, Beth, I tell myself that you could not possibly shock me more—and yet you do!'

'I am sorry!' Beth said, feeling contrite and secretly vowing not to tell Charlotte any more of the encounter. 'You know I am desperate to reclaim Fairhaven!'

'Not so desperate, surely, that you would do anything to take it back!' Charlotte sat back and patted the seat beside her. 'This obsession is ridiculous, Beth! The island was lost to our family years ago—leave it in the past, where it belongs!'

Beth did not reply. She had learned long ago that Charlotte was practical by nature and did not share the deep mystical tug of their heritage. Beth could remember standing on the cliffs of Devon as a small child and staring out across the flat, pewter sea to where a faint smudge on the horizon signified the island that they had lost. The tales of her grandfather, the dashing Charles Mostyn, and his struggle with the dastardly George Trevithick, had captured her child's imagination and never let it go. Lord Mostyn had lost the island through treachery and, fifty years later, Beth had vowed to take it back and restore the family fortunes. In her widowhood, a woman of means, she had twice offered George Trevithick, the Evil Earl, a fair price for the island. He had rejected her approach haughtily. But Beth was persistent and she had fully intended to repeat the offer to his grandson, the new Earl. It was one of the reasons that she had come up to London. Fate, however, had intervened...fate, and her own foolish impulse.

But perhaps it had not been so foolish, Beth

thought. Whatever the circumstances Fairhaven was hers now, won in fair play. And she intended to claim it.

'What sort of man is Marcus Trevithick, Beth?' Charlotte asked casually. 'What did you think of him?'

Beth jumped. She was glad of the lamp-lit shadows and the firelight, for in the clear daylight she did not doubt that her face would have betrayed her.

'He is perhaps of an age with Kit, or a little older,' she said, glad that she sounded so casual herself. 'Tall, dark… He has something of the look of the old Earl about him.'

'The Evil Earl,' Charlotte said slowly. 'Do you think that his grandson has inherited his character along with his estates?'

Beth shivered a little. 'Who knows? I was scarce with him long enough to find out.'

'Yet you must have gained some impression of his nature and disposition?' Charlotte persisted. 'Was he pleasing?'

Pleasing? Who could deny it? Beth remembered the strength of Marcus's arms around her, the compelling demand of his lips against hers. He was a man quite outside her experience. But he was also a liar and a cheat. She saw again his mocking smile. She turned her hot face away.

'No, indeed. He was a proud, arrogant man. I did not like him!'

Charlotte yawned and got to her feet. 'Well, I am for my bed.' She bent and dropped a soft kiss on Beth's cheek, pausing as she straightened up. 'You did not tell Lord Trevithick your name?'

'No,' Beth said, reflecting that that at least was true.

'And though you were with Kit, you were masked.' Charlotte sounded satisfied. 'Well, at least he will not know your identity. For that we must be grateful, I suppose, for it would cause the most monstrous scandal if it were known that you had attended the Cyprians' Ball! People would assume—' She broke off. 'Well, never mind. But perhaps you will think twice in future before you play such a hoyden's trick again!'

The door closed softly behind her. Beth lay back on the cushions and let out her breath in a huge, shaky sigh. Charlotte was in the right of it, of course—it would be very damaging for it to become known that she had been at the Cyprians' Ball. And what Charlotte did not know was that whilst she had not given Trevithick her name, he had seen her face without the mask. Beth stared into the fire. Well, it mattered little. She would send Gough to call on the Earl's man of business in the morning, and once the title to Fairhaven was in her pocket, she would leave for Devon without delay.

Even though he had said he would not honour his bet, Beth could see no reason why Marcus Trevithick would decline to surrender the island to her, for it could not be worth much to him. He had lands and houses far more valuable and there was no sentimental reason for him to hold on to the least important part of his estate. If he persisted in his refusal, however, she was still prepared to pay him, and, Beth thought with satisfaction, one could not say fairer than that. She had heard that his pockets were to let and she was certain that he would see the sense of the matter.

She raked out the embers of the fire, doused the lamp and went upstairs to bed. It should have been easy to put the matter out of her head but for some reason the memory of the encounter—the memory of Marcus Trevithick—still lingered as she lay in her bed. She told herself that she had seen the last of him, but some unnerving instinct told her that she had not. Then she told herself that she did not wish to see him again and the same all-knowing voice in her head told her that she lied.

Chapter Two

'A gambler, a wastrel, a rake and a vagabond!' the Dowager Viscountess of Trevithick said triumphantly, ticking the words off on her fingers.

There was a short silence around the Trevithick breakfast table. The autumn sun shone through the long windows and sparkled on the silver. There were only three places set; one of Marcus's married sisters was coming up from the country for the little Season but had not yet arrived, and the other had gone to stay with friends for a few weeks. Only Marcus, his youngest sister Eleanor and the Dowager Viscountess were therefore in residence at Trevithick House.

'A vagabond, Mama?' Marcus enquired politely. 'What is the justification for that?'

He thought he heard a smothered giggle and looked round to see Eleanor hastily applying herself to her toast. Although she appeared to be the demurest of debutantes on the surface, Marcus knew that his sister had a strong sense of humour. It was a relief to know that the Viscountess had not crushed it all out of her during Marcus's years abroad.

'Traipsing around the courts of Europe!' the

Viscountess said, giving her son a baleful glare from her cold grey eyes. 'Drifting from one country to another like a refugee…'

Marcus folded up his newspaper with an irritable rustle. He had a headache that morning, no doubt from the brandy that he and Justin had consumed the night before, and Lady Trevithick's animadversions on his character were not helping. In fact, he was surprised that she had not added drunkard to the list.

'I scarce think that a diplomatic mission accompanying Lord Easterhouse to Austria constitutes vagabondage, Mama,' he observed coolly. 'Your other charges, however, may be justified—'

'Oh, Marcus, you are scarcely a wastrel!' Eleanor protested sweetly. Her brown eyes sparkled. 'Why, since your return from abroad I have heard Mr Gower say that the estates are already better managed—'

'Enough from you, miss!' the Dowager Viscountess snapped, chewing heavily on her bread roll. 'You are altogether too quick with your opinions! We shall never find a husband for you! As well try to find a wife for your brother! Why, Lady Hutton was saying only the other day that her Maria would be the perfect bride for Trevithick were it not that Hutton would worry to give her into the care of someone with so sadly unsteady a character! So there is no prospect of *that* fifty thousand pounds coming into the family!'

Marcus sighed. It was difficult enough having a parent who was so frank in her criticism without her holding the view that he was still in short coats. How Eleanor tolerated it, he could not imagine. He knew that if he had been in her shoes he would have taken the first man who offered, just to escape Lady

Trevithick. Marcus was also aware that his friendship with Justin did not help either. The Dowager Viscountess had never got over her disapproval of her nephew and barely acknowledged him in public, a sign of displeasure that Justin cheerfully ignored. Families, Marcus thought, could be damnably difficult.

As if in response to that very thought, Penn, the butler, strode into the room.

'Mr Justin Trevithick is without, my lord, and enquiring for you. Shall I show him in?'

Marcus grinned. 'By all means, Penn! And pray send someone to set another cover—my cousin may not yet have partaken of breakfast!'

The Dowager grunted and hauled her massive bulk from the chair. 'I have some letters to write and will be in the library. There is the possibility that Dexter's daughter may be a suitable wife for you, Marcus, but I have some further enquiries to make!'

'Well, pray do not hurry on my account, Mama!' Marcus said cheerfully, gaining himself another glare from his parent and a covert smile from his sister. 'Miss Dexter would need to be very rich indeed to tempt me!'

'Marcus, you make her much worse!' Eleanor whispered, as the Dowager Viscountess left the room. 'If you could only ignore her!'

'That would be difficult!' Marcus said drily. 'I curse the day she appointed herself my matchmaker!' His expression softened as it rested on his sister. 'How you tolerate it, infant, I shall never know!'

Eleanor shook her head but did not speak and, a second later, Justin Trevithick came into the room. He shook Marcus's hand and gave Eleanor a kiss.

'Eleanor! I'm glad that Lady Trevithick did not whisk you away—'

The door opened. 'Her ladyship requests that you join her in the library, Miss Eleanor,' Penn said, in sonorous tones. 'Lord Prideaux has called and is with her.'

Eleanor gave her cousin and brother a speaking glance, then dutifully followed Penn out of the room. Marcus gestured towards the coffee pot. 'Can I offer you breakfast, Justin? And my apologies for my mother's transparently bad manners at the same time?'

Justin laughed. 'Thank you. I will take breakfast— and for the rest, please do not regard it! The only thing that concerns me is that Lady Trevithick considers Prideaux more suitable company for Eleanor than myself! He is a loose fish, but then, I suppose his parents were at least respectably married!'

'So were yours,' Marcus commented.

'Yes, but only after I was born!' Justin leant over and poured some coffee. 'How do you feel this morning, old fellow? Must confess my head's splitting! That brandy was nowhere near the quality it pretended!'

'The coffee will help,' Marcus said absently, reflecting that the brandy had proved to be the opposite of his mysterious adversary of the previous night. She had been Quality masquerading as something else and today he was determined to get to the bottom of that particular mystery. He had told Justin an expurgated version of the whole tale the previous night over the maligned brandy bottle, and his cousin had been as curious as he as to the lady's motives. Justin had been closer to the fifth Earl than Marcus because their grandfather had taken Justin up deliberately to spite his elder son, but despite his far greater knowledge of the old man's estates and fortune, he could throw no light on why anyone would want the island of Fairhaven.

The door opened for a third time as Penn came in. 'Mr Gower is here to see you, my lord. He says that it is most urgent.'

Marcus frowned, checking the clock on the marble mantelpiece. It was very early for a call from his man of business, but if Gower had managed to find him rooms well away from Albemarle Street, then the earlier the better. Remembering the previous night, his frown deepened. There was another reason why Gower might have called, of course...

'Thank you, Penn, I will join Mr Gower in the study shortly,' he said.

The door closed noiselessly as Penn trod away to impart the message. Justin buttered another roll. 'Shall I wait here for you, Marcus, or do you prefer to join me at White's later?'

Marcus stood up. 'Why don't you come with me to see Gower?' he suggested. 'I have the strangest suspicion that this relates to the business last night, Justin, and I would value your advice.'

His cousin raised his eyebrows. 'Your mysterious gamester, Marcus? Surely she does not really intend to claim Fairhaven!'

'We shall see,' Marcus said grimly.

Mr Gower was waiting for them in the study, pacing the floor with an impatience that set fair to wear a track through the rich Indian rug. He was a thin, aesthetic-looking man whose pained expression had come about through years of trying to make the irascible old Earl see sense over the running of the Trevithick estates. There was a thick sheaf of papers in his hand.

'My lord!' he exclaimed agitatedly, as the gentlemen entered. 'Mr Trevithick! Something most untoward has occurred!'

Marcus folded himself negligently into an armchair. 'Take a seat and tell us all, Gower!' he instructed amiably. 'What has happened—has one of the housemaids absconded with the silver?'

Mr Gower frowned at such inappropriate levity, but he took a seat uncomfortably on the edge of the other armchair, placing his shabby leather briefcase at his feet. Justin strolled over to the window, still eating his bread roll.

'This morning I had a call from a gentleman by the name of Gough who has chambers close to mine,' Mr Gower said, still agitated. He shuffled his papers on the table. 'He is a most respected lawyer and represents only the best people! He came to tell me of an agreement between one of his clients and yourself, my lord, an agreement to cede the title deeds to the island of Fairhaven, which is—'

'I know where it is, thank you, Gower,' Marcus said coolly. He exchanged a look with Justin. 'Gough, is it? Did he tell you the name of his client?'

'No, sir,' the lawyer said unhappily. 'He told me that his client expected—*expected* was the precise word used, my lord—that I would have the deeds to the island ready to hand over immediately. Naturally I told him that I could do no such thing without your consent, my lord, and that you had issued no such authorisation. He therefore suggested...' Mr Gower shuddered, as though the suggestion had been made with some force '…that I call upon you to gain your approval forthwith. Which I am doing, sir. And,' he finished, apparently unable to stop himself, 'I do feel that I should protest, my lord, at the cavalier manner in which this transaction appears to have been handled, putting me in a most difficult position with a fellow member of my profession!'

There was a long silence. 'You are right, Gower,' Marcus said slowly. 'The whole matter is damnably out of order and I apologise if it has put you in a difficult situation.'

'But the island, my lord!' Gower said beseechingly. 'The deeds! If you have an agreement with Mr Gough's client—'

'There is no agreement,' Marcus said. He heard Justin draw breath sharply, but did not look at him. 'Tell Gough,' he said implacably, 'that there is no agreement.'

'My lord…' Gower sounded most unhappy. 'If there is any way that such a contract could be proved, I do beg you to reconsider!'

Marcus raised one black eyebrow. 'Do you not trust me, Gower?' he asked humorously. 'At the very most it could be construed as a verbal contract and there were no witnesses.'

Gower blinked like a hunted animal. 'None, my lord? Can you be certain of that?'

A smile twitched Marcus's lips. 'Perfectly.'

'But even so…' Gower glanced across at Justin. 'A verbal contract, my lord…'

'I think Mr Gower feels that you should honour your pledges, Marcus,' Justin said, with a grin. 'Even in a game of chance—'

'A game of chance!' Gower looked even more disapproving. 'My lord! Mr Trevithick! This is all most irregular!'

'As you say, Gower,' Marcus murmured. 'Have no fear. Gough's client will never sue. I would stake my life on it!'

Justin grimaced. 'Can you be so sure, Marcus? She sounds mighty determined to me!'

Gower, who was just shuffling his papers into his briefcase, scattered them on the carpet. 'She, sir, *she*?' he stuttered. 'Good God, my lord, not even the old Earl would have indulged in a wager with a female!'

'He was missing a trick then,' Marcus said coolly, 'for I found it most stimulating!' He rose to his feet. 'Good day, Gower. Give Gough my message and if you find his instructions are that he persists in his claim, refer him direct to me. Penn will show you out!'

'Marcus,' Justin said, once they were alone, 'do you not consider this a little unsporting of you? After all, the girl won the bet, did she not?'

'She did,' Marcus conceded. He met Justin's eyes. 'Truth is, Justin, I would like to meet her again, find out about this passion she has for Fairhaven. It intrigues me.'

'And this is how you intend to flush her out?'

'Precisely!' Marcus grinned suddenly. 'I could go to Kit Mostyn and ask for his help, of course, but I would wager he will not grant it! So…if I refuse to honour the bet, my mysterious opponent may show her hand again!'

Justin's lips twisted. 'You're a cunning devil, Marcus! But what is your interest in the lady herself?'

Marcus's grin deepened. 'That depends—on the lady and who she turns out to be!'

'And you would recognise her again?'

'Oh, yes,' Marcus said slowly. 'I would recognise her anywhere, Justin.'

'Pull your chair up a little closer, my love,' Lady Fanshawe instructed her goddaughter, gesturing her to move to the front of the theatre box. 'Why, you will not be able to see anything at all from back there! But do not lean out too far! It is not good to lean excessively, for the gentlemen will stare so! Oh, pray do look, Beth!' Lady Fanshawe leant as far out of the box as she could without falling. 'It is Mr Rollinson and Lord Saye! I do believe they will call upon us in the interval!'

Beth edged her chair forward an inch and leant backwards at the same time. She had every intention of effacing herself until she was practically invisible. The invitation to the theatre was a longstanding one and could not be avoided, for Lady Fanshawe had been her mother's closest friend. That was the only reason why Beth had come to Drury Lane that evening, although the play, Sheridan's *The Rivals*, would normally have been sufficient to tempt her out. Normally, but not now. The matter of Marcus Trevithick and her ill-conceived wager with him had suddenly become so very difficult that she had no desire to risk meeting him again.

Beth chanced a glance over the edge of the box at the crowded auditorium below. Fortunately it would be easy to be inconspicuous in such a crush. People were milling around and chattering nineteen to the dozen: dandies, ladies, courtesans... Beth drew back sharply as a passing buck raised his quizzing glass at her in a manner she considered to be odiously familiar. Lady Fanshawe did not notice for she was waving excitedly to an acquaintance in the crowd.

It was already very hot. Beth fanned herself and looked around idly. Kit had escorted her again that evening but as soon as they had arrived he had left her in Lady Fanshawe's company and could now be seen in a box to the left, chatting to a very dashing lady in green silk with nodding ostrich feathers. Lady Fanshawe had taken one look and remarked disapprovingly that one met with any old riff-raff at the theatre and that Kit need not think to foist his *chère amie* on their attention! Beth had been a little curious, but had tried not to stare. She thought that the dashing lady looked rather fast but, given her own performance at the Cyprians' Ball, she was scarcely in a position to comment.

As time wore on without mishap, Beth started to relax a little. She felt comfortably nondescript in her rose muslin dress. She had chosen it deliberately because it was so unremarkable and she had tried to disguise herself further with a matching rose-pink turban, but Charlotte had positively forbidden her to leave the house looking such a dowd. Beth sighed. It was a terrible shame that Charlotte could never accompany them, but her cousin had had a fear of crowds ever since she was a girl and the glittering hordes that thronged the *ton*'s balls and parties terrified her. It was odd, for Charlotte was perfectly comfortable in society she knew, and could travel and visit amongst friends quite happily, but she was never at ease with strangers.

Beth watched as Kit took a fond farewell of his companion and turned to rejoin them for the start of the play. He was just making his way back to their box when Beth saw that his attention had been firmly caught by a slender young lady, very much the debutante, who was just taking her seat opposite. Intrigued, Beth watched as the young lady saw Kit and faltered in her conversation. For a long moment the two of them simply gazed at each other, then the girl gave Kit a half-smile and turned hesitantly away. Beth smiled to herself. Kit seemed smitten and she must remember to quiz him on the identity of the young lady…

She froze, all thought of Kit and his romantic entanglements flying from her mind as she saw the gentleman who had entered the box behind the girl. She recognised his height, the arrogant tilt of his head. She could even imagine those smooth, faintly mocking tones that she had last heard at the Cyprians' Ball, but which had positively leapt from the page of the letter he had sent her via Gough earlier in the week:

'My dear lady adventuress…'

Beth's fan slipped from her shaking fingers and she leant down to retrieve it, trying to shrink into the shadows. Bent almost double, she groped around on the floor and tried to think quickly at the same time. How was she to avoid Marcus Trevithick seeing her when their boxes were almost opposite each other? If she tried to leave now, would she be able to slip away or would she only draw more attention to herself? She cursed the pale pink dress, which had seemed such a good idea earlier but in the dim light seemed to glow like a beacon.

'What are you doing down there on the floor, Beth, my love? Are you feeling unwell? Do you wish to return home?'

Beth straightened up hastily as Lady Fanshawe's

carrying tones threatened to attract the notice of the whole theatre.

'I am very well, I thank you, dear ma'am. I had only dropped my fan…' Her words trailed away as, under some strange compulsion, she looked across the theatre and directly into the dark eyes of Marcus Trevithick. There could not be the slightest doubt that he had recognised her. He held her gaze for a long moment, a smile starting to curl the corners of his mouth, then he inclined his head in ironic salutation.

The play started at last and Beth forced herself to look at the stage and nowhere else. This proved difficult as a wayward part of her seemed to want to look across at the Earl of Trevithick all the time and she had to fix her gaze firmly on the actors instead. She soon discovered that she was one of the few people in the whole theatre who was giving their undivided attention to the stage. The chatter about her scarcely faltered and it seemed that most of the fashionable crowd viewed the play as a diversion from the main business of the evening. Eventually the noise began to grate on Beth, who inevitably found her concentration interrupted. After that it was easy for her thoughts to wander back to the tangle in which she found herself.

When Gough had come to her five days before and told her that the Earl was refusing to honour his bet and give Fairhaven to her, she had been annoyed but not particularly surprised. She had sent the lawyer back to offer a price that she felt was more than fair and had waited, confident that Trevithick would agree this time. It had come as a nasty shock when Gough returned the next day, out of countenance, to relate that he had seen the Earl in person and that her offer had been spurned. Further, the Earl was demanding in no uncertain terms that his client identify herself and discuss the matter with him face to face. This Beth declined to do, but she sweetened her refusal with a far more tempting sum of money. She could afford it and he… Well, she had thought that he would seize the chance to make such a profit. Instead, Gough had delivered the letter.

My dear lady adventuress,

Your offers intrigue me but you should know that I will only do business with you directly. If you choose not to identify yourself it makes no odds; I shall soon know your name and your direction. Then, even if you do *not* choose it, I shall seek you out…

After that, Beth had not set foot outside the house for two days. Glancing across at Marcus Trevithick now, she acknowledged that she had not felt afraid, precisely, more angry and outmanoeuvred. She had won the wager, but he held all the cards. He was not only refusing to give her Fairhaven, but he was also refusing to *sell* it to her, and if he discovered her identity he could ruin her by having it whispered abroad that she, a respectable lady, had attended the Cyprians' Ball. She knew that the wisest thing was to withdraw her offer and retire from the lists, but it seemed that Marcus Trevithick was not prepared to let her do so. She was angry with him, but she was furious with herself for giving him the advantage.

'Do you care to take a walk during the interval, Beth?' Kit enquired, from beside her. 'It might be pleasant to stretch our legs…'

Beth came back to the present, looked around and realised that the curtain had come down at the end of the first act. She glanced across at Marcus Trevithick and saw that he was already moving purposefully towards their box. So much for her half-formed hope that he would not dare accost her there! She took a quick breath.

'A walk? Yes! No...I am not sure... Yes!'

Kit looked understandably confused. 'What the deuce is the matter with you, Beth? You're as edgy as a thoroughbred mare!'

Beth grabbed his arm. She could see that Marcus had been delayed by an acquaintance, but he was still watching her with the concentrated attention of a predator. There could be no question that he meant to approach her.

Beth took one last look and hurried out of the box. 'Yes, by all means! Let us walk! This way!'

She steered her cousin out of the doorway and plunged into the corridor outside, making for the place where the crowd was thickest.

'Steady on, Beth!' Kit protested, as he was buffeted on all sides. 'You'll have us trampled in the crush!'

It was inevitable that such tactics, whilst they might delay matters, could not put them off forever. It was only a matter of minutes before someone recognised Kit and stopped him for a word, whilst the pressure of the crowd pulled Beth from his side before she had even noticed. Seconds later she looked round and realised that her cousin was nowhere in sight. Marcus Trevithick was, however.

He was leaning against a pillar just a few feet away from her, arms folded, as though he were prepared to stay there all night. His black gaze was watchful and faintly amused. Beth felt her breath catch in her throat. For one moment it seemed as though the press of people would whisk her past him, but then he stretched out one hand in a negligent gesture and caught her arm, pulling her to his side.

'Well, well! My mystery lady—at last! Have you any idea of the balls and routs I have endured these past few days in the hope of catching sight of you, ma'am?'

There were prying eyes and ears all around them. Beth strove to keep her face blank and give nothing away, though her heart was hammering.

'Good evening, my lord! I am sorry that you have put yourself to such trouble on my account!'

Marcus gave her a look of brilliant amusement. 'Thank you! It was worth it, however, for now I have found you again!' He tucked her hand through the crook of his arm and steered her out into the corridor. The crowd had lessened now and they could stroll along without too much difficulty. Beth looked around for rescue, but none was immediately forthcoming.

'I only wanted to speak with you, you know,' Marcus said reproachfully. 'I was utterly intrigued by your offer and wished to discuss the matter with you—'

'Is that not why you employ a man of business, my lord?' Beth asked, keeping her bright social smile in place. 'To relieve you of such onerous tasks?'

'Generally. But this would hardly be onerous.'

Beth found the warmth in Marcus's tone difficult to resist. She glanced up through her lashes and saw that he was smiling at her. It made her feel strangely hot and cold at the same time and she almost shivered. She made an effort to gather her scattered senses.

'If you had but honoured your wager, my lord, such a situation would not have occurred!'

'True.' Marcus bent closer and she felt his breath stir the tendrils of hair by her ear. 'But that would have defeated my object—of seeing you again, sweetheart!'

Beth stopped dead and glared at him. 'Do *not* call me that!' she hissed. 'You must know I am no...no lightskirt for your tumbling!'

Marcus grinned. 'Then why behave like one, ma'am? A dignified request to buy Fairhaven might have elicited a more dignified response!'

Beth could have wept with frustration. What had started as a light-hearted idea—to visit the Cyprians' Ball—had caused more trouble than she could ever have imagined. She wondered what on earth had possessed her to dance with Marcus Trevithick and to further the masquerade. At the time the opportunity to trick him out of Fairhaven had seemed too good to miss, amusing, clever even. She had congratulated herself on her ingenuity—and on her courage! Now she could see that the wager had been the product of too much wine and excitement. She tightened her lips in exasperation.

'It was an impulse! Which I now bitterly regret!'

'Understandably. If you are indeed the lady you pretend to be, what could be worse than a version of the events of that night circulating amongst the *ton*? Dear me, ma'am, it does not bear thinking about!'

Beth coloured up furiously. 'You would not do such a thing!'

'Why not?'

Marcus's tone was mild, but when she glanced up at his face Beth saw that he was watching her intently. It was exactly the problem that Charlotte had hinted at, the one that Beth had not even anticipated. If the Earl of Trevithick let it be known that he had had an encounter with a lady indecorously disporting herself at the Cyprians' Ball, no one would believe in her innocence. And yet some instinct told her that he would not do that to her. Her troubled grey gaze scanned his face and she saw the hard lines soften a little as a smile came into his eyes. Suddenly she was acutely aware of him; of the smooth material of his sleeve beneath her fingers and the hard muscle of his arm beneath that, of the warmth of his body so close to hers and the disturbing look in his eyes.

'Just tell me your name,' he said softly, persuasively.

'Beth, my dear! There you are!' Beth jumped and swung round, tearing her gaze from Marcus. Lady Fanshawe was bearing down on them, her good-natured face wreathed in smiles. Her gaze moved from her goddaughter to the Earl of Trevithick and her smile faltered slightly in surprise, but she recovered herself well.

'Oh! Lord Trevithick, is it not? How do you do, sir? I had no notion that you knew my goddaughter!'

Beth was aware of a sinking feeling as she watched Marcus bow elegantly over Lady Fanshawe's hand. She knew that her godmother, voluble as ever, was about to give her identity away completely.

'It is so delightful to see that the younger generation has ended that tiresome estrangement between the Mostyn and Trevithick families!' Lady Fanshawe burbled. 'I have never quite understood the cause of all the trouble, for it was an unconscionably long time ago and over some trifling matter such as a lost battle—'

'Or perhaps a lost island, ma'am!' Marcus said smoothly. Beth felt his dark gaze brush her face and deliberately evaded his eyes. 'In fact, I was hoping that your charming goddaughter—' there was just a hint of a query in his voice '—might tell me more about our family feud, for I confess it fascinates me!'

Lady Fanshawe beamed, accepting Marcus's other arm as they strolled slowly back towards the box. 'Oh, well, Beth will be able to tell you the whole story, I dare say! All the Mostyns are steeped in family history from the cradle!'

'I see,' Marcus said slowly. Beth could feel him moving closer to his goal, but for some reason she felt powerless to intervene and direct the conversation into other channels. And Lady Fanshawe was so very good-natured, and seemed pleased that the Earl was showing such an interest…

'You must know the family extremely well, ma'am,' he continued.

'Oh, indeed, for Davinia Mostyn, Beth's mama, was such a dear friend of mine, was she not, Beth, my love? It was such a tragedy when Lord and Lady Mostyn were killed in that horrid accident! But then Kit inherited the title and Beth married Frank Allerton…'

Beth felt Marcus's arm move beneath her fingers. She caught her breath.

'You did not tell me that you were Sir Francis's widow, Lady Allerton,' Marcus said gently, smiling down at her. She could see the triumph in his eyes. 'He was a fine man and a great scholar. His treatise on hydrostatics formed part of my university studies. I remember his work well.'

'Thank you,' Beth murmured, looking away. 'Sir Francis was indeed a fine academician.'

They had reached their box now and discovered that the second act of the play was about to start. Kit was already in his seat and looked up, startled, to see both his cousin and Lady Fanshawe escorted by the Earl of Trevithick. The two men exchanged a stiff bow, and then Marcus took Beth's hand in his.

'I should deem it an honour to call on you, Lady Allerton,' he murmured, his gaze resting on her face in a look that brought the colour into her cheeks. 'I understand that you are staying in Upper Grosvenor Street?'

Beth hesitated. 'We are, but—'

'Then I shall look forward to seeing you shortly.' He bowed again. 'Good evening, ma'am.'

Beth bit her lip as she watched his tall figure make its way back to the party in the Trevithick box. It seemed that the Earl was difficult to refuse. And now that Lady Fanshawe had told him everything he needed to know, his position was well nigh unassailable. With a sigh, Beth tried to direct her attention back to the play. She wondered what his next move would be.

'I am not at all sure about these newfangled artists,' Lady Fanshawe sighed, pausing in front of a landscape painting by John Constable. 'Only look at those odd flecks of light and the strange *rough* technique. There is something not quite finished...indeed, not quite *gentlemanly* about it!'

Beth laughed. She rather liked Constable's atmospheric landscapes and they gave her a longing for the countryside and the fresh sea air. It was pleasant to be able to escape the bustle of the London Season for a little and step through an imaginary window into another landscape, even if they were in fact in the Royal Academy and Lady Fanshawe was starting to complain that her feet were aching.

'Why do you not take the seat over there, ma'am, if you are fatigued?' she suggested, gesturing to a comfortable banquette placed over by the window. 'I shall not keep you long, but I should just like to see Mr Turner's collection in the blue room. If you would grant me five minutes…'

Lady Fanshawe nodded, sighing with relief as she took the weight off her feet. 'Take as long as you wish, my love,' she said, sitting back and closing her eyes. 'I suggest we call in Bond Street on our way home. Far more to my taste, but one must be seen here, you know!'

Smiling, Beth wandered through to the second gallery. There was quite a fashionable crowd present, bearing out the truth of Lady Fanshawe's statement on the social importance of attending the exhibition. Beth paused before a picture of seascape and gave a small, unconscious sigh. The water was a stormy grey and the clouds were building on the horizon, and far out to sea there was an island…

'Daydreaming, my lady?' The voice, deep and slightly mocking, caught Beth by surprise. She turned her head sharply to meet the quizzical gaze of the Earl of Trevithick. She could feel a vexatious blush rising to her cheeks and looked away swiftly. It was irritating enough that she had spent the last three days waiting for him to call on her, with a secret anticipation that she had not acknowledged even to herself. She had just begun to relax and think that he had forgotten her, when here he was.

'How do you do, my lord.' Beth smiled politely. She tried not to notice how superbly elegant Marcus looked in a coat of green superfine and the fawn pantaloons that clung to his muscular thighs. 'I hope that you are enjoying the exhibition?'

Marcus took her hand. 'To tell the truth, I came here with the sole intention of seeing you, Lady Allerton. I called in Upper Grosvenor Street and was told that you would be here, and I hoped to persuade you to drive with me. It is a very pleasant autumn day and my curricle is outside.'

Beth hesitated. 'Thank you, my lord, but I am here with Lady Fanshawe—'

'I am sure she could be persuaded to entrust you to me.' Marcus smiled down at her. 'That is, if *you* wish to come with me, Lady Allerton. You might not want to break a centuries-old feud, after all!'

Beth could not help laughing. 'How absurd you are, my lord! I believe I might take the risk, but...'

'I know!' Marcus looked apologetic. 'You are quite out of charity with me because of my ungallant refusal to grant you Fairhaven! But now, Lady Allerton...' he bent closer to her '...now you have the opportunity to persuade me! Will you take the challenge?'

Beth looked at him. There was a definite gleam of provocation in his eye. She frowned.

'It seems to me, my lord, that you have the best of both worlds! You have nothing to lose whereas I may wear myself to a shred trying to convince you of my attachment to Fairhaven and still have no influence over you!'

A wicked smile curved Marcus's lips. 'Believe me, Lady Allerton, you have made quite an impression on me already! I would put nothing outside your powers!'

Beth blushed and looked away. 'Pray do not tease so, my lord.'

'Must I not?' Marcus offered her his arm and they started to walk back through the gallery. 'It is difficult to resist. So, will you take my challenge?'

Beth paused. 'I will drive with you. That would be most pleasant.'

'Very proper. You are not always so proper, are you, Lady Allerton?'

'However, I could withdraw my acceptance. Any more of your mockery, my lord—' Beth looked at him severely '—and I shall do so!'

Marcus inclined his head. 'Very well! We shall instigate a truce! You are a most determined person, Lady Allerton. It is quite unusual.'

'Unusual, perhaps. Most certainly imprudent.' Beth spoke wryly. She was thinking of Charlotte and her strictures on her conduct. 'I think it comes from being an only child, my lord. I was much indulged and given my own way. It bred stubbornness in me, I fear. And then, my late husband…'

'Yes?' Marcus slanted a look down at her. Beth sensed that his interest had sharpened and she managed to stop her runaway disclosures just in time.

'Well, he was very kind and indulgent too… generous to me… I was most fortunate.'

'You must have been a child bride,' Marcus observed lightly, after a moment. 'After all, you are scarce in your dotage now! How long have you been widowed, Lady Allerton?'

Beth turned her head so that the brim of her bonnet shielded her from his too-perceptive gaze. Something about this man made her feel vulnerable, as though he could read into her words all the things she did not say.

'Sir Francis died two years ago. Yes, I was very young when I married. My parents had been killed in an accident and I...' Her voice trailed away. She did not want to reveal how lonely she had felt, uncertain if she was making the right decision in marrying hastily. On the one side had been security and on the other... On the other, she had felt as though she was throwing away all her youth and future by marrying a man older than her father. Yet Frank had been a kind husband, as kind to her as to a favourite niece. All she had lacked was excitement.

'I see,' Marcus said, and Beth had the unnerving suspicion that he did indeed see a great deal.

'My dears!' Lady Fanshawe had watched them approach and now rose to her feet, wincing slightly. She greeted the Earl as though he was a family friend of long standing, which Beth found slightly unnerving. She watched with resignation as it took Marcus all of a minute to persuade Lady Fanshawe to his plan.

'If you have offered to take Lady Allerton up with you I am all gratitude, my lord,' Lady Fanshawe trilled, 'for I am sorely in need of a rest! I was intending to call at Bond Street, but fear I do not have the energy! This picture-viewing is unconscionably tiring!'

They went out of the Academy, Marcus calling a hackney carriage to convey Lady Fanshawe home before handing Beth up into his curricle. It was a fine, bright day for autumn and the pale sun was warm. It was pleasant to be driving slowly through the fresh air of the Park, although it seemed to Beth that they were obliged to stop every few yards to greet the Earl's acquaintances. She knew few people in London, so had little to contribute to this social ritual, and after a while she had been introduced to so many new people that her head was spinning.

At last, when they reached a quieter stretch of road, Marcus turned to her with a rueful smile. 'Forgive me. To drive at the fashionable hour precludes sensible conversation!'

'You seem to have a vast number of friends in London, my lord,' Beth said non-committally, thinking of the elegant ladies who had appraised her with curiosity-hard eyes and the sporting gentlemen who had looked her over as though she was a piece of horseflesh.

Marcus smiled. 'I certainly know a lot of people, but as for friends—' he shook his head '—I could count them on the fingers of one hand! But I almost forgot, Lady Allerton...' His gloved hand covered Beth's and her pulse jumped at the contact. 'I cannot count you my friend, for we are sworn enemies, are we not? Will you tell me more about the feud?'

'Oh, the feud...' For a moment, gazing into those dark eyes, Beth was all at sea. She had forgotten all about it. Then she pulled herself together. This was the point of the whole exercise, after all. Somehow she had to persuade Marcus Trevithick of the importance of Fairhaven to her, and becoming distracted by his company was not going to help at all. She pulled her hand away and saw him smile at the gesture.

'I believe that the feud between the Trevithicks and Mostyns dates back to the Civil War, my lord.' Beth cleared her throat and tried to sound businesslike. 'The Mostyns were on the side of the King and the Trevithicks were for Parliament. When Sir James Mostyn went into exile with Charles II, the Trevithicks took the chance to steal—I mean to seize—Mostyn land.'

'Steal will do,' Marcus said lazily. 'I fear the Trevithicks always were thieves and scoundrels, Lady Allerton! But they prospered as a result!'

'To profit by the misfortune of others is not honourable!' Beth said hotly. 'Even worse, at the Restoration, the Mostyns regained a little of their former estate, but the Trevithicks managed to persuade the King of their good faith and were not punished!'

'I can see that you have a very strong sense of fair play, Lady Allerton!' Marcus observed. 'Sadly, the way the Trevithicks prospered is the way that fortunes are often made—through double-dealing!'

Beth looked severe. 'That is no recommendation, my lord!'

'No, I can see that my ancestry is doing me little service here. I sense that worse is to come as well. Pray continue!'

Beth glanced at him doubtfully. Although his tone contained its habitual teasing edge, he was looking quite absorbed. She shifted uncomfortably.

'I hope that the tale does not bore you, my lord?'

'Not in the least! I am all attention!'

Beth realised that this was true. Marcus had loosened his grip on the reins and the horses, very well-behaved thoroughbred bays, were trotting at a decorous pace along the path. All of Marcus's attention was focused on her and as soon as Beth realised it she became acutely aware of the warmth of his regard and the disturbingly intent expression in those dark eyes.

'Well, yes…anyway… For a hundred years the Trevithicks prospered and Mostyns struggled, but they still held Fairhaven Island.' Beth glared at Marcus, forgetting for a moment that he had not been personally responsible for wresting it from her grandfather. It was easy to fall back into the stories of her childhood, the enthralling tales of Trevithick treachery. 'Then my grandfather inherited the estate and came up against your grandfather, my lord, the fifth Earl, George Trevithick.'

'Ah, the Evil Earl. I have heard much of his exploits. They say that in his youth he was in league with the wreckers and the smugglers and the pirates and anyone who could help him make an illegal profit.'

'I have no doubt. What is certainly true is that our grandfathers were implacable enemies, my lord, and had sworn to take their fight to the death. One stormy March night my grandfather was sailing for Fairhaven, not knowing that the Earl had already landed there and that the wreckers were waiting for him. There was a gale blowing and in the dark my grandfather did not realise that the shore lights were not placed there by his servants but were a trick of the enemy.' Beth took a deep breath. 'His ship ran aground and all hands were lost, along with the chest of treasure the ship had been carrying. My grandfather was the only one to escape ashore, but he was ambushed by the Evil Earl and cut down in the fight. Then the Earl stole his sword, the Sword of

Saintonge, that had been in the family for centuries, and took the island into the bargain! Now, what do you think of that, my lord?'

Beth finished, out of breath, and looked at Marcus expectantly. It was a tale for a dark, stormy night rather than a bright day in the park, and it was difficult to believe that either of them were the descendants of men who had struggled to the death for supremacy only fifty years before. That conflict had been ruthless and atavistic, belonging to a previous and less civilised time. Beth allowed herself to consider the man who sat beside her, looking every inch the sophisticated society gentleman. She wondered suddenly just how much of that image was a façade, for she already knew from her dealings with Marcus that if one scratched the surface there was something infinitely more ruthless beneath. As for herself—how far would she go to regain Fairhaven? The stubborn tenacity of the Mostyns was in her blood. Perhaps both of them were true to their ancestry after all.

Marcus encouraged the horses to pick a bit of speed, then turned to Beth with a smile. 'What do I think of it? I cannot deny that it is a tale that reflects no credit on my grandfather. Yet I have some questions for you, Lady Allerton. What was Lord Mostyn doing sailing in such dangerous waters at night? Why did he have his treasure with him? Was there not something slightly suspicious about his own actions?'

Beth stared. In twenty years she had never questioned the detail of the story. She remembered Maddy, her nursemaid, telling her the tale at bedtimes, by the light of the candle in the nursery at Mostyn Hall. She had imagined the perfidious, flickering light of the wreckers' lamp on the cliff, the smashing of the ship's timbers as it broke up on the rocks, the glint of gold as the family treasure tumbled into the depths of the sea... It had never occurred to her to wonder why her grandfather had been carrying so much money on his journey, nor what he had been doing sailing to Fairhaven on a stormy night. Until Marcus had spoken, she had not even thought of it.

Beth wrinkled up her nose, looking at him thoughtfully. 'I must concede that it is odd...'

'Indeed. One is tempted to go to Fairhaven to discover the truth of the whole story!' Marcus flashed her a smile. 'Would you accompany me, Lady Allerton, if I invited you to join me on Fairhaven Island?'

Beth looked scandalised. 'Accompany you? I should think not, my lord! A most improper suggestion!'

Marcus laughed. 'A pity. Yet I do not doubt your loyalty to the notion of regaining Fairhaven for your family.'

Beth clenched her gloved hands together in her lap. 'It is something that I feel I must do, my lord. My grandfather's ghost is unquiet...'

Marcus smiled at her. 'I hope you do not feel that in order to lay the ghost you must foster the quarrel!' Once again he transferred the reins to one hand and put the other over hers. 'I have a feeling, my lady, that you and I might settle this feud once and for all.'

This time Beth let her hand rest still under his. 'I hope that we may, my lord,' she said, deliberately reading nothing into his words. 'Might I suggest that you accept my offer for Fairhaven as a first step? It is a very generous offer...'

'It is.' Marcus let go of her and picked up the reins

again. 'Too generous. Fairhaven cannot possibly be worth such a sum.'

Beth shrugged a little. 'How does one assess sentimental value, my lord? To me, Fairhaven is priceless.'

Marcus smiled. 'I understand that,' he said slowly. 'Fairhaven has become your passion, has it not, Lady Allerton? I wonder just what you would do to achieve that obsession.'

Beth stared at him. Despite the fact that his words only echoed what Charlotte had said to her previously, it was disconcerting to hear them from a relative stranger. It was even more disconcerting to read the double meaning behind them. She looked at him very directly.

'I am not sure that I understand you, my lord. Are you rejecting my offer?'

'I preferred your original one,' Marcus said coolly.

Their gazes locked. The sun disappeared behind a grey cloud and suddenly the wind was chill. Beth shivered inside her pelisse, but it was not entirely from the cold.

'Are you offering me *carte blanche*, my lord?'

Marcus laughed out loud. 'You are very frank, my lady! I was under the impression that the boot had been on the other foot! You set the terms of our wager—'

'You lost the wager,' Beth said swiftly, 'and it is because you did not honour your stake that I am offering so much more!'

'You are offering more financially, I suppose. As I said, I preferred your original—more personal—offer!'

Beth could feel herself blushing and was vexed.

She knew he was deliberately provoking her and was determined to stay calm. It was difficult, however, particularly as a tiny corner of her mind was acknowledging the attractions of such a course of action. To offer herself to Marcus in return for Fairhaven Island. It was immoral. It was iniquitous. And it was definitely tempting…

She frowned.

'The wager was a means to an end, my lord! It is not my usual mode of behaviour to offer myself as part of a bargain!'

'I see.' Marcus had allowed the curricle to come to a halt under the bare branches of a spreading oak tree. 'In that case it was a remarkably dangerous wager.'

'It was.' Beth held his gaze. 'However, if I had lost, I had only to refuse to honour my stake—as you did, my lord!'

'Touché!' Marcus laughed again. 'I must confess myself disappointed, Lady Allerton. I was hoping that you might be persuaded—'

'Were you? You cannot know me very well, then, my lord!' By now there was a warning glint in Beth's eye. 'I have told you that I am no courtesan! I wish you take me home now, if you please!'

'Very well!' Marcus's tone betrayed amused admiration. 'I will not tease you any further, my lady. And if it is true that I do not know you well, time can at least remedy that situation!'

The thought gave Beth little comfort. In the first place, she had a strange and disturbing conviction that Marcus did in fact understand her very well, for all his teasing. As for his pledge to know her better, her instinct told her that that could be a very perilous enterprise indeed.

Chapter Three

Another country dance came to an end and Beth applauded enthusiastically and accepted the escort of her partner back to Lady Fanshawe's side. It was very hot in the Duchess of Calthorpe's ballroom for there were at least two hundred guests and the event was assured of the accolade of being a crush. The Duchess had chosen white as her theme to create the impression of approaching winter, and it was ironic that the temperature resembled that of the tropics. Hundreds of white candles added to the heat in the ballroom, creating such a fire risk that footmen were stationed about the room with buckets of water.

'Are you enjoying yourself, my love?' Lady Fanshawe fanned herself vigorously. 'It is such a sad crush in here, I declare there is barely a spare rout chair to be had! And all this white is quite dazzling to the eye!'

Beth giggled. As well as the white candles there were filmy white draperies that were threatening to catch fire and droopy white lilies that evidently preferred a cooler climate.

'You are in looks tonight, my dear,' Lady

Fanshawe continued. 'That lilac muslin is very pretty and stands out well amongst the debutantes. Poor girls, I fear they will melt into the draperies!'

'In more ways than one!' Beth agreed, gratefully accepting a glass of lemonade from Mr Porson, who had been partnering her in the previous dance. He was a worthy young man and he showed signs of lingering at her side, which Beth did not particularly mind. At least she felt safe with him.

'Mr Porson, do you think—?' she began, only to raise her eyebrows in surprise as the young man shot away with barely a word of farewell. Kit Mostyn came up and took the vacated rout chair at his cousin's side.

'Good gracious, Kit!' Beth said crossly. 'What sort of reputation do you have that scares away my innocent admirers? Poor Mr Porson was only indulging in conversation!'

'I doubt that it was my arrival that scared him off,' Kit said drily. 'The Earl of Trevithick has just come in, Beth. Porson won't want to be seen trespassing on Trevithick's ground!'

Beth glanced quickly at the doorway and looked away equally quickly, conscious that plenty of people were watching her. She was unhappily aware that she had become the talk of the town during the previous ten days, all as a result of Marcus Trevithick's attentions. They had driven in the park twice, attended a concert and fireworks at Vauxhall, met at a musical soirée and danced at a couple of balls. That had been sufficient to set tongues wagging and it seemed to Beth that Marcus had done nothing to quell the speculation. He had behaved entirely correctly towards her on all occasions, and yet Beth was aware of something beneath the veneer of convention, something entirely more exciting and dangerous in his attitude towards her.

The interest of the *ton* was piqued because of the family feud and also because the Dowager Viscountess of Trevithick had made her disapproval of Beth very plain. Only the previous night, the Dowager had cut her dead at the opera and Beth had decided that she would have to avoid Marcus in future. This was not entirely because of his mother's attitude but also because of some belated sense of self-preservation. Beth knew that she found Marcus all too attractive and she had heard something of his reputation and did not want to become another conquest. Now, however, her resolution put her in an awkward situation, for to shun Marcus's company at the ball would be remarked upon. Beth fidgeted, drumming her fingers on the arm of the chair as she tried to decide what to do.

She saw Marcus start to cross the room towards her. He had paused to speak to an acquaintance but Beth saw that although he was talking to the man, he was still watching her with a deliberation that was most disturbing. She got hastily to her feet.

'Kit, will you dance with me, please?'

Kit looked pained. 'Must I? If this is some elaborate charade to avoid Trevithick—'

'Kit!' Beth frowned at her cousin's lack of tact. 'How can you be so unchivalrous? Even if it is, I still need your help!'

Kit grinned at her. 'I only meant to warn you that Trevithick would not be fobbed off! By all means let us dance if we must!'

He took her arm and led her away from Marcus

Trevithick, joining the set that was at the furthest end of the ballroom.

'I saw you talking to Eleanor Trevithick when her mother's back was turned,' Beth said slyly, as they took their places. 'If you seek to warn me, perhaps you will take some advice in turn? I hope you do not have a *tendre* there, Kit, for you must be doomed to disappointment!'

She had the satisfaction of seeing a hint of colour come into Kit's lean cheek. He avoided her gaze. 'Don't know what you mean, Beth! Miss Trevithick is a charming girl, but I have no interest there!'

Beth smiled beatifically. 'Of course not! How foolish of me even to imagine that you did!'

'It's bad enough having Charlotte dispensing advice,' Kit said gloomily, 'without my honorary sister joining in as well!'

They danced in perfect accord, though Beth found that she had to concentrate on her steps rather more than usual. Her gaze was drawn with tiresome repetitiveness to the tall figure of Marcus Trevithick as he threaded his way through the crowd and joined his mother and sister over by one of the long terrace windows. It seemed that some strange compulsion made it well nigh impossible for Beth to ignore him, for even when she was not looking at Marcus she sensed exactly where he was. It was only when Justin Trevithick came up to the family group and he and Marcus headed towards the card room that Beth started to relax, but by then the dance was ending. Kit bowed to her, then hastened away to claim another lady for the boulanger.

Beth was about to rejoin Lady Fanshawe, when she saw Marcus emerge unexpectedly from the card room

again and start walking towards her through the
crowd. She immediately dived towards the door and
took refuge in the ladies' withdrawing room, where
she fretted and fidgeted for twenty minutes, uncertain
whether Marcus would simply be waiting in the corridor outside. He was not. Wrestling with a mixture
of relief and disappointment, Beth tiptoed back into
the ballroom and saw that Marcus was now dancing
with Eleanor. She made her way back to Lady
Fanshawe's corner of the room, only to find that her
chaperon had disappeared.

Beth sat down, feeling a little self-conscious. She
could see Kit, who was dancing with a plump debutante in a pink gown, but was looking over her shoulder all the time at Eleanor Trevithick. So much for
his denials of an interest there! Beth smiled to herself.
It seemed that she and her cousin were both caught
in the same trap.

The crush in the ballroom was lessening now as
some of the guests moved on to other engagements,
and without the camouflage of the huge crowd Beth
felt strangely vulnerable. She watched as the dance
ended and saw Marcus look around and fix on her
with an almost uncanny accuracy. In a candlelit room
of a hundred and fifty people it seemed unreasonable
that he was able to pick her out so quickly, but she
did not feel she had time to stop and think about the
implications. She started to edge towards the doors
that led out on to the terrace, then paused, thinking
that it would probably not be a good idea to wander
out into the dark, especially on a cold autumn night.
If Marcus decided to follow her they would end up
playing hide-and-seek in the gardens and who could
say where that would end. Glancing over her shoul-

der, Beth saw that he was getting closer to her, moving with a purposeful intent that was most disconcerting. She skittered along the edge of the dance floor, almost tripping over in her attempts to put some more distance between them. What she really needed now was someone to ask her to dance. Someone, anyone…

'Would you care to dance, Lady Allerton?'

Beth turned sharply, her grateful acceptance withering on her lips as she looked up into the smiling face of Justin Trevithick. Out of the frying pan and into the fire. She was certain that Justin had seen her trying to avoid Marcus, but she was also aware that she could not refuse to dance with him without seeming dreadfully rude.

'Oh, Mr Trevithick! I…yes…thank you, sir…'

Beth had met Justin several times in the previous ten days and had taken to him immediately, liking his sense of humour and easygoing manner. Just now, however, she was wishing him at the bottom of the sea. Dancing with Marcus's cousin was getting too close to Marcus for comfort. She looked round and saw that Marcus was now speaking to a fashionable matron in striped red and white silk. He looked engrossed and suddenly Beth began to feel rather silly. Perhaps Marcus had never intended to approach her at all and all her diversions had served no purpose other than to make her look foolish. Probably she was flattering herself by imagining that he had ever shown any real interest in her.

Justin was waiting, a look of speculative amusement in his eyes. Beth hastily wiped all expression from her face and gave him her hand. She was pleased that she managed to keep up a tolerably bright conversation throughout the polonaise, only faltering slightly when she observed Marcus and the stripily clad matron disappearing through the door together. That was that, then. Evidently Marcus had found company more to his taste and had retired to enjoy it in privacy. Beth felt even more out of countenance at the unedifying jealousy that swept through her.

At the end of the dance, Justin guided her off the floor and into the refreshment room.

'May I fetch you a glass of lemonade, ma'am?' he suggested. 'It may be a tame sort of beverage but is just the thing in a hot climate like this! If you take a seat in this alcove I will undertake to be back directly.'

Beth sank gratefully onto the window seat. It was fresher here with a pleasant draught of air that cooled her heated face. She rested her head against the stone window casing and closed her eyes. The noise of the ball swirled around her but she took no notice.

'Your lemonade, Lady Allerton.'

Beth jumped so much that she almost banged her head against the stone. The voice was not Justin Trevithick's, but the deeper tones of his cousin the Earl. Sure enough, Marcus was standing before her, a glass of lemonade in one hand, watching her with the same quizzically amused expression that he had been wearing all evening. Beth felt at a disadvantage and tried to get to her feet, but she found that Marcus was standing too close to her and that any movement would bring her into physical contact with him. This did not seem a very good idea, so she leant back instead and took the lemonade from him with an assumption of ease.

'Thank you very much. How do you do, Lord Trevithick?'

Marcus gave her his devastating smile. 'I am all the better now that I have finally caught up with you, Lady Allerton! I thought that I would never achieve it!'

'I was expecting your cousin's company—' Beth began.

'And did not want to have to tolerate mine instead? I fear I persuaded him to exchange places with me.' Marcus shrugged lightly. 'Now that I finally have you to myself, Lady Allerton, I would be obliged if you would keep still for at least a minute! I would like to speak with you!'

Beth shifted guiltily on the window seat. There was little chance of her escaping anywhere since Marcus was now leaning against the alcove embrasure and comprehensively blocking her retreat.

'In that case you had better sit down,' she said coolly, 'and cease looming over me in that threatening manner!'

Marcus grinned and sat down next to her. 'I will do as you ask on the understanding that you will not run away! What has all that ridiculous rigmarole been about this evening—dodging out of rooms, hiding away, avoiding even looking in my direction—?'

'When I did look in your direction I thought you most preoccupied!' Beth said tartly, before she could stop herself. 'I am surprised that you noticed me at all!'

Marcus laughed. 'I collect that you are referring to me stepping aside with a lady just now? That is my elder sister, Lady Grace Walters. She found the heat too overpowering in the ballroom and needed some fresh air.'

Beth looked away, feeling foolish. 'I am sure that I do not care—'

'Well, you do, or you would not have quizzed me about it!' Marcus sat back on the window seat and stretched his long legs out in front of him. 'And you still have not answered my question, Lady Allerton. What was all that play-acting for?'

Beth flushed. 'I thought it best to avoid you,' she said candidly, trying to look him in the eye. 'There has been so much speculation about our...' She hesitated, trying to think of the right word to describe their relationship.

'Our friendship?' Marcus supplied helpfully.

'Friendship. Yes, thank you. So much speculation about our friendship, my lord, that I thought it best to subdue it by—'

'By creeping about like an actor in a bad play? You have caused so *much* speculation tonight by your strategies for avoiding me that I am amazed you are not aware of it!'

'Well, if it comes to that, you have hardly suppressed the gossip by cornering me in this alcove!' Beth said, firing up. 'It seems to me that you positively enjoy stirring up scandal, my lord!'

Marcus shrugged his broad shoulders. 'I confess that I seldom regard it. As you should not, my lady! Why should the tabbies concern you? I am minded to kiss you here and now and see what the scandalmongers make of that!'

Beth recoiled slightly. 'Do not jest, my lord!'

'Why should I be jesting? You did not object to kissing me before!'

Beth blushed scarlet. 'My lord! Kindly lower your voice—'

'Come and speak with me in private, then. I want to talk to you about your offer for Fairhaven. It is time that we settled the matter.'

Beth gave him a very direct look. 'I do not believe you, sir! This is just a trick! In fact, I do not trust you! At all!'

'Why not?' Marcus grinned. 'Because the last time we were private together we shared more than just a conversation—'

Beth waved her hands about in mute appeal. 'I believe you must be inebriated to speak thus, my lord—'

Marcus captured both her hands in one of his. 'Not in the slightest! But if you will not speak with me, come and dance with me instead!'

He had already pulled her to her feet and was steering her through the crowded room with one hand resting lightly in the small of her back. Beth was sharply conscious of his tall figure close beside her, so close that her skirt brushed against his thigh as they walked. She tried to move away a little but found that the press of people forced them together. She could feel the warmth of his touch through the thin muslin of her dress, and suddenly she felt hot and vulnerable. It was no state in which to begin a dance, and when Beth heard the waltz striking up she almost turned tail and fled.

'No need to look so terrified, sweetheart,' Marcus murmured in her ear. His voice was warm and persuasive. 'I promise to behave!'

A strange shiver went down Beth's spine. She did not dare look at him. She reluctantly moved into his arms and felt only slightly relieved when Marcus held her at an irreproachable distance from his own body and made no attempt to draw her closer.

They started to circle the floor in time to the lilting rhythm of the music. The faces of the guests spun past them, curious, avid, amused, sharp, and spiteful... It seemed to Beth that the music was whirling faster and faster and that the flickering candlelight washed over them like a kaleidoscope of black and white. Marcus's face was in shadow, his expression inscrutable, almost distant. Yet despite his apparent coolness Beth could feel a current of heat running between them, intense and strong. She shivered again, convulsively.

Beth had intended to keep a decorous distance between them and to avoid the intimacy of conversation during the waltz, but some compulsion made her glance up into Marcus's face as they completed their second circuit of the floor. His gaze met hers for a split second and now it was dark and heavy with a passion he made no attempt to conceal. Beth caught her breath on a little gasp and almost lost her footing. Immediately Marcus's arms tightened about her, pulling her into sudden and shocking contact with his body. His cheek brushed hers, hard against the softness of her skin, causing a feeling of helpless, wanton warmth to flood through her. Beth shuddered in his arms, unable to prevent her body betraying her with its trembling. She saw Marcus's lips curve into a smile, felt his own body harden with arousal against hers and thought that she might well faint with shock and sheer, sensual delight, there in the Duchess of Calthorpe's ballroom in front of one hundred and fifty people. It was terrifying but also strangely exhilarating all at the same time, and she was thoroughly confused. She did not risk looking at Marcus again.

The music was ending, the waltzing couples slowing down, breaking apart and walking away. The chatter rose around her and the room suddenly seemed brighter. Beth tried to break free of Marcus's grip, intent only on putting a little distance between them, but he held on to her, keeping her close.

'You must give me a moment...' his voice was husky '...if you are not to embarrass me...'

The colour flamed into Beth's face. She allowed him to guide her skilfully to the edge of the dance floor, where she plied her fan and desperately tried to think of an innocuous topic of conversation. Her mind was dazed, cloudy with desire, and all she could think of was what had happened between them and how she was still trembling with an echo of the passion she had seen in his eyes.

'It is very warm,' she said uncertainly, and was relieved to see amusement replace the sensual heat in Marcus's face.

'Certainly it is very hot in here,' he drawled, 'and between us, Lady Allerton, I should say that it is almost too hot for comfort!'

Beth's gaze flew uncertainly to his face, but before she could answer, Justin Trevithick appeared, escorting Lady Fanshawe. Beth was tolerably certain that Marcus's cousin had summed up the situation with one comprehensive glance, for his gaze moved from her face to Marcus's and his eyebrows rose fractionally as he picked up on the tension between them. Fortunately Lady Fanshawe was decidedly less perceptive.

'There you are, my dear! You know that we are

promised to Lady Baynton's rout and positively must put in an appearance before the night ends!' She beamed at Marcus and Justin. 'Do you gentlemen wish to accompany us, or do you have other plans?'

Beth felt Marcus's gaze rest on her. It was not difficult to imagine just what other plans he might have for her. She schooled her face to remain blank, annoyed that he seemed to be able to make her blush at the slightest provocation.

'Thank you, ma'am, but I believe we are for White's,' Justin was saying, with a smile. 'May we escort you to your carriage?'

It felt cold outside after the stifling heat of the ballroom. Beth drew her velvet cloak more closely around her and tried not to shiver. Marcus kissed her hand before helping her up into the coach, and murmured that he hoped to call on her the following day. She was almost at a loss for a reply, half-longing to see him again, half-afraid of the feelings he could evoke in her.

As she settled back in the coach, Beth reflected that it seemed strange now, but she realised that she had barely given a moment's thought to physical passion in her whole life. She had married almost from the schoolroom and had considered herself happy with Frank Allerton, but he had rarely troubled her for his marital rights and had treated her with all the indulgence of a fond parent. No hint of passion had disturbed the even tenor of their relationship. From the vague comments that Charlotte had occasionally made, Beth had realised that there could be a great deal more to marriage than she had shared with Frank, but she had largely dismissed such matters as simply not for her. She had met a few personable men during her widowhood and had even enjoyed the company of some of them, but had never felt moved to indulge in a love affair. She realised now that she had even begun to believe that she was simply not very interested in love.

Then Marcus had kissed her and it felt as though a whole new side of her personality, both emotional and physical, had been brought to life. Curled up in a corner of the carriage, listening vaguely to Lady Fanshawe's chatter, Beth reflected that Marcus had awoken something she had not even been aware was sleeping: a hunger to experience emotion and passion in vivid detail.

And it was the first of these that was the problem. If she had only wanted to take a lover, matters would have been simple. Marcus was there and he was eminently suitable, eminently desirable as a lover. Beth felt the warmth steal over her again. It was a tempting thought, yet she knew that she could not accept it. Newly awakened, her feelings were craving satisfaction as much as her body was, and the thought was terrifying. Against her better judgement she liked Marcus. She enjoyed his company, his conversation, his humour. She knew she was in danger of loving him, too quickly, careless of the risk. It was in her nature to be impulsive, but on this one occasion she had to be more careful and protect herself against this danger. For though she knew Marcus wanted her, she could not be confident that his feelings were engaged any more deeply than that. It hurt her to think it, but she knew she was right.

'Would you mind if we do not go on to Lady Baynton's rout, dear ma'am?' she asked Lady

Fanshawe in a small voice. 'I am a little fatigued and would prefer the quiet of going home.'

Her godmother shot her a concerned look. 'Of course, my love. You do look rather done up! I suppose that it is country living—you are simply not prepared for such a dizzy round of events as we indulge in here in town!' Lady Fanshawe fidgeted with her reticule. Her voice changed a little. 'Beth, dear, I do not mean to pry, but I feel I should warn you about the Earl of Trevithick…'

Beth shifted slightly on the seat. 'There is no need to warn me, ma'am,' she said sadly. 'No need at all.'

'Beth, I do declare you are in a brown study this morning!' Charlotte Cavendish put down the dress she was holding and viewed her cousin with a puzzled eye. 'I asked you if you preferred the mauve or the green and you said both! Are you not feeling in plump currant? You need only say if you wish us to stop!'

Beth shook herself. They had been wading their way through the dizzying pile of goods sent round that morning by the Bond Street modistes. There were dresses, shawls and spencers, scarves and tippets, stockings and petticoats, gloves, fans and hats. The crimson saloon looked like an eastern bazaar and Beth felt utterly unequal to choosing anything from the selection. Not that her mind was on the task in hand. Not at all. She had spent the best part of the night and most of the morning dwelling on Marcus Trevithick; on his high-handed manner and his infuriatingly mocking tone, on the dark face that could soften into a warmth that took her breath away, on the forceful attraction of a man who was quite beyond her experience. Any minute she was expecting—hoping—that the bell would ring and he would have fulfilled his promise to call on her. And at the same time she was thinking that to foster any hopes of him was the greatest folly.

'The pale blue suits you to perfection, Lottie,' she said hastily, admiring the way that the figured silk mirrored her cousin's bright eyes, 'and I would take the ivory muslin and the grey as well.'

'That is all very well for me, but what about you?' Charlotte questioned. 'You do not seem very interested, Beth, and this is the finest that Bond Street has to offer!'

Beth let a pale green scarf float through her fingers and stood up, moving over to the window. 'I am sorry. I think I am a little tired from last night. We were back very late, you know, and I did not sleep particularly well.'

Charlotte frowned a little. 'I wish I could come with you to all the parties and balls, Beth! Lady Fanshawe is the sweetest person imaginable, but I am not entirely sure she is up to snuff! Why, she told me she was hoping that Sir Edmund Netherwood might make an offer for you, when everyone knows he is the most tiresome old fortune-hunter and has been through three wives and their dowries already!'

Beth giggled. 'You need have no fears on that score, Lottie!' She sobered. 'All the same, it would be so much more fun if you could accompany me about town. I do not like to think of you sitting here on your own whilst Kit and I set the town by the ears!'

'Speaking of which, Lady Fanshawe said that you met with the Earl of Trevithick at the ball,' Charlotte said casually, examining the stitching on a fine pair of kid gloves. 'She said that he was most attentive, Beth!'

Beth blushed. She looked away, down into the street, where a flower-seller was just setting up a stall on the corner opposite.

'Yes... I... Well, I could not really avoid him...'

'Oh, Beth! Did you really want to?'

Beth raised troubled grey eyes to her cousin's blue ones. 'No, not really.' She spoke in a rush. 'I like Lord Trevithick a great deal, Lottie, but I am afraid...'

Charlotte was folding up the material, but now she let her hands rest in her lap. 'Afraid? Of how you feel about him?' she asked shrewdly.

Beth nodded, avoiding her gaze. 'He is just so very different from Frank!'

Charlotte laughed. 'I should say so!'

The doorbell shrilled, making them both jump. Carrick, the butler, strode into the room, carrying a flat packet wrapped in brown paper and tied with string. He proffered it to Beth.

'This parcel has arrived from the Earl of Trevithick, madam. There is also a note...'

Beth shot Charlotte a startled look, and then tore open the envelope. Inside was a single sheet of paper, written in the strong scrawl that she had come to recognise:

Dear Lady Allerton

I enclose your winnings. I have every intention of regaining them in time, however. Pray do not flee London for Devon before I have time to call upon you.

Until then,

Trevithick

The note drifted to the floor as Beth slit the parcel with her letter opener. Her fingers shook slightly.

Inside was a document, dated that very morning, granting the Island of Fairhaven in the Bristol Channel to Elizabeth, Lady Allerton, and her heirs in perpetuity. Again, it was signed in a strong black hand with the one word, Trevithick. There was also a bundle of other papers, some of them ancient manuscripts written in Latin on paper so old and thin that the light shone through. Beth riffled through them in disbelief, seeing the history of her beloved island so suddenly and unexpectedly in her hands.

Charlotte had picked up the note and was reading it. She looked doubtfully from the letter to Beth and back again.

'Oh, no! I cannot believe that the Earl is prepared to humour you in this mad obsession!'

Beth could not quite believe it either. 'I suppose that it does not matter to him,' she said, a little breathlessly. 'He has so many other estates more valuable. Fairhaven has only its sentimental worth, and that only matters to me!'

'I wonder what he means by saying that he intends to regain Fairhaven,' Charlotte said thoughtfully, 'and what he wants in return for his gift!'

Beth looked up, startled.

'Why, nothing! He is paying his debt, that is all! He lost the wager—'

'Do not remind me of it!' Her cousin pursed her lips. There was a twinkle in her eye. 'Sometimes you are so naïve, my love! In my experience there is no such thing as something for nothing! Ten to one, Trevithick has some kind of bargain in mind! It might be that he seeks your good opinion, which would be reassuring, or it might be that his intentions are dishonourable.'

Beth could feel herself blushing again. She had not told Charlotte that the Earl had already offered her *carte blanche*, for she knew it would only fuel her cousin's fears. 'Oh, no, I cannot believe—' She met Charlotte's sceptical gaze. 'Well, perhaps…'

'You know you suspect it yourself!' Charlotte said drily. 'What exactly happened during that wager, Beth?'

Beth felt herself blush harder. 'Why, nothing! Only…' She evaded Charlotte's penetrating gaze. 'I suppose he did…does…perhaps admire me a little…'

'Quite so. That being the case, I think you should be careful. Trevithick is not a man with whom to indulge in an idle flirtation! He is far too dangerous!'

Beth was momentarily distracted. 'Is he? I was not aware that his reputation was *so* bad.'

'You never are,' Charlotte said, with a sigh. 'Remember that fortune hunter who tried to attach your interest at the Exeter Assembly? You thought him a very pleasant fellow, as I recall—'

'Oh, but he was not in the least like Lord Trevithick!'

'No,' Charlotte said, opening the door, 'he was harmless! Just take care, Beth!'

She went out. Beth picked up all the documents and walked over to the window seat, sitting down in the mid-morning sun. Outside the street was busy with vendors and passers-by.

She put the papers down on her lap and gazed out at the jumbled spires and rooftops stretching into the distance. It felt very claustrophobic to be cooped up in London in the autumn. It was a season in which to ride across the fields and feel the sharp breeze on her face, to stand on the cliff tops and look out across the sea, to walk along the beach and hear the hiss of the waves on the sand.

Beth looked down at the papers again. She realised that she felt decidedly odd, but could not work out why. Perhaps it was the shock of having her heart's desire suddenly thrust into her hands, or that the pleasure of owning Fairhaven had overcome her. But it did not feel like that. She realised that she had wanted Marcus to talk to her about it, to tell her what he intended. Now she felt oddly cheated. She had what she wanted but she was uncomfortable about it. And she was not entirely sure why.

The reading room at White's was very quiet that morning and it was proving a most pleasant oasis of calm for Marcus after an eventful breakfast at Trevithick House. The Dowager Viscountess, mindful of her elder son's behaviour at the ball the night before, had rung a peal over him for his lack of filial duty. It was her expressed view that the Trevithicks had not fostered a feud with the Mostyns for two hundred and fifty years simply for Marcus to disregard it by paying attention to a fast little widow, no matter how rich. Marcus, incensed to hear his mother speak so slightingly of Beth, had thrown down his napkin and departed the house forthwith, fortunately bumping into Justin in St James's. The two of them had retired to White's where Justin promptly fell asleep and Marcus buried himself in the *Morning Chronicle*. After half an hour, Marcus stirred his cousin with his foot. 'How much did you win last night, Justin? When I left you were ten thousand guineas up against Warrender. Did you make enough to pay off that voracious opera singer you had in keeping?'

'Twenty-five thousand, all told,' Justin muttered, without opening his eyes. He slumped down further in his chair. 'I took the money and Warrender took the girl off my hands! She was sweet, but too much of a handful!'

Marcus laughed. 'Seems you struck a good bargain! So, are you clearing your decks in order to settle down, old fellow?'

'Devil a bit!' Justin yawned. He opened his eyes and squinted at Marcus. 'Thought you were the one about to be caught in parson's mousetrap!'

Marcus raised his eyebrows. 'Are you trying to marry me off by any chance, old chap? Only last night you were singing Lady Allerton's praises!'

'No harm in marrying a fortune,' Justin said laconically, straightening up. 'Good money but bad blood in that family! Not that the Trevithicks should criticise the Mostyns! Pirates and thieves, the lot of them!'

'Call me fastidious, but I would not care to marry for money,' Marcus said slowly.

Justin bent a perceptive look on him. 'Ah, but you wouldn't be, would you, Marcus? Never seen you more smitten, old fellow! After all, you've never given away an island before, have you?'

Marcus smiled, but did not trouble to reply. Justin knew him too well to be fooled, but equally he had no intention of discussing his matrimonial plans just yet. He shifted a little in his chair as he thought of Beth. He would call on her in a little while and take her driving. He wanted to talk to her about Fairhaven, make her promise that she would not rush away from London to inspect her new property. His smile deepened as he imagined how excited she would be to have the island in her possession. It pleased him to make her happy and it was a feeling he was not accustomed to. He had always been generous in a careless, casual way, but this protective desire to take care of someone else was entirely new. He grinned. Damn it, he must be getting old, wanting to marry and set up his nursery...

A servant was approaching them with a folded note on a silver tray. The man's face wore a rather pained expression, as though he had been entrusted with an errand that was in poor taste.

'Excuse me, my lord. A person by the name of Gower is without. He asks if you might spare him a moment of your time...'

Marcus raised his eyebrows. He had seen Gower only the previous day when his man of business had reluctantly presented him with the deed of gift by which Marcus had signed Fairhaven away. Gower had begged him to be prudent, to reconsider, to wait... And Marcus, impatient to make Beth happy, had signed the document and sent it round immediately, ignoring Gower's advice. He knew that something untoward must have happened for Gower to seek him out at White's. Wondering if it was to do with Fairhaven or some completely unrelated matter, Marcus felt his own apprehension growing.

The man of business was waiting for him out in the street, turning his hat round between his hands in the gesture he always employed when he was worried or nervous. On this occasion Marcus judged him to be both of these things.

'My lord,' he said jerkily, looking from Marcus to Justin and back again, 'forgive me for disturbing you, but the matter was most urgent. I would not have troubled you else—'

'That is understood, Gower,' Marcus said shortly. 'What is the difficulty?'

'My lord…' Gower looked unhappy. 'There are documents I feel you should see, matters that have come to light—'

'Matters to do with Fairhaven Island?' Justin interposed, his gaze keen. Marcus felt his heart sink as Gower nodded his head.

'Matters concerning Fairhaven—and Lady Allerton, I fear, sir.'

'Well, we cannot stand here in the street discussing it,' Marcus snapped. 'Gower, your rooms are more appropriate than Trevithick House. We will go there.'

They walked to Gower's rooms in Chancery Lane in an uneasy silence. Gower ushered them into his office and a clerk who had been working at the desk moved unobtrusively away. Gower carefully moved some stacks of papers from the chairs and invited the gentlemen to take a seat, but Marcus ignored the suggestion.

'Thank you, I prefer to stand,' he said tersely. 'Now, what is this matter that is of such import, Gower?'

Gower resumed his seat behind his large mahogany desk. He moved a few documents to the right, picked one up, put it down again, then moved the pile left. Marcus felt his nerves tightening.

'For God's sake, man, just get on with it—'

He saw Justin shoot him a warning glance and tried to get a hold on his temper. Shouting at Gower would do no good and the man was only doing his job anyway. Marcus knew that he needed a pernickety lawyer to attend to all the matters that held no interest for him, but when he wondered what Gower was about to tell him about Beth he felt the cold seep through him like water on stone.

'Yes, my lord,' Gower said expressionlessly. He settled his half-moon spectacles on his nose. Behind the lenses his eyes gleamed palely. He picked up the document on the top of the pile and cleared his throat.

'On the matter of Fairhaven Island, my lord… Several weeks ago, when you first mooted the possibility that you might cede the island to Lady Allerton, I instigated some investigations—' Gower's pale eyes flashed '—all in your best interests, my lord.'

'Of course,' Marcus said politely. He resisted the impulse to take the lawyer by the throat and shake him. 'Pray continue, Gower.'

'Yes, my lord. I discovered that the possibility of a sale of Fairhaven had first been suggested some twenty years ago, when Sir Frank Allerton approached your grandfather, the late Earl.'

Marcus shifted impatiently. 'What of it, Gower?'

The lawyer shuffled the papers again. 'It seems that Sir Frank was a notable mineralogist, my lord, and suspected that there might well be valuable resources on the island, mineral deposits that would justify the cost and difficulties of mining there.'

Justin gave a low whistle. 'There cannot be many substances that would be worth such an effort, Gower.'

'No, sir.' Gower permitted himself a small, prim smile. 'Naturally enough, Sir Frank did not inform the late Earl of his precise interest in Fairhaven, but information that subsequently fell into my hands…' the lawyer looked slightly shifty '…suggested that the substance under discussion was gold.'

Marcus expelled his breath sharply. He did not speak, but turned away to look out of the dusty window. There were some pigeons pecking in the gutter opposite. In the room behind him he heard Justin say carefully, 'Would you say that Sir Frank was well informed on the mineral potential of the Devon area, Gower?'

Marcus swung back round. 'Of course he was,' he said abruptly. 'Why, even I know that Sir Frank Allerton was a distinguished expert on such matters! In addition to work in his native county, he was looking to develop the Somerset coal field and held considerable concessions in the Cornish tin mines—'

'Concessions which his widow still holds,' Gower finished quietly.

Marcus leant on the desk. 'Very well, Gower. I believe you have reached the crux of your story, have you not?'

The lawyer looked unhappy. 'Perhaps so, my lord.' He took a deep breath. 'My lord, I do wish you to know that I am only looking after your best interests—'

'It is understood,' Marcus said tersely. His mouth was set in a grim line. 'Please go on.'

'Very well, my lord. As you are aware, your grandfather did not choose to sell Fairhaven to Sir Frank, claiming that he had only just wrested the place from the ''cursed Mostyn brood'', as he put it, and had no wish to give it up so easily. He had neither the money nor the inclination to explore the island's potential himself, but was content to leave it unexploited for the following years.' Gower looked up. 'There is an ancient castle there, my lord, as well as a farm and a rudimentary village. If you recall, your uncle St John Trevithick holds the living there and he and your aunt Trevithick live in the castle. I last visited it some two years ago, when your factor, Mr McCrae—'

'Please get to the point, Gower,' Marcus said wearily, subsiding into the chair opposite Justin. He saw his cousin's look of concern and flashed him a brief smile. 'Forgive my abruptness, but what is really of concern is the nature of your allegations against Lady Allerton.' He stopped and looked at the lawyer. 'For I believe that you have some.'

'Yes, my lord,' Gower said again. The paper in his hand shook slightly. 'Some two years ago, shortly after the death of her husband, Lady Allerton petitioned the Earl to buy Fairhaven.'

Marcus raised his eyebrows. 'Yes? She has told me as much.'

'Indeed, my lord.' The lawyer's voice was dry. 'She approached your grandfather twice, in point of fact, and after he refused her offer a second time, she wrote to tell him that she would resort to whatever methods necessary to gain the island. I remember the Earl laughing and saying she was a spirited little filly with more mettle than the rest of her family put together! But for all that he thought it unbecoming that such a young lady should involve herself in business matters, for all that she brought her lawyer with her— the self-same man whom Sir Frank had always used to negotiate his mining ventures.'

Justin shifted uncomfortably. Marcus's eyes narrowed on the lawyer's face. 'I do not find that in any way surprising, Gower. If the man were acting for Sir Frank it would be natural for Lady Allerton to retain his services in matters relating to the estate. It does not mean that she retained an active interest—'

He broke off at the look on the lawyer's face. 'No, my lord,' Gower said lugubriously. 'However, when Lady Allerton was out of the room, the man apparently told your grandfather quite openly that it was their intention to pursue Sir Frank's ambitions on Fairhaven. Lady Allerton still retains the same lawyer,' he added quietly, 'a gentleman by the name of Gough, as you know, my lord. As soon as you mentioned to me the matter of the wager for Fairhaven I was suspicious, my lord, and even more so when I discovered that Gough was involved.'

Marcus let out a long breath. He could see both Gower and Justin watching him with similar sympathetic looks and felt the anger rise in him. It seemed that he had made a fine fool of himself over Beth Allerton and was in danger of appearing even more foolish by his unwillingness to believe badly of her. He remembered the passion with which she had spoken of her love of Fairhaven, the way she had related the tales of her childhood, her fervent intention to regain her patrimony. It seemed that it had all been assumed to hide a more avaricious reason, a convenient tale to make him sympathise with her, to bewitch him, as she had done so subtly, with her smoky grey eyes and her soft, sweet body and her conniving mind. He clenched his fists.

'Is there any more, Gower?'

'Only that I have heard this very morning that

Christopher Mostyn has been approaching various backers for a new commercial venture,' the lawyer said slowly. 'It was then that I felt I had to lay all this matter before your lordship. I understand that Lady Allerton signed over all active interests in her late husband's business to Lord Mostyn, although she shares in the profits.'

'And the plans,' Marcus said grimly. 'Could this new venture be the mining of Fairhaven, Gower?'

'I do not know, my lord,' the lawyer said truthfully, 'but it might well be.'

There was a silence.

'It does not look good,' Justin said carefully, after a moment. He put a hand on his cousin's arm. 'I am sorry, Marcus…'

Marcus shook him off and stood up. 'There is no need. Gower, I am obliged to you for your information. Justin…' he turned to his cousin '…we have a call to make, I think. In Upper Grosvenor Street. I will take back the deeds to Fairhaven and give that devious little witch a piece of my mind!'

Chapter Four

'Excuse me, my lady.' Carrick, Beth's butler, had come into the red drawing room and was looking rather dubious. 'The Earl of Trevithick is here and is asking—rather strongly, my lady—that you should receive him.' The butler's frown deepened. 'There is another gentleman with him, a Mr Justin Trevithick. I was somewhat concerned, my lady, that the Earl was inebriated, for he was most forceful in his demands for entry.'

Beth put her book down and looked at Charlotte in some consternation. The clock stood at ten minutes to two, which seemed somewhat early for a gentleman to be in his cups. It also seemed somewhat out of character.

'I cannot believe that the Earl is foxed, Carrick,' she said forthrightly, gaining a squeak of disapproval from Charlotte at her unladylike language, 'so perhaps I should see him to ascertain the reason for his behaviour.' She turned to her cousin. 'Shall I receive Lord Trevithick in the green study, Charlotte, so that you need not be disturbed? I do not wish you to have to receive two strangers so unexpectedly.'

Charlotte stood up, smoothing her dress with nervous fingers. 'Thank you, Beth, but there is no difficulty. If the Earl is inebriated I would rather be with you to prevent an unfortunate scene—'

The words had scarcely left her lips when the door was flung open with a crash as Marcus stalked into the room, closely followed by Justin, who was looking slightly less than his usual imperturbable self.

'My apologies, ma'am,' Marcus drawled, sketching a slight bow in Charlotte's direction. 'I have no wish to discompose you, but I have an urgent need to speak with Lady Allerton and I was afraid that I would have taken root to the spot by the time your butler saw fit to return!' He turned to Beth and she recoiled slightly from the expression on his face. There was a furious light in his eyes and a very grim set to his jaw. The change from the attentive suitor of two nights before to this hard and angry man was almost impossible to believe.

As she stared at him in bemusement, Marcus said silkily, 'I am glad to find you at home, Lady Allerton, and not halfway to Devon to claim your ill-gotten gains! Will you grant me a private interview or must I rehearse my quarrel with you in front of your cousin and a host of servants? I have no difficulty in doing so, you understand, but Mrs Cavendish might find it somewhat distasteful...'

Beth drew herself up. The reference to her ill-gotten gains puzzled her, for had Marcus not sent her the deeds of Fairhaven only that morning, and with a perfectly amicable note into the bargain? She wondered briefly if Carrick had been correct and Marcus was drunk, but it took only one glance to see that he was stone cold sober. Sober but very angry. It was frightening.

'I have no notion to what you refer, my lord,' she said a little shakily, 'nor have I any wish to hear your impertinent accusations! I think you must be either drunk or mad to speak like this, and I suggest that you return when your temper has cooled!'

Justin caught Marcus's arm. 'Lady Allerton is in the right of it, old chap! Cool reason is better than hot heads! Let us retire for now—'

Marcus ignored him. He crossed the room to Beth and stopped an unnerving foot away from her. She could see the anger and dislike clear in his face.

'Well, ma'am?' he challenged softly. 'What is it to be? A private discussion or a public quarrel? The choice is entirely yours!'

Beth heard Charlotte draw a protesting breath and saw Justin Trevithick move protectively to her cousin's side.

'Beg pardon, ma'am,' she heard him say in an undertone. 'Dreadful intrusion, I know, but there is no reasoning with him when he is like this. The Trevithick temper, you know. The old Earl was renowned for it…'

Beth's gaze flickered to Charlotte and back to the compelling anger in Marcus Trevithick's face. She drew breath to give Marcus a blistering set-down, but Charlotte spoke first.

'Beth dear, it does seem that the Earl has some pressing matter to discuss with you. Perhaps you could take him into the study, whilst Mr Trevithick stays here with me? Carrick, would you bring tea?'

The prosaic suggestion seemed to restore some sense of normality. The tight rage lessened slightly in

Marcus's face and he walked over to the door and held it open for Beth with studious courtesy. Carrick moved away with his customary composed tread to fetch refreshments. Beth saw Justin take Charlotte's hand and start to introduce himself formally, then the door closed behind them with a snap and she was alone in the hall with Marcus.

'If you would step this way, my lord,' she said, a little faintly, gesturing towards her book room, 'I am sure that we can resolve this problem, whatever it may be…'

The study faced south and had a warm fire burning. Earlier that morning Beth had taken the deeds to Fairhaven and placed them on the desk, intending to read them thoroughly in the evening. She had wanted to see Marcus first and talk to him about his gift. And now it seemed that she had the opportunity, but not exactly as she would have wished it…

She saw Marcus's gaze go to the pile of papers and saw a frown crease his forehead as though he wanted to snatch the deeds up and simply walk off with them. For a moment her mind was filled with the ludicrous picture of them tugging on opposite ends of the papers until they tore across and fluttered to the ground. And for what? She was still utterly confused about the nature of his quarrel with her.

Marcus drove his hands into his jacket pockets. 'Lady Allerton, I have come to ask for the return of the deeds to Fairhaven Island,' he said, in tones of measured dislike. 'It seems that you have obtained them under false pretences and so our agreement, such as it was, is null and void. The wager, the gift…' his dark gaze dwelled on her face for a moment in a look that made Beth feel curiously vulnerable '…everything. I do not expect to see you again or have any further debate about the ownership of the island.'

Beth sat down weakly in the nearest chair. She raised her eyes to his face. 'I do not understand you, my lord. You made me a free gift of the island only this morning—'

Marcus spoke through his teeth. 'It was a mistake. I am rescinding it.'

The indignant colour sprung into Beth's face. 'But you cannot do that! There is no reason— Why, how dishonourable can you be? First to renege on the wager and then to cancel your gift—'

Marcus came across and bent over her chair. His furious dark eyes were only inches from hers. 'If we are talking of honour, I would like to know how a woman who lies and cheats could possibly know anything of such a quality!' He turned away from her, his movements so full of repressed rage that Beth quailed. 'I have heard about your plans to exploit Fairhaven for financial gain! So much for your touching protestations that you were wishing to regain your lost patrimony! And to think that I believed you—' He stopped and ran a hand through his disordered dark hair. 'Well, I was richly taken in, but not any more!'

Beth got to her feet. Her eyes were wide and puzzled. 'Truly, my lord, I do not understand—'

Marcus spun round and caught her wrist. 'Not understand? Do you deny that your late husband tried to buy Fairhaven because he wanted to mine gold there? Do you deny that you went to my grandfather and told him that *you* wished to buy the island for the same reason? Do you deny that your cousin is even now looking for investors for such a project, now that you have tricked me out of Fairhaven—?'

'Yes, I do deny it!' Beth wrenched her wrist out of his grasp. 'I knew nothing of Frank's business concerns, nor do I know anything of Kit's! I do not wish to! I want Fairhaven for all those reasons I told you, my lord, and as for telling your grandfather otherwise—' she swallowed a sob '—I never said anything of the sort!'

Her gaze searched Marcus's face and saw the unyielding disbelief there. She could tell that she was wasting her breath. 'It seems, however, that you have no wish to trust me,' she finished quietly.

Marcus moved over to the writing table. 'I will take these with me—'

Beth whisked across the room before he could reach for the deeds to Fairhaven, and inserted herself between Marcus and the desk, blocking his way. She put her hands behind her and leant back against the desk's smooth surface to steady herself. Marcus looked at her for a moment, then raised an incredulous eyebrow.

'So determined to keep your island, my dear? I have not forgotten exactly what it was you offered me when we made our wager! It seems you will do anything to achieve your ambition!' His gaze swept over her with contemptuous familiarity, from the black curls piled up on her head to the kid slippers peeping from beneath the hem of her pale blue muslin gown and Beth felt as though he was stripping her naked. He moved forward until she was completely trapped with the writing table behind her and Marcus in front of her. Beth drew back as far as she could, but she felt the sharp edge of the desk digging uncomfortably into the back of her legs. A second later she forgot all about the discomfort as Marcus moved in closer, so close that Beth could feel his thigh pressing against hers through the thin muslin gown. She drew an outraged breath.

'My lord, kindly let me go!'

Marcus smiled with wicked amusement. All his anger appeared to have gone now, replaced by a devilish enjoyment that Beth suddenly found even more frightening. She tried to lean away from him, but the desk behind her blocked her path completely, and when she attempted to slide sideways Marcus simply leant both arms on the desk on either side of her, effectively pinning her down. As Beth tried to arch away from him she saw his gaze drop to the neckline of her dress and linger there on the soft swell of her breasts.

'My lord!' Beth's voice came out as a desperate squeak. 'This is not fair!'

Marcus leant closer. She could feel his breath soft on her heated skin. He raised a hand and traced one lazy finger down her cheek, continuing down the line of her neck to her collarbone. His eyes were dark with desire.

'Would you have honoured the bet if you had lost, sweetheart? Would you?'

'No!' Beth gasped. She felt his fingers pause at the hollow in her throat, felt him stroke the pulse there.

'Your skin is all flushed.' Marcus's voice had sunk to a husky whisper now. 'You are as hot as you were the other night. I do not believe you, Lady Allerton. I think you are as shameless as you pretended to be at the Cyprians' Ball…'

Beth's gasp of fury was lost as his mouth came

down on hers. This time his kiss was hard and hungry, as demanding as the one at the ball had been gentle. He forced her lips apart and she felt his tongue invade her mouth and her senses spun under the onslaught. She brought her hands round to grip Marcus's arms, intending to push him away, but he leant his weight against her so that the table caught her behind the thighs and she was borne helplessly back, to lie amongst the scattered papers and rolling inkpot. She felt her dress gape and her hair come loose from its pins and fan out across the wooden surface, and she could neither struggle nor scream, for Marcus's weight was on top of her, holding her still, and his mouth still plundered the softness of hers.

It was only when his lips left hers, to follow the line his fingers had traced earlier and brush against the sensitive softness of her throat, that Beth realised she had no will to struggle anyway. The touch of his hands and lips was exquisite pleasure and she wanted more. She tangled her fingers in his hair and pulled his mouth back up to hers so that she could once again touch and taste him.

She had no idea how long they lay locked together before Marcus moved with single-minded concentration to strip the dress from her shoulders. Beth felt the little puffy sleeves slide down her arms to the elbow and a moment later Marcus had slid one warm hand inside the gap in her bodice and cupped her breast. Her involuntary moan was lost against his lips as he thrust his tongue deep into her mouth. His fingers found her hardening nipple and he pulled the bodice of her dress down before his mouth left hers to fasten over the pink tip he had exposed. Beth squirmed in delight and desperation as he bit down on her sensitised skin. There was an exquisite pain in the pit of her stomach and she was lost in the sensations of pleasure that he was creating. The remaining papers went flying from the desk as she writhed with excitement.

There was a sudden noise out in the hall and Marcus eased away from her with a purely involuntary movement. It was enough to bring Beth down to earth. Suddenly she was horribly aware of something digging into her back, of the papers scattered beneath her hands, the dress that had almost slipped to her waist. She wriggled again but this time in a desperate attempt to stand up, and Marcus stepped back and put out a hand to help her to her feet. Beth flinched away.

'Don't touch me!' All her horror at what she had done was in her voice. She could not believe it—could not believe her own behaviour and could not forgive him his. She saw Marcus recoil and knew that finally, she had the upper hand. She gestured towards the door. 'Lord Trevithick. Please leave. Now.'

She tidied herself with trembling fingers and watched as Marcus smoothed his hair and straightened his clothes. His eyes met hers and she saw that they were as dazed and dark with passion as she knew her own must be. Suddenly she wanted to throw herself into his arms, to make all well again between them, but she drew herself up haughtily and simply waited for him to go.

'Beth—' Marcus put out a hand to her, but Beth turned her shoulder and stared blindly out of the window. 'Beth, I am truly sorry—'

'No!' Beth's eyes filled with tears. She did not know whether he meant that he was sorry for his actions or for his earlier suspicions but whatever the case, she *did* know that she would cry in another instant. 'I do not want to hear it!'

She heard Marcus open the study door and she turned round quickly. Before he went there was something she had to say to him, something that had to be absolutely clear.

'Lord Trevithick.' Her voice shook. She could not help it. She took a deep breath and ploughed on. 'Lord Trevithick, I intend to travel down to Devon immediately. Fairhaven Island is mine and I am going to claim it.'

She watched with misgiving as Marcus straightened up and gleam of amusement came back into his eyes. He sketched an ironic bow. 'Very well, my lady. You are going to Fairhaven. I am going to Fairhaven. We shall see which of us manages to claim the island first!'

And before Beth could say another word, he was gone.

Charlotte was very good. She did not ask why Beth had ink stains on her blue muslin dress, nor why her hair, so prettily arranged *à la Greque* earlier in the day now looked as though it had been dragged through a hedge, nor even why her cousin chose to lock herself in her room for several hours, emerging pale and wan for dinner. She patted Beth's hand, told her that if she wished to discuss anything she was always happy to talk, and tactfully went off to the kitchen to confer with the cook about menus.

Kit joined them for dinner and seemed inclined to quiz Beth over her pallor and lack of appetite, but a well-aimed kick from his sister soon put paid to his questions. He was more voluble about the use to which the fine dessert wine had been put in removing the ink stains from a certain blue muslin dress, but when Beth pointed out that it was her wine cellar he did not pursue it. Beth herself felt inclined to take the rest of the bottle and drink it straight down, but her natural good sense suggested that she would soon feel the worse for it. Besides, she found dessert wine too sweet and reflected wryly that if she wished to become intoxicated for the first time in her life, she should find a more enjoyable way of doing so.

Beth felt miserable and as weary as though she had been awake for a week, but most of all she felt furious at the injustice of Marcus's behaviour. To make wild accusations and not even do her the courtesy of explaining them properly; to give Fairhaven to her only to try to take it away again; to behave in a less than gentlemanly fashion—but here she blushed hotly even in her thoughts and hastily turned her mind to something else.

After dinner, Beth sought Charlotte out in the red drawing room where her cousin was sitting placidly embroidering at her tambour frame. Charlotte was working on a piece of white muslin, sewing the hem with exquisite neatness, and Beth smiled a little as she remembered her own hopeless efforts at needlework. She plumped herself down next to her cousin, curling up and hugging one of the red velvet cushions.

'Charlotte, I have been thinking,' she began. 'I intend to leave London tomorrow and go home to Devon. I know that Kit has business to finish here, but I have no more taste for parties and balls, and it would be better to be home in good time for Christmas.'

She saw her cousin's penetrating blue gaze resting

on her and blushed slightly. 'Well, there is no reason to stay...'

'I know that you are doing this to avoid Lord Trevithick,' Charlotte said calmly, cutting her thread. 'I do not really understand the nature of your quarrel, Beth, for Justin Trevithick had too much delicacy to speak to me of it, but if you wish to run away from your troubles that is your affair!' She fixed her cousin with a severe regard. 'However, running away does not generally solve anything!'

Beth hugged her cushion harder. 'No, I know you are right! But I do not believe I can resolve my dispute with Lord Trevithick, for he is utterly indifferent to my explanations! Indeed, he scarcely gave me the chance to offer any! Oh!' All her pent-up frustration came out on the word. 'He is the most arrogant and tiresome man imaginable!'

'Strange, when his cousin is so courteous,' Charlotte observed, with a little smile. 'Mr Trevithick is all that one could wish for in a gentleman of quality!'

Something about her tone of voice struck Beth, despite her preoccupation. She gave her cousin a penetrating stare.

'Charlotte, are you developing a *tendre* for Mr Trevithick?'

Charlotte blushed. 'Certainly not!' she said with dignity. She bent her head over her tambour frame. 'Besides, we are speaking of your concerns, Beth, not mine!'

Beth had not missed the colour that stained her cousin's cheeks. She smiled. 'I would far rather talk of the impression that the *gallant* Mr Trevithick made upon you than the shortcomings of his kinsman, the Earl!'

'Humph!' Charlotte seemed put out of countenance for the first time. 'I know you are only seeking to distract me, Beth! Mr Trevithick was very charming, but I doubt that I shall see him again. Now...' she recovered herself '...you mentioned returning home to Devon, but did you intend to go to Mostyn Hall— or to Fairhaven Island?'

Beth narrowed her eyes. Her cousin's powers of perception were disturbing at times. 'Well, I confess I had thought to visit Fairhaven first... That is, the Earl granted the island to me, so it is mine now! And though he now wishes to rescind his gift, I do not see that I should make it easy for him...'

Charlotte selected another thread from the sewing box open on the seat beside her. 'I see. So what do you intend to do? Take Fairhaven by storm and defend it against him? Really, Beth! This is the nineteenth century! You are not in the Civil Wars now, you know!'

Beth got up and walked over to the window. She was not going to admit it, but there was something powerfully tempting about Charlotte's suggestion. Things must have been so much easier when one could round up an army of retainers and take the fight to the enemy. Perhaps she had been born in the wrong century but, army or not, she was determined to claim her island.

'It would not be like that, Lottie,' she said, with more confidence than she felt. 'I'll warrant that there is no tenant on Fairhaven—who would want to live in such an out-of-the-way place? And doubtless the villagers will be pleased to have someone take an interest at last...'

Feeling restless, she pulled back the red velvet curtain and looked out. It was dark in the street outside and the lamplighter and his assistant were making their rounds. The lamplighter had rested his ladder against the stand and passed the oil container down to his assistant for refilling. The boy was pouring oil slowly from the jug, his tongue sticking out of the corner of his mouth with the effort of concentration. Beth smiled a little.

'Anyway, I still have the deed of gift to Fairhaven,' she said slowly, 'signed by the Earl himself. It is a legal document and he would find it difficult to explain it away in a court of law—'

Charlotte looked horrified. 'You would not take this matter to the courts! Think of the cost! Think of the scandal, and all for what? Beth, surely you cannot mean it?'

Beth turned back to the candlelit room. 'No, Lottie. I would not go so far, but I do intend to claim Fairhaven.' She pressed her hands together. 'It is just that Trevithick's behaviour has been so *unfair* and I have the greatest dislike of being bested!'

'I had observed it,' Charlotte said, very drily. 'Oh, Beth, can you not just let it go? If you truly do not believe you can come to terms with the Earl of Trevithick, then concede gracefully and let us go home to Mostyn!'

There was a silence. The fire crackled and spat. 'Does that mean that if I were to go to Fairhaven you would not come with me?' Beth asked, after a moment. 'I know you disapprove, Lottie...'

Their eyes met. Charlotte looked pained. 'Oh,

Beth! Yes, I do disapprove! Most heartily! *Why* must you go?'

Beth looked unhappy. 'Because it is a point of principle. Because I cannot let him win!'

'Those are not good reasons!' Charlotte almost wailed. 'Of course Trevithick will win! He is the Earl and he holds the island and he has all the advantage! You are tilting against windmills!'

Beth's mouth set in a mutinous line. 'Perhaps so. But I have to try!'

Charlotte screwed her face up. 'Why? Such stubbornness is so unbecoming!'

Beth laughed. 'Stubbornness, impetuosity... Oh, Lottie, you have been trying to improve me this age! I do not know why you bother, for I shall never become more ladylike!' Her smile faded. 'But if you do not wish to come with me I shall understand. There is no reason for you to have to compromise your propriety just because I am a hoyden!'

Charlotte pushed the tambour frame away and got to her feet. 'What, am I to let you go jauntering about the countryside alone and in even more of a hoydenish manner? I shall go and start my packing!'

Beth rushed across the room and gave her an impetuous hug. 'Oh, thank you!'

Charlotte hugged her back. 'Do not thank me for being as foolish as you! Why, it will take us at least six days to get there at this time of year—'

'Oh, no, only three! And the weather is not so bad at present!'

'And the inns will be dreadful and the sea will be rough and like as not we will end locked in a dungeon! Oh, Beth...'

'There will be no difficulties,' Beth said, with far

more confidence than she was feeling. She did not think that this was the moment to tell Charlotte that the Earl of Trevithick had indicated that he too would be travelling to Fairhaven, so that another confrontation was inevitable. 'I have it all planned! I will ask Gough to formally register the transfer of the island from the Earl of Trevithick to myself, so there will be no questions about the legality of the situation! Gough will take care of everything!'

Charlotte looked unconvinced. 'It seems to me that there is every doubt! However, if Gough will deal with it, I suppose we may be comfortable on that score!' She brightened a little. 'Now, if we were to wait until your legal title to the estate was established…'

Beth shook her head. She knew that Charlotte was right; it was the most sensible course of action and by far the safest. She also knew that the Earl of Trevithick was eminently capable of opposing her at every turn and that the ensuing struggle might last for months. And possession was nine-tenths of the law…

'It would never serve, Lottie. I could be waiting for ever!'

Charlotte sighed, apparently accepting the inevitable. 'Very well! I suppose I shall have a few days on the road to try to change your mind!'

Beth smiled. 'I have it all planned out! Kit can keep the house open here for as long as he has business in town and meanwhile I will send to Mostyn Hall for some of the servants to join us on Fairhaven! We shall go across and tell the islanders that the property has changed hands—it will be exactly as though I had purchased the estate!'

'Not precisely,' Charlotte said drily. She looked at

Beth with deep misgiving. 'A disputed deed of gift is hardly the same as an acknowledged sale! However, I can see that there is no reasoning with you! This whole plan will go horribly awry! Mark my words!'

On the first night of their journey the inn, the Castle and Ball in Marlborough, was of good enough quality to meet even Charlotte's specifications. They had a neat private parlour, well away from the public tap, and a bedroom on the quiet side of the inn so that they would not be disturbed by the comings and goings in either the main street or the coach yard.

Charlotte had wanted to put up for the night at Newbury and had argued that there was no necessity to push on to Marlborough, but Beth had been adamant that they needed to cover as much distance as possible. Their departure had already been delayed by two days, for it had taken far longer than she had expected to make all the arrangements for their journey. Firstly she had had to discuss her plans with Gough, who had raised any number of legal queries about the deed of gift. Then she had had to send a messenger to Mostyn Hall to ask the estate manager to arrange for a group of servants to be ready to join them on Fairhaven once she gave the word. She could imagine the raised eyebrows that letter would cause when it was received. Finally she had to attend to her own packing and all the preparations for the journey, which all took twice as long as she had expected. Then, when they were about to depart, Kit had expressed his severe disapproval of the plan and all but threatened to forbid them to go. The quarrel that ensued had ended with him telling Beth that she was headstrong to the point of madness and with Charlotte telling both of them that they were as bad as each other. It had not been a good start to the venture.

Beth sighed. Downstairs in the inn parlour, a clock chimed seven. They had set off at eight o'clock that morning and had been travelling for almost nine and a half hours, with barely time to snatch a drink or something to eat when they stopped to change the horses. Charlotte had frowned at Beth's urgency and both of the girls had become increasingly tired and irritable as the day had worn on. However, when they had arrived at Marlborough, a pitcher of hot water, a change of clothes and the promise of a good meal had made them both feel much better, and Beth was looking forward to a peaceful night's sleep.

Charlotte stuck her head around the bedroom door. 'Are you ready to come down to eat, Beth? Our supper is on the table.'

The most delicious smell of roasting lamb filled the corridor and Beth's stomach gave an enormous rumble. She went gratefully into the little parlour and allowed the bowing landlord to escort her to her seat. The table was already laden with covered dishes, the candles were lit and the room had an altogether welcoming feel to it. Beth was glad to see that Charlotte seemed much happier now that they were settled and that the accommodation was everything that she could have desired.

Neither of them spoke for about ten minutes, for they were far too busy applying themselves to the food and drink. Eventually Charlotte accepted a second glass of wine and a second portion of lamb, and smiled across the table at her cousin.

'Thank goodness! I feel so much better! And this place is a most superior establishment! I was afraid that they would not treat us so well, travelling alone and without any gentlemen to bespeak rooms for us!'

Beth shifted a little on her chair. Like her cousin, she was aware that their arrival had caused some curiosity, travelling as they were with only a couple of servants and without an escort. She knew that it made Charlotte feel vulnerable and whilst she did not believe that they were in any danger, it was certainly more comfortable to have Kit's company when travelling. He had always been the one to bespeak rooms, arrange meals and deal with payment. Beth was in no way a retiring female, but she had not travelled a great deal and so had little experience to draw on. Fortunately the inns at which they planned to stay were all reputable ones and there was no doubt that her title and evident wealth were most useful in smoothing their way. She did not anticipate any trouble.

The dishes were removed and a fine apple pie brought in. Beth considered another glass of wine and regretfully decided that it would make her fall asleep at the table. Charlotte yawned prettily.

'May we travel a little less precipitately tomorrow, please, Beth?' she pleaded. 'I am shaken to pieces from the journey, for all that the coach is so comfortable! Surely we could stop at Trowbridge or Frome? There is no need for us to hurry in this madcap way!'

Beth toyed with a spoonful of pie. She had still not told Charlotte that the Earl of Trevithick had threatened to journey down to Fairhaven himself and that it was her main aim to reach the island before him. When they had left London that morning she had been reassured to know that Trevithick was still in the capital—Kit had seen him at a ball only the night before. Beth had begun to wonder if, in fact, the Earl did not intend to go to Fairhaven at all. He had never evinced any interest in the island for its own sake, and his only aim had been prevent her from claiming it. It was a matter of pride to him as well as to her. But perhaps, Beth thought, it was not important enough to him to come chasing after her. Only time would tell.

She reached for the cream jug and poured a little on to her remaining piece of pie.

'I had hoped to reach Bridgwater tomorrow night—'

'Bridgwater!' Charlotte seldom interrupted for her manners were too good. This time, however, she was staring at her cousin with incredulous eyes. 'Why, that must be all of eighty miles! Why on earth do we need to go so far in one day?'

Beth sighed. 'It is simply that I had hoped to reach Fairhaven as soon as possible.' She avoided her cousin's gaze. 'When we last met, the Earl of Trevithick indicated that he was intending—well, that he might be thinking of travelling to Fairhaven himself. So—'

'Trevithick going to Fairhaven himself?' Charlotte interrupted for a second time. She stopped eating and put her spoon down slowly. 'Why did you not tell me this before, Beth?'

Beth toyed with her food, still evading her cousin's eye. 'I thought you would only worry if you thought we were engaged in some sort of race. Matters were bad enough as they were...'

'Yes, but if Trevithick is going to be at Fairhaven that will not be so bad at all!'

Beth looked suspiciously at her cousin. For a moment she wondered if Charlotte had had too much wine, but although her cheeks were becomingly pink and her eyes bright, she did not appear inebriated.

'Whatever can you mean, Lottie? How could it possibly be a good thing for us both to be there together? We would come to blows within minutes!'

'Well…' Charlotte started to eat again. 'It will not be so much like an invasion this way, more a house visit—'

'House visit!' Beth stared. 'Good gracious, what can you mean? It will make things twice as bad!'

'Oh, surely not! For we may all sit down together and discuss the matter calmly!'

Beth stared all the more, wondering which of them was mad. 'Lottie, you saw what the Earl was like when he came to the house in London! How can you imagine that we would be able to discuss anything calmly?'

Charlotte frowned. 'Well, I realise that the Earl was suffering under some strong emotion then, but surely he is perfectly reasonable under normal circumstances!'

Beth grimaced. She could not imagine how their situation could be interpreted as normal and was afraid that Charlotte was clutching at straws. Should the Earl of Trevithick appear and throw a rub in their way, it would prove decidedly awkward. Beth's fervent hope by now was that the Earl would not care enough for Fairhaven to put himself to the trouble of going all the way to Devon in winter. The little Season was in full flow and Christmas was approaching and surely he had better things to do with his time than pursue a wild goose chase?

Before she could put this view to Charlotte, however, there was a rumble of wheels in the courtyard outside and the flare of carriage lamps in the darkness.

'Ostler!' a deep masculine voice shouted. 'Look lively there!'

Beth got up from the table and hurried over to peer through the diamond-paned windows. A curricle was standing in the yard outside, a superb vehicle in dark blue or green livery, with four elegant horses of a quality to match. As she watched, the driver handed his reins to his passenger and swung down from the seat. Beth's stomach suddenly felt hollow for all the excellent meal she had just eaten.

She turned back to Charlotte who had also started to look apprehensive.

'You may judge for yourself how reasonable the Earl of Trevithick is, Charlotte,' she said slowly, 'for I do believe that he is here now!'

In an excess of propriety, Charlotte had whisked her cousin away from the window, drawn the curtains tightly and ordered the servants to remove the dishes and to serve tea. She and Beth now sat in the wing chairs on each side of the fire, clutching a cup in their hands and looking at each other with ill-concealed nervousness. Both of them knew that good manners demanded that they make themselves known to the new arrivals. Neither of them had moved to do so.

The whole inn seemed to have come alive with the gentlemen's arrival. Beth could hear Marcus out in the yard, chatting with the grooms and ostlers and accepting many complimentary comments on the quality of his horses. Lights flared, doors banged and Beth reflected uncharitably that it was typical of the

Earl to make as much fuss as possible wherever he
went. She sipped her tea, wondering how on earth
Marcus could have reached Marlborough that night
and with his own horses. Then she told herself that
she did not want to know. She did not want to speak
with him and preferably she did not want him to know
that she was even there. Her appetite for a confrontation seemed to have vanished completely.

Beth heard Justin Trevithick's voice in the corridor
outside, bespeaking supper for two and rooms for the
night. Charlotte heard it too; Beth saw a hint of colour
come into her cousin's face as Charlotte busied herself pouring fresh tea. Then Beth heard the door of
the taproom open and a gust of laughter flow out, and
for a moment she thought that they were safe and that
the gentlemen had chosen to take a drink in the bar.
She was swiftly disabused.

'The ostler tells me that there are some other trav-
ellers staying tonight, landlord.' Beth heard Marcus's
voice sound from further down the corridor. She realised that the maid had left the parlour door slightly
ajar when she had removed the dishes. She crept towards it and put her ear to the crack.

'Yes, my lord.' The landlord spoke above the hub-
bub coming from the taproom. 'There are two ladies
staying with us.'

'Beth!' Charlotte whispered urgently from behind
her. 'What are you doing?'

'Hush!' Beth put her finger to her lips. 'I am trying
to eavesdrop—'

'Real ladies or the other sort?' Beth heard the
amusement in Marcus's voice. Evidently the landlord
did as well, for this time his tone was scandalised.

'Beg pardon, my lord, but I don't run that sort of a house! And these are very definitely real ladies!'

'My apologies.' Marcus had erased the amusement from his tone. There was a rustle of something and a mutter of thanks from the landlord.

'It is just that some friends of ours are on the road and we are trying to catch up with them,' Marcus continued. 'We traced them through the toll houses and the posting inns and wondered if they had already arrived here…' The rustle sounded again. 'Two ladies, young…attractive… The younger is very striking, with black hair and silver-grey eyes…'

Beth felt herself warming and pretended that she was hot with indignation that Marcus should be speaking so freely of her. She had a small suspicion, however, that it was his compliments that made her face glow. She was not totally immune to his admiration. And the landlord had evidently recognised her from the description. She heard him clear his throat and speak obsequiously.

'Yes, sir. I do believe you are describing our guests… A most beautiful young lady, sir. Most striking.'

Beth drew in her breath silently. She had not suggested to the staff in any of the inns that her journey was secret, so they had no reason not to give out information, particularly if Marcus smoothed the process with the kind of tip that she could imagine had just changed hands. The landlord was still talking, evidently anxious to please his open-handed visitor.

'The ladies have the private parlour, sir, so you will find them there. I dare say they may be retiring soon though, as they've already partaken of supper and have been travelling all day—'

'Of course they have,' Marcus murmured. Beth could tell he was coming closer. 'But I am sure that once they know we are here, the ladies may be persuaded to share their parlour with us…'

Beth shot away from the door like a scalded cat. Charlotte was watching her with a frown between the eyes. 'What is it, Beth?' she hissed.

Beth closed her eyes and opened them again sharply. 'Oh, Lottie, I think we should have retired when we had the chance—'

There was a step right outside the door, then Justin's voice came even closer at hand. 'Marcus, can you come out to the stable for a moment? Stephens tells me that there is a problem with one of the horses—'

A cold draught swirled through the parlour as the door to the courtyard opened and closed again. The gentlemen's footsteps could be heard outside on the cobbles. Without a pause for thought, Beth grabbed Charlotte's hand, pulled her from her chair and bundled her out of the room and up the stairs. Charlotte, out of breath and protesting, sank down on to the big four-poster bed as Beth closed the bedroom door behind them and leant against it, breathing hard.

'Beth! What on earth was all that about? Why could you not just greet Lord Trevithick in a civilised manner?'

Beth was not sure of the answer to that. All she knew was that she felt unequal to the task of confronting Marcus that evening and that any such meeting would have to wait until the morning when she would be stronger and better prepared. She did not have the first idea of what she would say to him or how the conflict between them might be resolved.

What she *did* know, however, was that she was certainly not going to agree to go tamely home just because Marcus had caught up with them already.

There was a knock at the door and Beth's heart jumped into her throat. The cousins looked at each other.

'Well, go on,' Charlotte said, a little impatiently. 'Pray answer! I cannot believe that even Lord Trevithick would beard a lady in her bedroom!'

Beth privately thought that that was exactly what Trevithick would do, but she went over to the door and peeped round. To her relief there was only the maid on the landing outside. The girl dropped a slight curtsy. She was carrying a tray with two beakers of steaming liquid, and now brought them into the room and placed them on the table by the window.

'His lordship's compliments, ma'am, and he wondered if you would both care to take a nightcap that is sovereign against the aches and pains of the road.'

Beth stared suspiciously into the cup. The smell was delicious, a mix of mulled wine and spices. Charlotte came across and stood looking over her shoulder.

'Oh, how thoughtful! Pray thank Lord Trevithick for his consideration!'

The maid dropped another curtsey and went out, and Charlotte, smiling, picked up one of the cups and took a sip. She gave a sigh.

'Oh, that is truly delicious! Beth, you must try some!'

Beth took a careful taste. The liquid was warm and soothing, easing away all the aches of the journey just as the maid had promised. Suddenly it seemed churlish to be suspicious of Marcus's motives. Beth drained the cup to the dregs.

Charlotte was yawning widely. 'Goodness, I feel tired! I am for my bed.' She gave Beth a kiss. 'Do not forget to lock your door, Beth—and I am in the next room should anything untoward happen! I am sure we can resolve this situation with Lord Trevithick in the morning. Goodnight!'

Beth closed the door behind her and after a moment bolted it. She hesitated over calling the maid but felt too weary to bother. She donned her nightdress in a somewhat haphazard fashion, and half-climbed, half-tumbled into the big bed. She had barely blown out the candle before she was asleep.

Chapter Five

Beth awoke feeling warm and comfortable. The room was full of sunlight and shifting shadow, and for a moment she was puzzled until she realised that she must have fallen asleep before she could draw the bed curtains. Certainly she remembered that she had felt extraordinarily weary the night before, which she supposed was no great surprise since she had been travelling for an entire day with little rest. Now, however, she felt miraculously restored and quite capable of dealing with the problem of seeing Marcus Trevithick again. She swung her legs over the side of the bed and hurried to ring the bell for some hot water.

It was whilst she was waiting for the maid to appear that she heard the clock downstairs in the parlour strike twelve. Beth paused in the act of brushing out her hair, then counted very carefully as the faint chimes of the church clock out in the square echoed the same twelve strokes. She put down her brush and flung open the bedroom curtains.

Her window looked out on to a small kitchen garden with rows of neat vegetables and a chicken scratching in the dust. The sun was bright and high, and Beth could feel its October warmth through the glass pane. High noon. There could be no doubt. She had slept for fifteen hours.

Beth frowned. She had been intending to breakfast no later than seven-thirty and be on the road by eight. If they were to reach Bridgwater that day... But there was no possible chance of reaching Bridgwater now, or even Glastonbury. They would be lucky to make thirty miles that day and meanwhile Marcus would be halfway to Devon. No doubt he was on his way already.

Beth's eye fell suspiciously on the cup that had held the mulled wine. She picked it up and sniffed the dregs. They smelled of nothing but the same delicious honey and spice scent that had tempted her the previous night. Sovereign against the aches and pains of the road, the maid had said, but perhaps they had been sovereign against more than that...

There was a knock at the door and the maid appeared, clutching a large pitcher of water.

'Good morning, milady! And a lovely day it is—'

'Is my cousin awake yet?' Beth asked urgently, dispensing with the greetings somewhat precipitately. 'It is far later than I had imagined and we had intended to be on the road hours ago!'

The maid, a large, untidy country girl, put her hands on her hips and surveyed Beth with a certain puzzlement.

'Lords lawks, ma'am, there's no need to go hurrying about the country on a lovely day like this!' Her accent was as rich and soothing as butter. 'Mrs Cavendish only woke a few moments ago—just like yourself, ma'am!—and ten to one you'll be needing some luncheon before you set out!'

Beth fidgeted with the curtain cord. Charlotte was a notoriously slow riser and if she had only just woken it would be at least an hour until she was ready to go. It was with difficulty that Beth restrained herself from rushing into her cousin's room and exhorting her to hurry up, but she knew there was no point in harassing Charlotte, who would proceed at her own unflappable pace.

The maid shot her a curious look, then started to pour the water into the basin. 'His lordship sends his compliments, ma'am, and asks that you join him in the parlour—when you're ready, of course.'

Beth paused. 'His lordship? Lord Trevithick is still here?'

'Yes, ma'am.' The girl lowered the pitcher. 'Some problem with one of his horses, so I'm told. Still, there's no rush, is there, ma'am? I'll tell him that you'll be down shortly!'

Beth sighed. However polite Marcus's request, she suspected it hid a rather more emphatic order and there was little point in resisting.

She came down the stairs fifteen minutes later, her travelling dress neatly pressed and her hair demurely plaited. The door of the parlour was closed and there was no sound within, and after a moment Beth decided that she had no wish to beard Marcus in his lair just now, and went out into the sunshine.

There was a busy market in Marlborough High Street and Beth resolved to take a look at the stalls that lined either side of the wide cobbled road. She was in no hurry. Charlotte would not be ready for ages and as far as Beth was concerned, the longer she put off her meeting with Marcus, the better.

Plenty of cottagers had brought their vegetables to market and turnips, onions and potatoes spilled out of baskets and across makeshift wooden trestles. Cheek by jowl with these were the vendors of bootlaces, nutmeg graters, cough drops, corn plasters and any number of necessities that Beth had never realised that she needed. She wandered along the row of stalls, pausing to chat with everyone and admire their produce and their children. A persuasive street trader almost convinced her that she would like to buy a small, mewling kitten—her heart was broken at the thought of it ending up in a drowning sack—but common sense suggested that it would not make a comfortable pet, particularly on a journey. It was whilst she was explaining to the trader that he must on no account sell the kitten to a bad home, that a gentleman paused beside them and Beth realised with a sinking heart that Marcus Trevithick had caught up with her at last. Her authoritative instructions wavered and faded away as she completely forgot what she had been talking about.

Marcus was watching her with an expression of amused indulgence in his eyes. He was bare-headed and in the bright sunlight his thick dark hair gleamed a glossy blue-black. He was immaculately dressed in buckskins and an elegant coat of blue superfine, and his Hessians had a mirror-polish that reflected the sun. As Beth watched, he handed the kitten's owner a coin and said gravely, 'Take the little creature to the Castle and Ball Inn. It can earn its keep catching mice in the stables.'

He offered Beth his arm. 'Good morning, Lady

Allerton. Have you completed your purchases, or are there more desperate animals that you wish to rescue? I noticed a small piglet at the stall on the left—if you do not buy it, it will surely end in the pot…'

Beth took the proffered arm a little gingerly. 'Thank you, my lord. I am not in a position to establish a sanctuary for animals at the moment and I do not believe I require any more candles, or boot-laces—'

'Or corn plasters or tin trays!' Marcus finished for her. He smiled down at her. 'It is tempting though, is it not? I have purchased a box of cigars and a carved walking stick and have no clear idea of how I came to part with my money!'

They were walking away from the bustle of the market now and down the hill towards where the river curled its lazy way through the fields. The water sparkled in the sunlight. Beth wondered how long it would be before one or other of them came to the point. After all, they could scarcely pretend that this was a chance encounter. Yet Marcus did not speak, and when she risked a glance at his face she saw that he was watching her with thoughtful consideration.

She paused on the bridge and looked down at the ducks splashing in the shallows beneath.

'Oh how pretty it is here!' she said impulsively. 'I would almost like to stay…'

She looked up, caught Marcus's eye, and bit her lip. She had no wish to give too much away.

Marcus leant back against the stone parapet and smiled at her.

'Is your journey too urgent to let you linger here?' he asked. 'Tell me, Lady Allerton, are you making your way home to Mostyn Hall—or, as I suspect, to Fairhaven Island?'

Beth held his gaze. 'We are travelling to Fairhaven!' she said. She raised her chin. 'Now that I have the deeds to the island I consider it my own! I told you that I would not give in easily, my lord!'

Marcus straightened up. 'Truth to tell, I should be immensely disappointed if you did,' he said softly.

The breeze rippled along the river and raised an echo of a shiver along Beth's nerves. A few dead leaves swirled down onto the water and floated away. She found that she could not look away from Marcus's compelling gaze, could not break the contact between them. Then Marcus shifted slightly.

'However, there are difficulties in your way,' he said. 'Did you expect that I would just let you sail to Fairhaven and stake your claim? I warned you that I would be travelling there myself!'

'I thought to get there first,' Beth said defiantly. The cold autumn wind had whipped the colour up in her cheeks. 'And I was not sure that you cared sufficiently for Fairhaven to put up a fight, my lord!'

Marcus laughed. 'But I have to defend my property against invasion—'

'Oh, do not be so melodramatic!' Beth snapped. She turned away from him, frowning down at the eddying water. 'The truth is that you do not wish to be bested, my lord! You care nothing for the island, but you have some cock-and-bull notion in your head that I cheated you in some way and you do not wish me to win!'

Marcus drove his hands into the pockets of his coat. 'It is true that at first I thought you had lied to me, Lady Allerton—'

An angry sparkle lit Beth's eyes. 'You have such a way with words, my lord! Pray do not spare my feelings! You made your opinion of me quite plain before!'

'And the evidence against you is very strong...' Marcus's gaze was thoughtful on her. 'If it were not that my own instinct is to the contrary, I should say that you had to be guilty.'

Beth turned her back on him. 'I do not wish to discuss this with you, sir. There is no point in doing so! You did not do me the courtesy of presenting your apparent evidence to me before, so I do not feel I need to listen to you now!'

Marcus shrugged elegantly. 'That is only fair, I suppose! So, how do we resolve this conflict, Lady Allerton? You wish to claim Fairhaven. I wish to prevent you from doing so. We are here together. So...'

Beth pressed her lips together. It seemed a frustrating and faintly ridiculous situation in which to find herself. She could rush back to the inn and leap into her carriage, but she could not prevent Marcus from following her. Similarly he could hardly force her to go home to Mostyn. It seemed that they had reached deadlock.

'This problem would never have happened if you had not got here so quickly!' she burst out. 'You were in London only yesterday morning, and yet you were here in Marlborough by nightfall and with your own curricle and team! It is not possible—' She broke off and looked at Marcus stormily as he started to laugh.

'I fear that your information is faulty, my dear! I was *not* in London yesterday morning.'

Beth frowned. 'But Kit said that you had been at Lady Paget's ball the night before!'

'That's true. After the ball, Justin and I drove through the night to Bradbury Park, a place I have close by Reading. We rested the horses for a few hours before pressing on to here. We did not wish you to get too far ahead of us, you see!'

Beth stared at him, anger and indignation warring within her. 'But how did you know where to find us?'

Marcus took a step closer to her. 'We could not be sure, of course, but when we asked at the post houses they were able to tell us of two ladies, travelling alone, who were anxious to press on with their journey.' He shrugged. 'It might not have been the two of you, of course, but given that you had told me you would be travelling into Devon and I knew you would not wish to linger, it seemed likely.' He raised a hand and touched Beth's cheek. His voice grew softer. 'Besides, you are very memorable, you know, sweetheart. At least three of the landlords knew exactly whom I was describing when I spoke of the beautiful lady with ebony black hair and smoky silver eyes!'

Beth gazed at him, trapped equally by the warmth of his regard and the softly mesmerising tone of his voice. In all her life she had never ever considered herself to be beautiful and had certainly never imagined that anyone else would think so. She broke the contact with an effort and turned away, resting her clasped hands on the parapet of the bridge and feeling the chill of the cold stone through her gloves. She did not want this confusion of her senses. It undermined her resolve to oppose Marcus and made it so very difficult to be angry with him. It simply was not fair. She deliberately recalled his behaviour in London, his lack of trust and his unfair accusations, and then she felt able to harden her heart.

'I do not believe your compliments sincere, my lord!' she said coldly. 'Indeed, I have the gravest suspicion that you are not to be trusted at all! That mulled wine that you sent up to us last night—can it be a coincidence that both Charlotte and I slept the clock round?'

Marcus was laughing again. 'I can only assume that you slept so well because you were tired, Lady Allerton, and no wonder if you will dash about the countryside at such speed!'

Beth smiled sweetly in return. 'And what a fortunate thing for you, my lord, when one of your own horses had gone lame and needed a rest! On your own admission you would not have wanted us to get too far ahead of you!'

'Indeed,' Marcus agreed affably, 'for how could we escort you if that were the case?'

Beth stared at him. The breeze was ruffling his silky dark hair and there was the beginning of a smile curling the corners of his mouth. She frowned a little. 'Escort us? What new nonsense is this?'

'It is an idea I have just had.' Marcus's smile grew. 'Would you not be far more comfortable on your journey with Justin and myself to smooth out any difficulties?'

Beth raised her eyebrows. In some ways the answer was a definite yes, but in others there was no doubt that Marcus's company was the last thing she sought, the most unsettling thing imaginable. Besides, it was simply not possible when they were adversaries.

'Well, it is most kind of your lordship to offer us escort, but—'

Marcus's hand covered hers on the stone parapet.

'Please don't refuse me, my lady. It would be my pleasure.'

Beth looked up at him and away quickly. The conventional words were given a completely new meaning by the sensual intensity in his eyes. She tried to slide her hand from beneath his.

'It would not be appropriate, my lord. How could you escort us? After all, we are in competition to reach Fairhaven first and can hardly travel together!'

'Need we be rivals?' Marcus queried softly. His fingers tightened over hers. 'I am sure we can find another solution…'

Beth held her breath. 'Such as?'

'Well…' Marcus looked thoughtful. 'With autumn so far advanced you might reconsider a sea voyage. Then we could escort you home to Mostyn for Christmas—'

Beth wrenched her hand from his. 'Oh, I understand your motives very well, my lord! You wish to persuade me to give up my quest! Well, I have already told you I shall not! Nor have I forgotten the slighting way you spoke to me when last we met! You are the last person whose escort I should accept on any journey, I assure you!'

She whisked past him and took the path up the hill towards the High Street, trying to hurry without the indignity of slipping on the cobbles. She was all too aware of Marcus's step close behind, his hand steadying her when she nearly lost her footing on some damp leaves, as she had known she would. By the time she reached the road, her cheeks were flushed with exertion and she felt hot, bothered and cross. Marcus, in contrast, was sauntering beside her, looking cool and infuriatingly amused.

Beth stalked across the road, narrowly missed being crushed by a cart that was clattering between the market stalls, and shot in at the door of the Castle and Ball with the intention of sweeping Charlotte up and driving off immediately. As she paused briefly in the corridor, she heard Charlotte's voice and pushed open the door of the private parlour.

Charlotte and Justin Trevithick were seated at the table partaking of luncheon. There were two other places set and an array of cold meats, cakes and fruit on dishes before them. As Beth burst through the door, Charlotte looked up and smiled at her. She looked pink and pretty and turned her glowing face to her cousin.

'Beth! And Lord Trevithick! Pray join us for some luncheon!' She drew out the chair beside her and smiled at Beth. 'The most excellent news, Beth! Mr Trevithick and his cousin are to escort us for the rest of the journey! What do you think of that?'

'This is ridiculous!' Beth grumbled, leaning back against the carriage's comfortable green velvet cushions and glaring out of the window at the passing scenery. 'How can we possibly be involved in a race to claim Fairhaven Island if we are accepting the escort of the very gentlemen we wish to outrun? Really, Charlotte! I never heard anything so foolish!'

Charlotte surveyed her placidly. She suddenly seemed much happier and Beth sighed inwardly with resignation. Charlotte did not have the temperament for risk or competition and now that she had the Earl and, more importantly, Justin Trevithick, to take care of all arrangements, she was much more comfortable.

'I do not see why we needed to become involved

in a silly race in the first place,' Charlotte said comfortably. 'Everything will be so much better now!'

Beth wriggled crossly. 'Certainly it will, for unless we can shake off the Earl we shall not be going to Fairhaven at all and shall end by going quietly home!' She looked out of the window, saw Marcus pull alongside on a raking black hunter, and hastily looked away. She wished that she had selected a book to pass the time, but it was such a lovely day that she had wanted to look out at the view. Unfortunately, the view seemed to consist of Marcus most of the time.

Justin Trevithick had taken the reins of the curricle for the time being and Marcus had chosen to ride. It was impossible for Beth not to observe that he had a magnificent seat on the horse and that he rode with an authority and elegance that was instinctive. She turned her gaze away from him and concentrated rather fiercely on the pretty Wiltshire scenery. Even though most of the trees had lost their leaves by now, it was still an attractive scene. It was a fresh day with a pale blue sky and the countryside shone in the weak warmth of the sun. It had not rained for several weeks, so the road was dry and the going good. The cows grazed in the fields and they rolled through several villages where the children played at the cottage gates. Charlotte dozed on the seat opposite. Beth reflected that she was the only one who seemed to be sitting underneath a private rain cloud.

They passed another tollbooth and drew up at the next inn to change the horses. Marcus appeared at the carriage door.

'Lady Allerton, it is such a fine day that I wondered if you would care to drive with me? I am leaving the hunter here—it belongs to the Castle and Ball anyway, and Justin is happy to take a turn in the carriage. What do you say?'

'Oh, do let Lord Trevithick take you up, Beth!' Charlotte said, before Beth could decline. 'You know you would prefer to be out in the fresh air and you are well wrapped up.'

This was true, but Beth could not help wondering how much Charlotte's eagerness owed to the prospect of spending some time with Justin. Marcus was holding out a hand to help her descend from the carriage and appeared to have taken her acquiescence for granted. Beth could not be bothered to argue, at least not for the time being.

They had some steaming hot coffee to warm them, but Charlotte declined a hot brick for her feet, saying that the day was mild enough for it not to be required. Nevertheless, when Marcus handed Beth up into the curricle, he was solicitous for her comfort, wrapping a blanket around her and ensuring that she had scarf, gloves and hat to keep her warm. Soon after they set off Beth realised that there was a great difference from travelling in the carriage; the speed was exhilarating, but it did generate a breeze, and because there was no shelter in the curricle it was considerably colder.

They had gone several miles when Marcus broke the silence and turned to her with a smile. 'I hope you are enjoying the journey, Lady Allerton! If you are too cold you need only to say, and I shall hand you up into the carriage again.'

Beth turned her glowing face to his. 'Oh, no, indeed, this is most enjoyable!' She looked around. 'Everything is so much more immediate, somehow, when one is in the open air! And Wiltshire is such a very pretty county…'

'It is,' Marcus agreed gravely. 'Do you know this area at all, Lady Allerton?'

'Oh, no, for I have travelled little and then only on the way to London and back.' Beth looked with lively interest at some curiously shaped little hills that lay close to the road.

'Only look! What odd-shaped mounds! I believe that these must be the mysterious barrows and hills that I have read about! They date from…oh, thousands of years ago! Is that not intriguing!'

Marcus laughed. 'It seems that history must be your subject, Lady Allerton! Was it an interest that you shared with your late husband?'

Beth turned her face away. For some reason she felt vulnerable when she spoke to Marcus about her marriage to Frank Allerton. It was as though no matter how little she said, Marcus could always see what lay beneath her superficial answers. Not that she had anything to hide, she told herself sharply. Her marriage had been no worse and no better than many others, May and December perhaps, but developing into mutual respect, if not love.

'Oh, Frank had little interest in the arts,' she said lightly, 'whilst I had no aptitude for mathematics or the sciences!'

'Complementary interests can be stimulating, however,' Marcus observed. 'There is much to talk about.'

'I suppose there could be.' Beth knew she sounded uncertain and for some reason honesty prompted her to add, 'Frank was too wrapped up in his studies to have much time to discuss matters with me.'

'Did you not find that disappointing?' Marcus enquired. Although Beth was not looking at him, she sensed that he was watching her rather than the road.

'Not particularly. A lady does not expect...' She glanced at him and her voice trailed away at the look in his eyes, for she was sure that she could see pity there.

'Surely it is reasonable—desirable—to hope for a certain sharing of interests? Life would be damnably lonely otherwise.'

Beth felt a strange pang inside her. She *had* been lonely at Allerton during the long weeks when Frank was absent, and even when he had been at home they had shared nothing more than an undemanding companionship. Marcus's words had given her a sudden glimpse of a different world, an existence where ideas were discussed and shared, giving mutual enjoyment. It was the sort of relationship that Charlotte had once described, something far beyond Beth's experience. Suddenly she felt as lonely as she had ever done at Allerton and she tried to cover it with a light laugh.

'Your ideas are somewhat unconventional, my lord! I can think of any number of married ladies and gentlemen who would be appalled by your suggestion that they speak to each other!'

Marcus smiled. 'Perhaps I ask a lot of the lady I would marry... An elegant and informed mind as well as gentleness, wit and charm! Am I then unlikely to find such a paragon?'

'Impossible!' Beth looked away. Marcus's references to his future wife made her feel peculiarly out of sorts.

'And since Sir Francis's death have you not felt inclined to remarry, Lady Allerton?' Marcus persisted. 'Doubtless you must have met plenty of gentlemen eager to persuade you?'

Beth shrugged, trying to hide her discomfort. 'Oh, I have no inclination to wed! I have my home and my cousins and plenty to interest me! What else could I want?'

It was a rhetorical question, but Beth wished she had not asked it when Marcus answered quite seriously.

'Companionship? Love?' His voice dropped. 'Passion?'

Beth shifted a little. 'Oh, love and passion are the most ephemeral and unreliable of things!' she said, with what she hoped was a worldly-wise air. 'I do not look for happiness there! Besides, I believe my nature must be cold—'

She saw Marcus raise his eyebrows in disbelief and almost immediately regretted her words. The memory of the kisses that they had shared seemed burnt on her mind. She looked about quickly for a distraction.

'What town is this that we approach, my lord? Can we be in Trowbridge already?'

They chatted easily until they reached the next stop, when Marcus insisted that, as darkness was falling, Beth should resume her place in the carriage to avoid becoming cold. She did not demur, changed places with Justin, and an hour later they arrived at the King's Arms in Shepton Mallet.

The King's Arms was much smaller than the inn in Marlborough, but it was a handsome building, clean and well cared for. Beth saw Charlotte nodding her approval as Justin escorted her inside, but then Beth thought Charlotte was wont to approve everything at the moment. Beth herself found that her earlier good mood had vanished as they settled into their room. She had wanted to press on to Wells, but Marcus decreed that they had gone far enough; she wanted to set off bright and early the next day whilst Marcus had already observed cheerfully that there was no hurry to be away in the morning.

During dinner, the other three chatted whilst Beth sat quietly and mulled over the frustrations of the situation. She could see no way of shaking off Marcus and Justin and getting ahead of them again, but on the other hand it seemed nonsensical to accept their escort all the way to Fairhaven. Such a course of action could never result in her claiming the island, for she would be there as Marcus's guest and not as the new owner. That was assuming that they had not worn down her resistance in the meantime, of course—Beth was determined that not even the combined persuasion of the other three would persuade her to go tamely home to Mostyn Hall.

She had to admit that Marcus had outmanoeuvred her, but only for the time being. She would think of a plan to escape him, of that she was quite determined.

The idea came to her after dinner, whilst she and Charlotte were waiting for the gentlemen to rejoin them to partake of tea. Charlotte had been asking idly how it was that Marcus and Justin had caught up with them so quickly and Beth had explained that they had travelled through the night. And whilst she was speaking she had suddenly thought that if Marcus could do that, so too could she... All that was required was that Fowler, the coachman, should be ready—and should keep the secret.

Beth had considered asking Charlotte to come with her and had reluctantly rejected the idea. Her cousin was so much happier now that she had Justin Trevithick's escort and Beth knew that she would kick up such a fuss at the plan that it would not be worth mentioning. It was in no way desirable to plan to travel alone, without either escort or companion, but Beth argued to herself that she would be able to reach the coast the following day, take ship for Fairhaven, and that would be that. She would have Fowler to protect her and plenty of money to ease her passage, and Marcus would not find out until it was far too late. The plan was perfect.

Before retiring, she went out to stables to apprise her coachman of the new arrangements and the need for secrecy. Fowler had been in the Mostyn family for many years and was accustomed to receiving orders unquestioningly, but even he commented that it was a powerful bad idea to be travelling at night in winter, and it took a lot of persuasion on Beth's part to convince him. Eventually he went off to the tack room, muttering under his breath, and Beth crept back inside the inn intending to sit out the night until two of the clock.

Although it was not yet late, Beth could discern a certain change of atmosphere in the inn. The gentility that had been so apparent during the early evening had now vanished. Earlier the corridors had been cleanly swept and bright with lamplight. Now they were gloomy and full of smoke, the stale smell of beer hung in the air and the sound of loud voices and coarse laughter, both male and female, roared from the bar. Beth scuttled in from the courtyard and made for the stairs, taking care to keep in the shadows, for she was not sure where Marcus was now and she had a particular reason for not wishing to draw attention to herself.

She had only ascended three steps, however, before she saw the shadow at the turn of the stair and checked as a man came down towards her. Her heart sank. Naturally it had to be Marcus Trevithick. It really seemed that there was no escaping him.

Marcus and Justin had evidently settled down in privacy to enjoy their port, for Beth registered that Marcus had discarded his jacket and loosened his stock. The pristine whiteness of his shirt seemed only to emphasise the bronze of his face and the unreadable darkness of his eyes. Beth felt her heart start to race as a mixture of guilt and some other more disturbing emotion stirred within her. She swallowed hard. She considered trying to slip past Marcus without having to stop for tiresome explanations, but knew it was a vain hope. Sure enough, as they drew level, Marcus put out a hand to block her escape up the stairs.

Beth instinctively stepped back and felt the hard wood of the banister against her back. In the dim light she could see nothing of his expression but felt rather than saw the intensity with which his gaze rested on her flushed face. She wondered if he and Justin had been drinking copiously. Not ten minutes previously she had hoped that they would be so sunk in their cups that they would not notice or suspect her escape. Now it seemed that that was all too likely—and rather dangerous.

'A moment, Lady Allerton.' Marcus spoke silkily. 'I have just been up to your room to check that you and Mrs Cavendish had everything for your comfort and I was concerned to find you absent. I cannot believe that it is appropriate for you to be wandering the corridors of an alehouse alone at this time of night! Whatever can have prompted you to venture out like this?'

Beth raised her eyes to his face in a look that she hoped was innocent. 'I was merely checking that all was well with my servants and carriage for the onward journey, my lord,' she said.

There was a pause. Marcus was still looking at her quizzically and Beth had the unnerving feeling that he was not convinced.

'I see. Well, I shall be very happy to attend to such matters myself and spare you the trouble.' Marcus shifted slightly and Beth backed away as far as she could. It had the reverse effect from the one she was trying to achieve, for Marcus took hold of her arm and drew her closer to him. 'Be careful that you do not fall over the banisters, my lady. They are a little rickety.'

Beth pulled her arm away. 'I am perfectly safe, I thank you, my lord.'

'I would dispute that,' Marcus said, giving her a smile. His gaze appraised her with disconcerting thoroughness. 'I think I should see you to your room, Lady Allerton. This inn is no place to be loitering alone. It has a somewhat…raffish…clientele in the evenings.' As if to underline his words the taproom door opened and a couple fell out into the corridor, laughing and amorously entwined. Beth looked away.

'There is no need to come with me,' she said a little abruptly. 'I can find my own way! Goodnight, my lord!'

Marcus stepped back and she brushed past him and

hurried up the remaining steps. When she looked down, he had reached the bottom of the stairs but he was still watching her and the mocking light was back in his eyes. He raised a hand.

'Goodnight, then, Lady Allerton! Sleep well!'

'And you, my lord!' Beth said politely.

Marcus's grin widened. 'Oh, Justin and I will no doubt sleep like tops once we have polished off our brandy!' He disappeared down the passage and Beth heard the parlour door close behind him.

She let out the breath she had been holding, and slumped against the banister, moving quickly away as it creaked protestingly under her weight. What to do now? She was certain that Marcus suspected something, but there was no chance that she would give up her scheme. It was tonight or not at all. Beth sped away up the stairs to pack her trunk and put her plan into action.

It was pitch black. Beth crept down the stairs, feeling for each tread and clutching the banister tightly so that she should not fall. Every creak of the steps sounded like a thunderclap and she was sure it was only a matter of moments before a door was thrown open above and she was discovered. Her trunk seemed very heavy and she could feel it nudging against her leg and threatening to push her down into the darkness beneath as she tried to steal silently down to the hall.

There was no sound in the passage but for the scratch of a mouse in the wainscot and the uneven tick of the parlour clock. Beth tiptoed to the door and drew back the bolt stealthily. She could see a faint light shining in the stables but there was no sound and the carriage was certainly not waiting in the yard for her. Perhaps Fowler had decided it would cause less of a stir to set off only when she was ready. Beth shivered. The moon was riding high amidst the stars and a cold breeze was swinging the weathervane on the stable roof. It was a frosty night.

Beth slipped out of the door and across the yard. The moonlight was very bright and it was easy to pick her way past the water trough and in at the darkened stable door. One torch still burned at the far end of the stables. A couple of the horses heard her approach and shifted in their stalls, bumping against the wall. There was the chink of harness. Beth paused, then went through the wide doorway into the coach house.

Here also a torch still burned, high on the wall. Her carriage was standing in the middle of the cobbled floor, exactly where it had been five hours previously when she had come to give Fowler his instructions. The door was open but of the coachman there was no sign and it was quite evident to Beth that she would be going nowhere other than back upstairs to bed. Fury and disappointment swept over her. It had been such a good opportunity to get ahead, with Marcus and his cousin no doubt dead to the world and unlikely to wake for hours. For a moment she toyed with the idea of harnessing the carriage horses herself and driving off, but she knew it would not serve. She had taken a gig out alone on more than one occasion but the idea of driving a coach and four was clearly unworkable. She almost stamped her foot in frustration.

Just as she was turning to leave the coach house Beth heard a sound emanating from inside the carriage itself. She froze, staring into its dark interior. There was no movement, but then the sound came again, a soft scraping that turned her blood cold. Someone was inside.

For a moment Beth wanted to turn tail and flee, but then she was seized by the conviction that the unfortunate Fowler must have fallen asleep about his work—or, worse, was dead drunk and was even now sleeping off his excesses in her coach. She marched up to the carriage steps and peered inside the open door.

'Fowler! Wake up at once! How dare you sleep when I require you to be working—?'

Strong hands grabbed her and pulled her inside the coach before she even had the chance to finish her sentence. All the breath was knocked out of her so that she could not have screamed even had she wished. In a hair's breadth of time she found herself tumbled on the velvet seat, pinned under a hard masculine body. She struggled and the cruel grip tightened, forcing her back against the cushions until she could not move. It was too dark to see anything of her assailant and her hair was blinding her anyway as it came loose from its plait and fell about her face. She drew a ragged breath, intending to call out or at the very least make a small yelping noise, but she suddenly froze, overwhelmed by the message that her senses were passing to her. Her assailant was none other than Marcus Trevithick.

Beth could hear him breathing and could smell the faint aroma of smoke and brandy that overlaid the more elemental scent of his skin. As soon as this impinged on her she felt herself weaken hopelessly in a way that was both inappropriate and unhelpful to her current circumstances. She let her breath out on a shaky sigh.

'Lord Trevithick!'

Immediately the ruthless grip eased and Beth heard the sound of flint striking sharply. A flame flared, then settled to a warm glow. Beth sat up and looked around.

The interior of the carriage, which was not particularly large in the first place, looked even smaller and oddly intimate in the glow of the lantern. Marcus adjusted the wick, then sat back in the corner. He was watching her with a mixture of amusement and calculation.

'That was…interesting, Lady Allerton. How did you recognise me?'

Beth had no intention of telling him, just as she had no intention of allowing him to gain the advantage. She edged towards the doorway and his hand immediately shot out and took her by the wrist.

'Not just yet. I believe you have some explaining to do!'

'I!' Beth looked him straight in the eye. 'It is your actions that require explanation, Lord Trevithick! Lurking in darkened stables, attacking innocent women…'

'And all in the middle of the night!' Marcus finished laconically. 'You start, Lady Allerton! Or perhaps I can help you?' His voice took on a sardonic inflection. 'When we last met you had apparently been checking on the welfare of your coachman. Perhaps you are repeating the exercise? To my mind it shows an unconscionable consideration for one's servants to come out to visit them at two in the morning!'

Beth sighed angrily. 'That was not my intention, as well you know.'

Marcus shifted on the seat. He was still holding her wrist and Beth had the unnerving impression that he would not let go of her until she came up with an adequate explanation. It was likely to be a long wait.

'So your intention was—what, precisely?'

Beth flushed at his tone. She was conscious that her hair was tumbled about her face and that Marcus was looking at her in a speculative manner that just made her feel all the more self-conscious.

'By what right do you quiz me anyway, my lord?' she demanded. 'It is not your place to question my conduct!'

There was a loaded silence, then Marcus shrugged. 'I suppose not, Lady Allerton. And as a matter of fact I do know the reason for your appearance here. You had asked your coachman to be ready to depart in the early hours, no doubt wishing to gain a march over us!' He smiled politely. 'I am sorry that your plan has failed, but, you see, Justin and I felt that Fowler was deserving of several glasses of the best brandy as a reward for the work he had done today, and alas...' He shrugged. 'It has such a detrimental effect on one's ability to drive a coach in the dark!'

Beth's eyes narrowed furiously. 'I see that you are intent upon corrupting my servants, my lord, as well as laying violent hands upon my person!'

Marcus was still smiling with infuriating calm. 'It was in your best interests, Lady Allerton! Driving in the dark is not a good idea and I was anxious to save you from harm. I believe that there is a frost tonight and the going might have been slippery. As for laying hands on you, well—' his gaze swept comprehensively over her '—I confess that it is tempting...'

Beth tried to pull away from him. 'I did not mean now.'

'I am well aware of what you meant.' Marcus looked rueful. 'However, you have put the idea into my head…'

Beth tried to draw away. The thought of Marcus fulfilling his threat gave her a feeling of nervous excitement that she tried hard to quell. She summoned up her most severe tone.

'This is foolish, my lord! We are in a carriage in a stables in the middle of the night…'

'True,' Marcus said, sighing. 'By all means let us be sensible and go back inside the inn.' He let go of Beth's hand and she immediately felt both disappointed and cross with herself. Marcus picked up the lantern, jumped down from the carriage and held a hand out politely to help Beth descend.

'Take care, Lady Allerton. It is dark and the steps are steep.'

Beth was never sure whether she slipped first or if he tugged on her hand, but as soon as the words were out of his mouth, she lost her footing on the carriage steps and fell into his arms. This did not appear to cause Marcus any problems; he held her pressed close against him for a second, a second during which Beth became acutely aware of the strength of his arms and the hardness of his body against hers. Then he slowly let her slide down the length of him so that her feet were once more on the cobbles but the rest of her body was still in startling proximity to his. Beth tried to step back and regain her balance, but Marcus simply moved closer so that her back was against the side of the carriage and he had a hand against the panelling on either side of her.

'My lord!' Beth's voice came out as a squeak.

'Yes, my lady?' Marcus's voice was barely above a whisper. His lips grazed the skin just beneath her ear, sending shivers rippling all over her body. He raised one hand to brush her hair gently back from her face.

'You said you would not!' Beth tried to sound authoritative but knew she simply sounded dazed. 'You said you would not lay a finger on me—'

Marcus stepped back a little and spread his arms wide in an exaggerated gesture of surrender. 'I am not doing so.'

Beth frowned slightly. 'Then…'

Marcus bent his head and kissed her.

It was like putting a flame to tinder. Beth's lips parted instinctively as his mouth came down on hers, its first light and persuasive touch deepening swiftly into passion. She reached out to him and his arms closed about her, holding her tight and fast. Beth gasped at the sensation of sensual pleasure that swept through her and Marcus took immediate advantage, tasting her, teasing her, exploring her with a languorous expertise that left her weak with delight. A wave of heat washed over her that had nothing to do with shame and everything to do with a more primitive emotion.

Beth struggled against the compelling demand of the kiss, the invitation to lose herself in the intense web of desire that surrounded her. She had almost forgotten that they were in a stables in the middle of the night; almost, but not quite. She had no intention of allowing Marcus to seduce her in the hay, which she was sure he would do without any compunction at all. She freed herself and Marcus reluctantly let her go.

'What is it, sweetheart?'

Beth frowned. 'It is just that it is not right, my lord!' She cast him a fulminating look. 'We are meant to be at odds—we *are* at odds—over Fairhaven and it is simply not appropriate for you to—' She broke off hopelessly. In the torchlight she could see a faint smile curving Marcus's mouth and it quite made her forget what she was talking about.

'To kiss you?'

'Yes! To kiss me and to make me forget…things.'

'Things?'

Marcus stood back for her to precede him through the coach house door.

'Things such as the reason why I was angry with you in the first place—apart from the matter of Fairhaven, I mean.'

'Ah.' Marcus sounded pensive. 'I think we may put that behind us now.'

'Well, I do not! If I could remember what it was…' Beth tried to marshal her scattered thoughts, but they remained obstinately elusive. 'When I do remember—'

'Beth? What on earth is going on?'

It was Charlotte's plaintive voice, emanating from the back door of the inn. 'I woke up and found you missing—'

She broke off as the light from Marcus's lantern illuminated their little group. 'Oh! Lord Trevithick! Good gracious! Whatever is going on?'

'I am sure your cousin will explain all to you, Mrs Cavendish.' Marcus politely held the inn door open for them. 'May I encourage you both to return to your chamber? And do not worry about an early breakfast! There is no hurry to depart in the morning.' He turned to Beth. 'Goodnight—again—Lady Allerton!'

'Whatever happened?' Charlotte whispered urgently, once they were back in their chamber and the door closed behind them. 'Beth, you are chilled to the bone and trembling! What were you doing in the stables—and with Lord Trevithick? I can scarce believe it!'

Beth told the story as concisely and unemotionally as possible, pausing only to allow for Charlotte's unavoidable exclamations.

'Fowler was apparently in his cups,' Beth said bitterly, as she reached the end of her tale, 'as a result of Lord Trevithick's generosity! And Lord Trevithick was in the coach, waiting for me!'

Charlotte gasped and pressed a hand to her mouth. 'Oh, Beth! What happened?'

'Nothing!' Beth said, shortly and untruthfully. 'Damnation! It was such a good idea.'

'Well, I do not think so,' Charlotte declared, 'and I can only be grateful that it has not come off! Driving off in the middle of the night! Whatever next!' Her gaze softened. 'Oh, let us talk about this tomorrow, for we are both tired and upset!'

Within ten minutes she was asleep again, but Beth lay awake for much longer. In part she was preoccupied with the infuriating failure of her plan, for she could not see how she would get another opportunity to get away. Her predominant thoughts, however, were of Marcus and of the devastating effect that he appeared to have on her. It made it even more imperative that she should escape him, and soon. She could not trust him and she could not trust her own reactions. Beth stared into the darkness of the bed canopy. Her body ached with an echo of the need that Marcus had aroused in her, a need that was both new and powerfully demanding. With a suppressed groan, Beth turned on her side and curled up. She was not accustomed to lying awake and suffering the pangs of frustrated desire and at that moment it was an experience she would happily have done without.

Chapter Six

The weather changed later that morning. The skies were grey when they set off from Shepton Mallet and by the time they reached Glastonbury the rain was falling and a strong westerly wind was blowing.

'I do not envy the gentlemen,' Charlotte said, peering out of the carriage window through the squally rain. 'Their curricle will be full of water! If the weather becomes much worse, I believe the roads will become waterlogged and we shall have to stop at the next inn.'

Beth did not reply. She had only had a couple of hours' sleep and was convinced that Marcus had roused them to set off at a particularly early hour because he knew she would still be half-asleep. Despite telling them that there was no hurry to depart, he had been knocking on the door at seven-thirty.

Beth felt tired and cross-grained but she did not want to vent her bad temper on Charlotte, who did not deserve it. They had already had one difficult conversation that morning; Charlotte had been hurt and reproachful that Beth had even considered leaving her behind. Once they had patched up that quarrel,

Charlotte had almost undone all the good work by trenchantly expressing the view that Beth's plan had been foolish, impulsive and utterly unworkable and Beth had had to bite her tongue hard to keep silent. It did not help that she knew there was a lot of truth in Charlotte's words. She knew she could be rash and impetuous, and that Charlotte considered her conduct unbecoming to a lady. She even accepted that she was thoroughly obsessed with Fairhaven and that that might also be considered inappropriate.

Beth wriggled crossly on the cushions. Today, for some reason, the carriage felt so much more uncomfortable. Her hours of insomnia the previous night had not led to any useful thoughts, either—she was still completely baffled as to how she might shake Marcus off and reach Fairhaven before him. Beth looked out at the pouring rain and sighed. Matters were not going at all to plan. The journey to Fairhaven, which had appeared so romantic and exciting to her only a few days earlier, had assumed a resemblance to a farce. Marcus held all the cards and she might as well give up now, which was no doubt what he intended her to do.

Then there was Marcus himself. She knew that the longer she was in his company, the greater her danger. She was as untried in love as a young debutante and no matter how fiercely she tried to defend herself against him, she was fighting her own feelings as well as him. She found him all too devastatingly attractive but, whilst she was certain he might try to seduce her, she had no confidence about reading his feelings. She stared glumly out at the rain. Perhaps Marcus even viewed her seduction as part of the challenge of the situation.

Just as she was thinking of him, the coach lurched to a halt and Marcus appeared at the window. His strong brown face was dusted with raindrops and his dark hair was plastered to his head. The rain was running in rivulets off his caped driving coat. Beth pushed the window down.

'Lady Allerton, Mrs Cavendish—the weather is far too inclement for us to continue. I have a friend living a short distance away in the village of Ashlyn. If you are agreeable, we shall call at the vicarage and beg shelter, at least until the storm stops.'

'Only fancy Lord Trevithick having a friend who is a clergyman!' Charlotte commented when the plan had been agreed and the carriage was in motion once again. 'He cannot be so dreadfully wicked if he keeps company with a man of the cloth!'

Beth laughed. 'Really, Charlotte! I sometimes think you are thrice as naïve as I, despite your greater years! There are plenty of clergymen far more wicked than Lord Trevithick will ever be!'

Charlotte looked affronted but did not argue. The coach had turned in at a neat entrance gate and was making its way up a drive to a substantial stone house, far grander than most of the vicarages Beth had known.

'I believe Lord Trevithick's friend keeps a certain style,' she commented, as they drew up outside the pedimented front door.

This impression was reinforced once they were inside the house. A neat housekeeper had gone to alert the Reverend March to their arrival and the visitors had time to admire the marbled hall, the sweeping stairway and the fine family pictures on the wall. Beth was just looking at a gold-framed portrait of a winsome child, when there was a step along the passage and a small gentleman hurried towards them, blinking myopically through thick reading glasses. His face broke into a smile of great sweetness as he saw Marcus, and he held out his hand.

'Marcus, my boy! How delightful to see you again! And Justin!' The Reverend March swung round on Justin Trevithick and shook his hand with equal enthusiasm. 'Your dear mother will be so delighted to see you! I was taking tea with her only the other day and she said it was high time you were bringing home a wife—' The Reverend broke off and peered at Beth and Charlotte. 'Upon my word, how remiss of me! Forgive me, ladies, I scarcely saw you there! My tiresome eyesight, you know… How do you do?'

Marcus stepped forward, smiling slightly. 'Lady Allerton, this is the Reverend Theophilus March who, for his sins, was once my tutor! Sir, may I present Lady Allerton and her cousin, Mrs Cavendish? We are travelling to Devon and have been in some distress from the weather, so thought to throw ourselves on your mercy…'

'Of course, of course!' Theo March seized Beth's hand and shook it firmly. 'Allerton? Cavendish? No relation of Hugo Cavendish, I hope, ma'am?'

'A distant cousin of my late husband's, sir,' Charlotte confirmed, looking slightly bemused. 'I have never met him myself.'

'Another of my tutees, I fear!' The Reverend Theo wrung his hands. 'A hopeless case! Quite wild and ungovernable as a boy and set fair to ruin himself as a man! You are to be congratulated on the fact that there is no close acquaintance there, ma'am!'

'I am sure that all your tutees drove you to distraction at times, sir,' Marcus said feelingly. 'I know that I was a sadly lacking in any academic ability!'

'Good at mathematics, but no application in Greek!' the Reverend Theo observed. He turned to Beth with a smile. 'I believe I knew your husband, Lady Allerton. A man of ideas, devoted to his studies. We were all very surprised when he married. Now, may I ask Mrs Morland to show you to your rooms? I am sure you will want a little time to rest before dinner.'

'I am sorry if you were offended by Reverend Theo's remarks,' Marcus whispered in Beth's ear, as Theo went off to call the housekeeper. 'He is tactless, but his heart is in the right place.'

Beth laughed. 'I did not take any offence and I am sure that Charlotte feels the same. Reverend Theo is quite a character, and more than generous in offering us all shelter!'

She saw Marcus relax slightly. 'I am glad you see it that way. He has offended many people from his pulpit, but the family is rich and owns the benefice and those who take him in dislike can find no way to remove him!'

Mrs Morland arrived then to show them all upstairs, and Beth found herself in a prettily appointed bedroom that faced south towards the Quantock Hills. The clock showed that there were several hours before dinner, and with a sigh of relief Beth removed her damp clothes and lay down to catch up on some sleep. The bed was soft and downy and before long she had drifted into a feverish dream where Marcus was pursuing her along a beach and into the sea itself. She woke up feeling hot and bothered and found herself tangled up in the bedclothes and feeling very little refreshed. It was now only a half-hour before dinner, and Beth forced herself to get up, wash her face and prepare to go downstairs. She had only brought one good evening dress with her, a confection of silver and lace, and though it was a little crushed it lifted her spirits to wear it. She called the maid to press the worst of the creases from the dress and arranged her own hair in a simple matching silver bandeau.

Everyone was already assembled in the drawing room and Beth was glad that she had taken trouble to repair as much of the ravages of the journey as she could. The gentlemen were elegant in their black and white evening dress and Charlotte always had the ability to look as immaculate as though she had just stepped out of a Bond Street modiste's. At her side, Justin Trevithick already looked proud and proprietorial and Beth smiled to herself. No matter what the other outcomes of the journey, that was one romance that she would wager would reach the altar.

Marcus came across to her side and took her hand. His gaze was admiring and Beth felt doubly glad that she had made an effort.

'Lady Allerton, you look very beautiful tonight. May I offer you a glass of Theo's excellent ratafia?'

It became apparent during dinner that the Reverend Theo kept an excellent wine cellar as well as a very good table. As dish succeeded dish, all accompanied by the most exquisite wines, the clergyman kept up an entertaining flow of conversation about parish life, then started to reminisce about Marcus's exploits as a youth. By the time that the gentlemen retired to take their port everyone was fast friends, and even Beth had almost forgotten that they were engaged in a contest for Fairhaven. The thought popped into her head as she was preparing for bed, but for once she dismissed it and as a result slept soundly and dreamlessly, leaving her worries to be confronted in daylight.

'I feel wretchedly sick!' Charlotte said miserably, the following morning. She was sitting up in bed and her pretty face was creased with pain and distress beneath her lace cap. 'It is all my own fault, for I knew I should not have had the sherry trifle last night! And now it has brought on the megrims and I have the most dreadful headache—' She winced as Beth pulled back the curtains a little and a bar of sunlight fell across the bed. 'Oh, Beth, pray do not! I fear my head will burst!'

Beth hastily pulled the curtains together again and went across to sit on the edge of the bed. It was a beautiful morning and she wanted nothing more than to be out in the fresh air, but she knew that Charlotte could not bear the light when she had one of her headaches. Besides, Charlotte was being more than generous in blaming the trifle. Beth suspected that it was the strain of the journey and the necessity of meeting new people that had done her cousin up and she felt more than a little guilty.

'Can I fetch you anything, dearest Charlotte? Some rose water or something to drink?' She saw the spasm that went across Charlotte's face as she shook her head. 'No? I shall leave you in peace, then.'

Beth went out and closed the door softly. When Charlotte was poorly it usually took at least a day for her to recover, so there would be no travelling to Devon that day. Beth knew that she would just have to be patient. It was not one of her usual virtues, but under the circumstances it was the only course. She hoped that the Reverend Theo would not mind prolonging his hospitality.

The house was very quiet. Beth went downstairs and into the breakfast room. Marcus was alone, sitting by the fire and reading a newspaper. He put this to one side immediately as Beth came in and stood up to hold her chair for her, his dark eyes intent on her face.

'Good morning, Lady Allerton. I trust that you slept well?'

'Exceptionally well, thank you,' Beth said truthfully. 'I am afraid, however, that my cousin is in poor health this morning and will be staying in her room.'

'I am sorry to hear it.' Marcus looked grave. 'It is a relief for me to find that you do not expect to move on today, however. Justin has gone to visit his mother over at Nether Stowey and the Reverend Theo has been called to the sickbed of a parishioner whom he assures me thinks himself at death door at least twice a month! It has become a ritual for them, I believe. Theo takes a couple of bottles of claret and the two of them sit drinking 'til the cows come home! I doubt we shall see him again this side of dinner!'

Beth looked at him a little uncertainly. 'Then we are…on our own?'

'To all intents and purposes.' Marcus's smile was faintly mocking. 'I will not inflict my company on you, Lady Allerton—not unless you wish it! Is there any possibility that you would like to spend the day with me?'

Beth hesitated, trying not to smile, but she could not prevent herself. It sounded a most attractive option. She reached for a piece of toast and buttered it slowly. 'Well, I could be persuaded…'

'Excellent!' Marcus smiled broadly. He handed her a cup of tea. 'Theo keeps as excellent a stable as he does a wine cellar, if you would like to ride!'

Beth's eyes sparkled. It was indeed too fine a day to sit inside and she relished the thought of a ride across country.

'Very well, then. I am sure we shall get on splendidly, my lord, provided that we do not quarrel over Fairhaven!'

Marcus smiled and got to his feet. 'Then we shall not mention it for the whole day!' He walked over to the door. 'Excuse me. I shall go to see to the saddling of the horses.'

As soon as Beth had finished her breakfast she hurried upstairs to change into her riding habit. The anticipation was buzzing through her body, as light and bright as the sunshine.

To spend a day with Marcus without the tension of Fairhaven between them seemed almost too good to be true. Maybe it was a temporary truce rather than a resolution of the conflict, but whatever the case, she intended to make the most of it.

They rode out all morning, taking an old green lane from Ashlyn towards the sea at Holford. They did not speak much. There was no need, for the sun was warm and the birds sang and the colours and wood smoke smell of autumn was all around them. Beth felt curiously content, more tranquil than she could ever remember. Her enjoyment sprang from the pleasure of Marcus's company, the warmth of his smile, the cadence of his voice and the light touch of his hand on her arm whenever he pointed out a view or something of interest. It was a more gentle feeling than the disturbing awareness that Marcus's presence habitually engendered in her, but Beth knew that under the calm surface ran the same attraction that was always between them.

After a while they started to speak more and Marcus told her a little about how he had felt when he had had to give up his diplomatic career to take over the responsibilities of the Trevithick estate. In return, Beth told him about Mostyn and her relationship with Kit and Charlotte. The time passed all too quickly and soon Marcus suggested that they return to Ashlyn for luncheon. It seemed a shame, but the exercise had given Beth an appetite and she reflected that they could always go out again in the afternoon. Or perhaps she might challenge him to a game of billiards, for she had spent many a long afternoon alone practising when Frank had been away from home and was tolerably certain that she could beat Marcus. She sighed. No doubt that was considered unladylike too.

Mrs Morland had set out a simple meal for them of bread, cheeses and Somerset cider; and as Charlotte was still prostrate with the migraine, Beth and Marcus ate alone. Marcus seemed preoccupied and quiet, and when Beth looked at him she thought he seemed rather stern. The thought was quelling. Perhaps the delightful morning had been a prelude to something more unpleasant—perhaps Marcus had only been kind to her because he was about to spring on her the fact that he was prepared to fight her through the courts before he let her have Fairhaven…

'Lady Allerton?' Marcus's quizzical tone recalled

her to the present. 'There is something I wished to say to you. I know we agreed that we would not mention Fairhaven today, but—'

Beth jumped to have her suspicions confirmed so promptly. She closed her eyes to ward off the blow.

'But I wanted to tell you that I will not oppose your quest to regain the island,' Marcus continued. 'You won Fairhaven in a just, if unorthodox, fashion…' there was an undertone of amusement in his voice '…and I know it means a great deal to you.'

Beth realised that she still had her eyes closed and opened them now, to see that Marcus was watching her with quizzical humour.

'Lady Allerton? Are you quite well?'

'I… Yes, indeed…' Beth floundered. It was the last thing that she had expected and it left her quite lost for words.

'That being the case,' Marcus continued, his tone steady, 'I would still like to escort you to the island in order to arrange a smooth transfer of the estate. I trust that that will suit you?'

'Oh, yes, of course…' Beth knew she sounded totally bemused. She simply could not believe that he had capitulated in such a way.

'Good!' Marcus smiled, getting to his feet. 'Please excuse me for a moment. I believe that Mrs Morland has a message from Theo…'

As he closed the door behind him, Beth sat staring at the panels, a lump of cheese still clasped unnoticed in her hand. Marcus's statement had been so unexpected that she had not gathered her wits to question him properly and already the doubts were creeping in. Could he be in earnest or was this just another cunning ploy to set her off her guard? She had been so certain that his tactic would be to try to persuade her to relinquish her claim and go home. Now she was thoroughly confused.

Beth nibbled the cheese absent-mindedly. Did she trust Marcus? He had played her false before. Yet she wanted to believe him. Her instinct told her to let go of her doubts and have faith in him, but that was dangerous, too dangerous for her to contemplate at the moment. It involved admitting to other emotions that made her feel totally vulnerable. Beth suddenly felt as though she was on the edge of a precipice where her own intuition was prompting her to step into the unknown but her natural caution was holding her back.

She sighed. If only Charlotte were not feeling ill she would go and ask for advice, but what was the point of that anyway, when she already knew what her cousin would say? Charlotte had never liked their escapade and would fall on Marcus's suggestion with cries of relief. Her advice could not be impartial. And there was no one else whom Beth could ask.

Still mulling over the problem, Beth went upstairs to see how her cousin was faring. Charlotte was asleep, so Beth came back down again. Mrs Morland was just crossing the hall as she reached the bottom step.

'Oh, Lady Allerton,' the housekeeper said, 'there is a message from the Reverend March. He anticipates being at Hoveton for the rest of the afternoon and begs your pardon.' She smiled. 'He especially asked that Lord Trevithick go down the wine cellar to select a particular claret to have with the dinner, plus a dessert wine and some more port! His lordship is down there now, if you were wondering where he had vanished to, my lady!'

'Thank you, Mrs Morland,' Beth murmured. She watched the housekeeper hurry off back to the kitchens and wandered slowly towards the drawing room, still turning the problem of Fairhaven over in her mind. It was as she reached the drawing-room doorway, when she actually had her hand on the door frame, that she was struck by an idea; an idea so outrageous, so daring, that she was not sure that even she would put it into execution.

There was Fairhaven and there was Marcus. She might trust him, or she might not…

Beth tiptoed down the corridor to the wine cellar. The heavy oak door was wide open, the cellar steps yawning below into darkness. Beth could faintly discern the flicker of a candle flame far in the depths of the vault and she heard the dusty scrape of glass on stone. Marcus was evidently engrossed in the task that Theo had set.

Only the previous night, when Theo March had been extolling the virtues of his wines, Beth had heard him joke that there was only one key to the cellar to prevent envious friends sampling his collection. That key was now in the door…

Beth stared. She crept forward and swung the door closed. It shut silently on oiled hinges. Beth turned the key, extracted it from the lock, and put it in her pocket.

A strange kind of madness took her and she almost laughed aloud. She ran up the stairs—she had not unpacked her trunk completely and now she threw her possessions in at random, squashing them down and slamming the fastening closed. She paused only to pen a hasty note to Charlotte and all the time she was listening intently, waiting for the inevitable shout from below that would show that she had been found out. None came. She hurried back down the stairs, her trunk bumping clumsily on every step, and shot out of the front door.

And all the while she was exulting in her escape and the fact that she had won.

It was only a step into Ashlyn village, but Beth hurried, glancing over her shoulder all the time, convinced that someone was watching her and about to ruin her plan. She had quickly considered and discarded the idea of asking Fowler to harness the carriage horses—that would take too long and be too noisy. Instead she was banking on the fact that there was a carter in Ashlyn who would be able to take her to Bridgwater.

At the forge she found exactly what she was looking for. An old cart was already standing waiting, half-loaded with sacks, the piebald cob chewing placidly on some hay whilst the carter chatted to the smith. Both of them looked up curiously as Beth hurried forward.

'Excuse me, sir! Can you take me to Bridgwater, if you please? I can pay you well…'

The carter was an elderly man and he was not to be hurried. He looked at the blacksmith, who gave him a significant look in return. He took off his hat, scratched his head, and put his hat back on again. Beth was almost dancing with frustration.

'Aye,' he said, after a long moment. 'I can take you there, missy.' He threw her trunk in the back, climbed slowly into the seat, leant down to give Beth a hand to scramble up beside him, then flicked the reins for the horse to set off. It seemed to Beth that the big cob was resentful of the sudden departure and moved with deliberate, agonising slowness.

'I believe it is but five miles to the sea?' she ventured, as they turned on to the road.

'Aye.'

'And we can go straight there?'

'Aye.'

Beth glanced over her shoulder. The village was receding, slowly, and no one was running down the main street and shouting after her. She started to relax a little. After all, there was only Charlotte and the servants at the vicarage. Charlotte was so poorly that she would not wake up for hours and the kitchen was well away from Theo's wine cellar. It could be some considerable time before anyone realised Marcus's predicament and even then she had the only key. It was heavy in her pocket.

As the cart lumbered down the country lane, Beth sat back with a sigh. The moment of exhilaration had gone, leaving her feeling oddly empty. She told herself that it was only because she felt so nervous at venturing off on her own, but her heart gave her another answer. They had been in complete accord, she and Marcus. It had been such a perfect morning. He had told her that he would not oppose her in the matter of Fairhaven. But...she had not trusted him. And she had ruined everything with her impetuous flight.

Beth gritted her teeth. She had won now. That was the important thing. The Reverend Theo would not return for hours and, even if he did, the door to the cellar was stout and could not easily be broken down. Marcus was trapped and she would definitely reach

Fairhaven before him now. It did not matter if he had
genuinely intended to give her the island or not, for
she had won.

Beth swayed backwards and forwards with the
movement of the cart and wondered what would happen next. In all likelihood Marcus would not even
trouble to follow her. Probably he would never wish
to see her again. Certainly he would never speak to
her, unless to haul her over the coals for her appalling
behaviour. And it had been appalling; Beth could see
that, now that she had plenty of time for reflection.
To have locked him in the wine cellar was bad
enough, but to somehow betray the memory of their
happiness that morning, to distrust him, that was her
real offence. She reminded herself that she had finally
outwitted him, but all she could think of was that the
price had been so very high. She found that she was
totally confused by her conflicting feelings and was
almost in tears.

They lurched their way along the country roads towards the sea. It became clear to Beth that her idea
of a direct journey and that of the carter was slightly
at odds—he detoured to several farms on the way to
unload his sacks and stood around chatting for what
seemed like hours to Beth. After a while the sun
dipped behind the clouds and a sharp wind sprang up,
bringing with it the first hint of rain. Beth huddled
down on the seat of the cart, but there was no shelter.
She was cold, for her gloves, hat and scarf were in
the trunk and the wind seemed to blow right through
her coat. By the time the carter dropped her on the
quay in Bridgwater it was getting dark and Beth felt
more miserable than she had done for a very long
time.

* * *

'How could she do such a thing?' Charlotte Cavendish wailed, pressing a small and inadequate lace handkerchief to her eyes. 'I know that Beth can be rash and impulsive, but she has never behaved like this before! Never!'

'Your cousin, madam, has all the self-restraint of a wayward child!' Marcus said, through his teeth. He was trying to remove some clinging cobwebs from his jacket and was tolerably sure that it would never be quite the same again. Certainly it was no longer a glowing tribute to Weston's tailoring.

'It is this absurd obsession with Fairhaven!' Charlotte lamented. 'I fear that it has quite taken over Beth's thinking! If only we could find some way to distract her attention—'

'I will give her something else to think about when I catch up with her!'

Marcus's gaze fell on Charlotte's apprehensive face and his own hard features softened a little. Mrs Cavendish had only risen from her sickbed a half-hour previously, and to find that her cousin had abandoned her and locked him in the cellar into the bargain was a shock that might have justifiably sent her into a fit of the vapours. Yet she was quite resolute, if pale, and Marcus admired her for that.

'Have no fear,' he said, in a gentler tone. 'I will find Lady Allerton and I will escort her to Fairhaven just as I had intended and I will also marry her! So you need have no concerns for propriety, Mrs Cavendish…'

Charlotte looked slightly winded at this rush of events. '*Marry* her! I cannot conceive why you would wish to do so, my lord—'

'Neither can I at this moment!' Marcus said feelingly. 'But it is inevitable, I fear! Would you be so good as to pass me those scissors, ma'am? There are several loose threads...'

Charlotte snipped assiduously for a moment. 'How did you remember the other entrance to the cellar, my lord?'

Marcus laughed. 'A relic of my misspent youth, I confess, ma'am! I remembered Reverend March once telling us that there was a passage from the cellar to the icehouse in the garden and one day when I was about fourteen I had sought it out. This time it seemed much smaller!'

Charlotte shuddered. 'Reverend March! Whatever will he say when he returns and finds the key to his wine cellar missing?'

'I leave you to smooth that over, ma'am!' Marcus said cheerfully. He looked up as Justin came into the drawing room. 'Is the curricle ready, Justin?'

'It's waiting for you,' Justin said, with a grin. 'I've sent a messenger to meet McCrae in Bridgwater, so he will be expecting you and will also have started to instigate a search. Don't worry, ma'am—' he turned swiftly to Charlotte '—I am sure Marcus will find Lady Allerton before she comes to any harm!'

Marcus clapped his cousin on the shoulder. 'Sorry to leave you so precipitately, old fellow, but I know you will deal admirably with Theo, and see Mrs Cavendish safely home.' He did not miss the look of guilty pleasure that passed between the two of them and smiled a little to himself. 'Mustn't let the horses chill! Oh, and Justin...' he paused in the doorway '...I'll wager that Theo will be more distraught at being debarred from his own wine cellar than by aught else! Pray tell him that I will send his key back to him as soon as I have wrested it from Lady Allerton's grasp!'

Although it was late afternoon and growing dark, Bridgwater quay was still busy with traffic from the river. Beth picked her way between barrels of herrings and piles of coal, trying to ignore the curious stares of the sailors and their occasional coarse remarks. She had thought that it would be a relatively easy matter to charter a boat to take her to Fairhaven, but now she realised that she had no idea where to start. There were plenty of ships tied up at the quay, but she knew she could not simply pick one, go aboard and ask the captain if he would take her to Fairhaven Island. Her trunk was weighing her down and seemed twice as heavy as it had done earlier. Eventually, when she had walked all the way down the North Quay and was wondering what to do next, she came to a brigantine whose captain was busy coiling a huge jute rope whilst his crew unloaded a cargo of lemons in big panniers. The captain looked up, smiled at Beth and touched his cap; emboldened by his courtesy, Beth hurried forward.

'Excuse me, sir. Could you tell me if there is a ship sailing past Fairhaven that might be prepared to land me there?'

'There's a ship sailing for Fairhaven on the morrow, ma'am,' the captain said, peering through the dusk. 'Moored just down the quay, past the square rigger. Over there, see—' And he pointed to a ship that was tied up some fifty yards away. 'Tidy craft, is that,' he said approvingly. 'Lovely job. Built originally as a French privateer, they say, and quite old now but as neat and as quick as they come...'

Beth stared, transfixed. The ship was very trim indeed and on the port side could be read the name *Marie Louise* next to a painting of seagull in flight. At the back of Beth's mind a voice echoed, the voice of her nursemaid all those years ago at Mostyn:

'Your grandfather had a beautiful ship called the *Marie Louise*, named for his French mother... It has a drawing of a seagull on the side, *La Mouette*, in French...'

So the evil Earl of Trevithick had stolen the ship along with the island and the sword. Beth let out a small gasp of shock and the captain looked at her in some concern.

'Are you feeling unwell, ma'am?'

Beth did not—could not—reply. She had seen two men, who were standing on the quay beside the *Marie Louise*, deep in conversation. One was thin and almost concave, dressed in an old-fashioned brown waistcoat and serviceable dark trousers. The other was tall and elegant despite his working garb of a rough frieze coat over his white linen shirt. The sea breeze ruffled his black hair. Beth pressed one hand to her mouth and took an instinctive step backwards, almost tripping over the coil of rope. Her movement caught the eye of the thin man, who caught his companion's arm and swung him round.

It seemed impossible to Beth that the man whom she had locked in a wine cellar only a few hours ago could be here on the quay at Bridgwater, seeing to the provisioning of what could only be his own yacht. How could Marcus possibly have escaped in the first place, let alone reached the port before her when she had a head start? All this went through her mind even while she spun around, ready to run away. Marcus was too quick for her. He had already halved the distance between them and when she bumped clumsily against a stanchion and nearly fell, Marcus's arm went around her, scooping her clear of the ground.

Beth gave a small sob of mingled fear, annoyance and strangely, relief. 'Lord Trevithick—'

'Lady Allerton?' Marcus sounded savage.

The thin man came running up, panting. 'My lord…'

'All right, McCrae.' Marcus's tone was clipped. He did not put Beth down. 'Would you call off the search, please? And take care of Lady Allerton's luggage. I will see you in the Sailor's Rest later…'

He looked down into Beth's face and she saw that his eyes were blazing with fury. She instinctively shrank back from the anger she saw there.

'As for you, Lady Allerton,' Marcus said smoothly, 'I will settle with you now! And in private! You are about to wish you had never been born!'

The inn was not like any that Beth had previously encountered in her travels. Although it was only late afternoon it was already full and smelled overwhelmingly of ale and tobacco. The noise was deafening— there was raucous laughter and loud conversation that quickly became lewd repartee when Marcus pushed his way thorough the throng, still carrying her.

'That's a pretty little moppet you have there, my lord, and no mistaking! When you've finished with 'er, pass 'er on…'

Beth struggled in Marcus's arms. 'Put me down at once, Lord Trevithick! How dare you subject me to the comments of these people—?'

'You have brought all this and more upon yourself

through your own behaviour,' Marcus said, through shut teeth. 'You will oblige me by keeping still, my lady, or I shall drop you into the nearest lap and let them have their way!'

This dire threat led Beth to turn her face into Marcus's shoulder, close her eyes and try to blot out the coarser comments of the crowd. In a moment the noise faded and Beth realised that they had left the taproom and were going upstairs. Marcus was carrying her with about as much consideration as a sack of potatoes—her feet bumped against the wall and she scraped one elbow painfully on the banister. She opened her mouth to protest, saw the look in Marcus's eye and closed it again.

Marcus pushed open the door of a tiny chamber and dropped her unceremoniously on to the bed. Beth bounced on the mattress and came to an undignified rest with her skirts all tumbled about her and her hair falling from its pins.

'Oof! Is it really necessary to treat me with such lack of consideration, my lord? And what can you mean by bringing me to this low place? I demand to return to Ashlyn at once—'

'No, madam,' Marcus said, still through gritted teeth. 'You were the one who was so determined to be here that you would take any steps to achieve it!' He kicked the door closed and turned to survey her, his glittering dark gaze raking her ruthlessly.

'I have no real wish to speak to you now, but there are a few things that I must say. Leaving aside your inexcusable behaviour in locking me in Theo March's wine cellar, you have the gross folly to try to run away and arrange passage for yourself to Fairhaven! Alone!' Marcus ran a hand through his hair. 'Have you any idea of the distress you have caused your cousin? Do you even care? You have no more sense than a spoilt brat and you deserve a good spanking!' Marcus drove his hands into the pockets of his coat as though to prevent himself from doing her an injury. 'I would administer one myself were it not for the fact that I should probably enjoy it far more than I ought!'

Beth blushed bright red. 'My lord!'

Marcus shot her a furious look. 'My lady? It is about time that someone told you a few home truths! You are easily the most infuriating and exasperating woman that I have ever met! Now, I am going to meet with McCrae to arrange tomorrow's sailing, and I shall be locking you in here for your own safety! Do you object?'

Beth stared at him, quite cowed into silence. 'I… Marcus, I am sorry—'

'I do not wish to hear it!' Marcus stalked over to the door, then turned back to her. 'Speaking of keys, I should be obliged if you would hand over the key to Theo's cellar—at once!'

Beth fumbled clumsily in her pocket, aware that Marcus was watching her efforts with the same angry, implacable regard. When she put it into his hand she heard him make a noise of disgust, and he took it from her without a second glance.

'We shall speak later, if I regain my temper sufficiently to do so without shouting!' he said, over his shoulder. 'In the meantime I suggest that you draw as little attention to yourself as possible. No leaning out of windows and begging for rescue! Do you really wish for that pack of villains to come upstairs for you? It is about time you learned some sense, Lady

Allerton!' And, so saying, he slammed out of the door and Beth heard the key turn with finality in the lock.

Marcus had not returned by eleven o'clock that night. Shortly after his departure a slovenly maid had appeared with a tray of greasy beef stew and Beth ate some half-heartedly whilst she listened to the noise swell downstairs as even more seafarers joined the throng gathered below. The tiny room was cold and dirty, but she had absolutely no wish to effect an escape and go straight from the frying pan into the fire. It was unnerving not knowing what Marcus intended. She did not believe that he had locked her in in order to take advantage of her, but she felt uncomfortably vulnerable.

She still could not understand how Marcus had reached Bridgwater before her, but then it seemed that there was a lot that she had overlooked. It was apparent now that Marcus had intended to sail for Fairhaven right from the start, either with or without her, for he had had a boat and a crew waiting. Beth stared miserably into the meagre fire. He had told her only that morning that he intended to escort her to the island, but she had only half-believed him. Yet perhaps his intentions had been honourable all along. She had already begun to regret her impetuous flight and particularly her lack of trust, and now she felt ashamed. But the damage was done. Marcus was deeply angered by her behaviour, and with good reason.

Beth shivered miserably. If Marcus had been acting honourably all along, her lack of trust would have been particularly wounding to him. Locking him up would hurt his dignity but distrusting him went deeper, much deeper. And just at the moment he was so angry he would not even let her apologise.

The fire had burned out and Beth slowly prepared for bed by the light of the one candle. The bedding looked none too clean and she was almost certain that she saw a flea jump from the mattress when she turned the sheets down, so she decided to lie under the bedspread and try to keep warm as best she could. This proved none too satisfactory; even fully dressed she was cold and uncomfortable, and had only drifted into a light doze when the door opened and Marcus came in.

'Lady Allerton? Are you awake?'

Beth opened her eyes and tried to discern whether or not Marcus was drunk. Certainly a strong scent of spirits had entered the room with him, but when the candle flame flickered briefly on the expression in his eyes, she saw that he was frowning and looked sober enough. His tone of voice was as abrupt as when he had gone out hours previously and Beth's heart sank as she realised that his temper had not improved. She struggled to sit up as Marcus sat down on the edge of the bed and started to pull off his boots.

'Oh, what are you doing—?'

Marcus shot her an irritated look. 'What does it look as though I am doing? I am coming to bed!'

Beth clutched the bedspread to her. 'Here? But what will people think?'

This time the look that Marcus gave her combined exasperation and a certain grim amusement. 'Believe me, Lady Allerton, none of the occupants of this ale-house care a jot for your reputation! They already believe that I have ravished you thoroughly and have been pressing me for the details!' He threw his boots into the corner of the room and started to unbutton his jacket. 'Besides, it seems a little late for you to be worrying about such things! A hoyden who dashes about the countryside barely chaperoned, who tries to run away in the middle of the night, locks gentlemen in wine cellars and wanders about a port alone after dark clearly has no consideration for propriety!' His frown deepened. 'Just tell me one thing—do you have so little faith in me that you disbelieve everything I say to you? I had thought that there was more trust between us than that!'

Beth stared at him in the candlelight. His face was set in hard, angry lines, but behind that she thought she glimpsed another emotion: hurt perhaps, or disappointment. It made her feel wretched, doubly so for mistrusting him and for causing him hurt. A big lump came into her throat and she looked at him, unable to speak. For what seemed like a long moment they stared at each other, then Marcus turned away with a sigh.

'Just why are you fully dressed and why are you *on* the bed rather than *in* it?'

Beth let out her breath on a sigh. Marcus was evidently so cross with her that he would find fault with anything.

'It is cold and there are fleas in the bed! Not that it is any concern of yours, Lord Trevithick! Why do you not sleep on your ship?'

Marcus laughed abruptly. 'What, would you have me leave you here all night unprotected? Is that the lesser of two evils?'

Beth turned away from him. 'Well, if you must stay, I am persuaded that you will find the chair comfortable enough.'

Marcus made a rude and derisive noise. 'Do not be ridiculous! And kindly move over! You are taking up all the space!'

Beth squeaked and rolled away quickly as the mattress sank under his weight. He was still in shirt and pantaloons, but he suddenly seemed too big and far too close. He was even closer once he had put out a lazy hand and pulled her back to his side. The treacherous mattress tumbled her into his arms.

'Why, you *are* cold...' Marcus's voice had softened as he felt the chill in her body and tucked it closer to his. He pulled the bedspread over the two of them. 'There, we shall warm up soon enough and be asleep...'

Beth was warming up far too quickly. Her head was on his shoulder and she could feel the heat of his skin through the thin shirt where the palm of one hand rested against his chest. His breath stirred her hair. The prospect of sleep now receded as she became acutely aware of every line and curve of Marcus's body against hers and felt the beat of his heart strong and steady against her ear. She had never gone to sleep in such a position before. Frank had never shared her bedroom and seldom her bed. On the infrequent occasions he had troubled her for his marital dues, he had left immediately afterwards.

Beth lay still, torn between arousal and comfort. She was keenly aware of Marcus's arm about her, his hand resting just below her breast. The awareness kept her awake whilst the corners of her mind started to cloud with warmth and drowsiness and comfort. Marcus turned his head a little and spoke drily.

'Try to breathe a little, Lady Allerton, or you may find yourself in difficulties. Unless...' his voice changed subtly '…your clothing is too tight to allow ease of breathing? If you wish to take anything off—'

Beth gave a protesting squeak and tried to pull away, but he held her tightly. 'Never fear. I do but tease you. But you should try to get some sleep, for the voyage tomorrow will take the best part of the day.'

Beth's eyes flew open. 'Tomorrow? So we do sail for Fairhaven?'

'Of course.' Marcus sounded sleepy. 'I said we would and so we shall.'

'But—'

'No buts…' He shifted slightly so that Beth's head was more comfortably pillowed on his shoulder. 'And no more discussion. I am exhausted, even if you are not. Talking can wait until tomorrow.'

Beth heard his breathing deepen almost immediately and realised that he had fallen asleep. Part of her, a very small part, was affronted that he could so easily ignore the fact that she was in his arms. Evidently he was used to being in such a situation, whereas she was tormented by his proximity. Another part of her mind was grappling with the implications of sailing for Fairhaven in Marcus's company the following day. She tried to think about it, but she was so weary with the events of the day that drowsiness overcame all resistance. At last she was warm, comfortable and safe, and she soon fell asleep.

Marcus awoke as the grey dawn light started to filter in through the bedroom window. The quay below was already noisy with the business of the new day. He opened his eyes and saw that they had both moved in the night; Beth was now tucked in front of him and they were lying very close and snug, like spoons. Her silky black hair was spread out on the pillow and in sleep her face was as clear and untroubled as a child's. Marcus smiled to himself. He had to admit that he had treated her very badly indeed.

When he had first seen Beth on the quay he had been so angry that he had not cared a jot about her feelings. As soon as she had tricked him and run away from Ashlyn he had known immediately what she intended and at first could not believe that she could be so foolhardy. He had thought that he had made it clear that he would take her to Fairhaven, yet clearly she had either disbelieved him or simply not wanted his company. Either way he was hurt and angry, but he was also worried. Very worried. A woman alone wandering around the quay at Bridgwater would soon find herself receiving several offers, none of which would be passage to Fairhaven. Passage to the nearest whorehouse, perhaps, and the invitation would be phrased in a way to brook no refusal.

He looked down at Beth's sleeping face. He wondered if she had even considered such a possibility or whether her obsession with reaching Fairhaven had blinded her to all good sense. She was no child to be unaware of the perils of journeying alone, though perhaps she had been so sheltered that she did not truly know what could so easily have happened to her. He had known it, and he had had men on every corner, in every inn, looking for her. He had been terrified that he would not find her in time, or that some accident had already befallen her on the way to Bridgwater.

Then he had seen her and his anger had increased tenfold because she was so obviously unharmed and

still unaware of the danger she was in. He had wanted
to take her and shake her hard, to force her to recognise her own folly, to punish her for the fear and
misery she had made him suffer. He had wanted to
kiss her and make love to her despite the hurt of her
betrayal. So he had locked her in and left her until
his anger had subsided, and then he had come back
and seen her and wanted her all over again…

Marcus shifted uncomfortably. Beth was pressed
against him, very soft and sweet, the curve of her
buttocks resting tantalisingly against his thighs.
Marcus was already half-aroused and now felt himself
harden further as he considered their relative posi-
tions. He reminded himself sternly that there were
several layers of clothing between them but this did
not help as it simply made him think of removing
them all. Then there were the fleas… That was better.
His tense body relaxed slightly. He had locked Lady
Allerton in a flea-ridden room in a rough alehouse on
the quay in Bridgwater and had spent the night with
her there. He smiled a little to think of the reaction
of the society gossips to such a story.

He smoothed the hair away from Beth's face with
gentle fingers and she turned her head slightly, snug-
gling closer to him. Marcus obligingly adapted the
curve of his body to hers. He knew there could only
be one ending to Beth's adventure now, now that she
was so thoroughly disgraced. It did not disturb him,
since it was what he had intended almost from the
first moment he had met her. How Beth would react
to his proposal was a different matter, however.
Marcus frowned. He was not at all sure if she would
accept him. Most importantly, she was still obsessed
with Fairhaven and he did not want to have to contend

with such a rival. So they had to go to the island and Beth had to find out the truth about her grandfather and then perhaps she could put the whole matter behind her and concentrate on the future. A future with him. Marcus sighed. It should have been easy but he had the deepest suspicion that it would not be. Where Beth Allerton was concerned, nothing was that simple.

Chapter Seven

Beth sat in the shelter of the wheel-house, out of the wind, a blanket tucked about her legs. Marcus had suggested that she stay below in one of the cabins and at first she had complied, but once they were clear of the land the wind had picked up and the boat had started to pitch alarmingly. Beth had soon started to feel nauseous and had moved out into the fresh air, where one of the crew had taken pity on her and arranged the makeshift seat from a few wooden crates. Now, although the horizon still dipped and soared with sickening regularity, Beth could at least feel the refreshing spray on her face and breathe deeply of the salty air.

She had quickly noted that Marcus seemed quite unaffected by the movement of the boat. He had been in the wheel-house for quite some time talking to the helmsman and he had also taken his turn at doing whatever job was required; casting off, trimming the sails or simply giving a hand to the other members of the crew. And she saw that the men appreciated it. There had been a quick compliment for his skill from one of the hands, and at least one glance between the crew that showed their approval. It was a side of Marcus that Beth had not seen before.

Unfortunately his attitude towards her was in stark contrast. She and Marcus had barely spoken that morning, except for one humiliating conversation over the stale bread and porridge that had constituted their breakfast in the inn. Beth had requested to be taken back to Ashlyn. Marcus had looked at her stonily and said that she could return there if she wished, but that he was travelling to Fairhaven and she might as well accompany him since she had gone to such an unconscionable amount of trouble to get there. That had been the end of the conversation and Beth did not dare question him further about the trip. His face had assumed the same forbidding expression that it had worn the previous night and she knew that she was still in deep trouble. When the meagre breakfast was over she had gone with him out on to the quay where the boat was waiting. They had cast off and now turning back was impossible.

Beth shivered a little within her fur-lined cloak. Ahead of them there was nothing to see but the grey of the ocean, and on the port side the land was slipping away, the hills of Devon growing smaller all the time. Marcus had said that it would take them the best part of the day to reach Fairhaven. To Beth that seemed as nothing after so many years of waiting.

After an hour or so she fell into an uneasy doze and woke feeling queasy and a little befuddled. The sun was peeping through thin cloud overhead and the wind was strong. A rich smell of stew filled Beth's nostrils and her stomach lurched. She turned away as Marcus appeared before her, his bare feet braced on the wooden deck, a plate of food held in one hand.

He took one look at her face and smothered a smile. Beth glared at him.

'Oh, dear, you look distinctly sickly, Lady Allerton…'

Beth tried to ignore the persistent smell of the stew but was forced to resort to holding her nose. She spoke with a distinct lack of dignity.

'Lord Trevithick, I would be obliged if you would go away! Now! And take that repellent plate of food with you!'

Marcus sauntered away, grinning. 'Pray call me if you require a bowl, ma'am!'

Within a half-hour Beth was too chilled to sit still any longer. She was tempted to go down to a cabin and try to sleep, but the thought of the enclosed stuffiness below decks made her feel even more seasick. Instead she wandered over to the rail and leant against it, staring into the flying spray below. She felt cold, sick and lonely, and it was a far cry from the way she had imagined arriving on Fairhaven Island.

Now that she thought about it, she realised that she had given very little thought to the practicalities of the journey. Her imagination had flown ahead of her, skipping over the difficult bits like a rough sea crossing, and had pictured some triumphant return to her grandfather's castle. She felt a little foolish. It did not help that Marcus had ignored her for the best part of the day and that his crew, apart from a few sympathetic glances, had left her to her own devices.

As much to occupy her mind as to keep warm, Beth wrapped her cloak closer and strolled around the deck, watching the seabirds that whirled and screamed in the ship's wake, scanning the horizon for land or for any other passing ships out of Bristol. The afternoon dragged by.

'Land ahoy!'

Beth had been staring at the sea for so long that she felt almost mesmerised by the time the call came. She swung round. Marcus was strolling towards her across the deck, a telescope in his hand. 'Fairhaven is visible from the starboard bow, Lady Allerton. Would you care to see?'

Beth went with him across to the rail, took the spyglass a little gingerly in her hand and searched the horizon. Sure enough, the great granite cliffs of the island were visible above the tossing of the waves. Everything looked grey: sea, sky, land. The clouds were lowering and clung to the island like a veil. But it was beautiful.

'Oh!' Beth handed the telescope back to Marcus, her eyes shining. 'I can scarce believe it! It looks very beautiful, my lord!'

There was a strange expression on Marcus's face, part amused, part rueful. 'If you think that, Lady Allerton, you must love Fairhaven very much indeed! To my mind it looks a damnably lonely place!'

He turned away to issue some instruction to the helmsman about avoiding the shoals around Rat Island and anchoring in Fairhaven Roads. Beth hardly paid attention. She was clinging to the rail as the island slowly grew bigger in front of her. Within minutes she was soaked by the spray and the drizzle that was falling from the grey sky, but she barely noticed. She was so close to achieving her dream of reaching Fairhaven that she had no thought for anything else at all.

As they grew closer the island took on a clearer

shape and Beth could even distinguish the chimneys of the castle and the roofs of the houses in the tiny village that huddled at the top of the cliff. The whole of the eastern side of the island was now spread out before them and Beth could see what Marcus meant— there were no trees, no shelter, only the plunging cliffs and the screaming seabirds.

'There are no trees…' she murmured, when he came back to her side. 'Does nothing grow here?'

'Colin tells me that the crops grow well enough,' Marcus said, nodding in the direction of Colin McCrae, 'and my aunt tends a small garden in the shelter of the castle walls. She always complains that the sheep take the greenest shoots!'

Beth frowned. 'Your aunt?'

'Why, yes.' There was a mocking smile curling Marcus's mouth. 'Did you imagine Fairhaven quite uninhabited, Lady Allerton? My uncle, St John Trevithick, has been the vicar of Fairhaven for donkey's years and his sister Salome keeps house for him at Saintonge Castle.' He gave Beth an old-fashioned look. 'Did you imagine that I was bringing you to a place quite beyond the pale? The truth is rather more prosaic, I fear!'

Beth looked away. She was not entirely sure what she had imagined, but her thoughts had not encompassed meeting any of Marcus's relations. She doubted that they would be pleased to see her. Certainly she had not supposed that she would be evicting a vicar who had served the community for decades, nor supplanting his spinster sister. It looked as though her image of Fairhaven as a bleak and neglected place had been embarrassingly at fault.

By now they had reached the shelter of the island

and the sea swell abated a little as they anchored in the lee of the great cliffs. A rowing boat was lowered and Marcus and Colin McCrae assisted Beth down the ladder to a place in the stern. It seemed the work of moments for two burly seamen to row them ashore and pull the boat up on the shingle of the beach. A cart was already waiting at the bottom of the cliff and they lurched up a rough track that seemed carved into the face of the rock, Beth clinging to the sides of the cart whenever they turned a corner and the wheels seemed to skim the thin air. Suddenly the walls of the castle rose before her, Saintonge Castle, built by her forebears so many years before. A lump came into her throat and for a moment she was afraid she would cry.

There was a reception party waiting for them at the bottom of the castle steps. It seemed that every man woman and child on the island had assembled to greet the new Earl. Beth became suddenly and devastatingly aware of the figure she must cut as she crouched in the back of the cart, her hair straggling from her bonnet in rats' tails and her soaking dress and cloak clinging to her body in a manner far too voluptuously revealing. No doubt the good villagers of Fairhaven would think the sailors had brought their concubine with them! As for what Marcus's relatives would make of her... Uncharacteristic reticence made her hang back, but it was too late, for Marcus was climbing down from the cart and had cheerfully swept her up in his arms, to deposit her right in front of the curious crowd. Beth suspected that he had done it on purpose.

'Marcus, by all that's holy!' A voice boomed from

behind them. 'I never thought to see the day! The lord moves in mysterious ways!'

Beth and Marcus both spun round. An elderly woman was descending the steps from the castle entrance. She was not fat so much as large, and recognisably a Trevithick from her very dark brown eyes, high cheekbones and the luxuriant dark hair that was coiled in a huge chignon in the nape of her neck. She was improbably dressed in pink satin with matching embroidered slippers, and a scarlet cloak was thrown carelessly about her shoulders and was now flapping in the strong wind. Beth found that she was staring.

'A plague upon this weather!' the woman said cheerfully, grasping Marcus to her and kissing him enthusiastically on both cheeks. 'Seven plagues upon it! My, my, how you've grown!'

'Aunt Sal,' Marcus said, grinning, 'it is such a pleasure to see you again!'

'And you, dear boy!' Salome Trevithick looked round and her bright brown gaze fell on Beth. 'Bless me, a stranger in the desert!' Then, at Beth's look of puzzlement, she added, 'Isaiah thirty-five, verse six, my dear.'

'Aunt Sal, this is Beth Allerton,' Marcus said formally. 'Lady Allerton, my aunt, Lady Salome Trevithick.'

'Welcome, my dear!' Salome Trevithick extended a hand sparkling with diamonds. She looked Beth over approvingly. 'A veritable angel, Marcus, albeit a rather sodden one!'

Beth blushed.

'Aunt Sal writes all my uncle's sermons,' Marcus explained in an undertone, 'so her conversation is always peppered with Biblical allusions! Indeed, she quotes the Bible at every available opportunity!' He raised his voice. 'Is Uncle St John not with you, Aunt? I was hoping—'

'Alas, St John has taken a journey into a far country,' Salome said, beaming. 'He has been called to the Bishop at Exeter, my dears. Apparently the poor man had heard that St John was drunk in the pulpit last month and demanded an explanation!'

'Nothing else to do on Fairhaven!' a voice from the back of the crowd shouted.

Marcus turned back to the villagers, who had been waiting with good-humoured patience. 'Thank you for such a warm welcome to the island!' His voice carried easily to everyone. 'It is good to be here at last, even on such an inclement day!'

'You should see the place in really bad weather!' the voice at the back of the crowd responded.

Everyone laughed. 'I am sure I shall!' Marcus said, grinning. 'For now, I am happy to see you all and to introduce Lady Allerton, who is to be the new owner of Fairhaven.'

To Beth's horror, Marcus pulled her to his side. 'I know that many of you will remember Lady Allerton's grandfather, Charles Mostyn, and be glad that the days of a Mostyn landlord are to return!'

A curious murmur ran through the crowd. Beth's smile faded as she saw the looks on the faces of the people in front of her. From smiling good humour they had moved to uncertainty and even sullenness. Some were muttering to each other and a few were watching her with undisguised hostility. Even Salome Trevithick looked stern. Beth bit her lip, conscious of their resentment but taken aback by the suddenness with which it had sprung up.

There was an awkward pause, then a woman who had been standing a little apart from the crowd bent down to murmur in the ear of the small blonde child beside her. A moment later, the girl had trotted forward and held out a wilting posy to Beth.

'Welcome to the island, my lady,' she whispered.

Beth forgot about the strange hostility of the crowd and her own dishevelled state. She smiled at the child, then crouched down to take the flowers and give her small admirer a kiss. The little girl looked at her with huge, considering blue eyes for a moment, then smiled back, stuck her thumb in her mouth and ran back to her mother. Another murmur ran through the crowd, this time of guarded approval.

'Prettily done,' Salome Trevithick said gruffly, grasping Beth's elbow and helping her to her feet. 'Suffer the little children to come unto me! Matthew nineteen, verse fourteen! Let me show you to your room, Lady Allerton. You look in sore need of some refreshment!' She linked her arm through Beth's and steered her up the castle steps. 'Some of the islanders have long memories, I fear, Lady Allerton. But ashes to ashes, I always say, and never speak ill of the dead!'

Before Beth could ask her to explain this strange pronouncement she found herself inside the castle and forgot everything in admiration of the sheer splendour of it all. Saintonge Castle had originally been built in the thirteenth century, but within the huge, window-less walls, a more modern dwelling had been fashioned. The stone-flagged entrance hall was neither as shabby nor as bare as Beth had imagined it, but was hung with rich tapestries and decorated with polished silver. Salome ushered her upstairs, to an opulent suite of rooms set into the southern wall of the castle. There was a huge bedroom with a wide window that looked out over the sea, a sitting room with a most comforting fire, and a modern bathroom with the biggest bath Beth had ever seen. She went back into the bedroom and walked over to the stone casement, standing by the window to look at the huge sweeping panorama of the sea. She gave a little sigh.

'Oh, how beautiful!'

'Bless you, my child!' Lady Salome said, moist-eyed. 'It is indeed a lovely place! Now, I shall send Martha McCrae to you in a little while to see if you need anything. She is the mother of that delightful child who greeted you outside!' She paused. 'Martha will bring you dinner in your room tonight, for we do not eat *en famille* until tomorrow. I thought you might be too tired for company!'

'Thank you!' Beth said gratefully. She did indeed feel worn out with travelling and trying to absorb new experiences. Lady Salome smiled and went out, red cloak flying, and Beth sank down on to the window seat to look out, entranced, across the bay.

She was still sitting there half an hour later, when Martha McCrae knocked at the door and came timidly into the room, bearing a supper tray.

'Is everything to your liking, my lady?' The housekeeper sounded a little strained.

Beth turned to her with a smile. 'Oh, of course! It is entirely delightful! I am just so taken aback by the beauty of the whole island!'

Martha McCrae smiled shyly. Unlike her blonde daughter, she had soft brown hair and kind brown eyes. Her complexion was very pale and freckled, and her face wore an unmistakably worried air. Beth wondered what could be making her so nervous.

'Have you lived on Fairhaven for long, Mrs McCrae?' she asked, anxious to put the woman at her ease.

The housekeeper nodded. 'A little while, Lady Allerton, but not as long as Lady Salome and the vicar. I came here as a bride six years ago, when the old Earl took Colin on as his estate manager here.' She wiped her hands down her apron in a sudden, nervous gesture. 'It has not always been easy—the winters are hard and the Earl—well, I believe that he forgot about us being here sometimes.' She sighed. 'That is why we thought... When we heard that the new Earl was finally coming here, we hoped—' she broke off and resumed '—we hoped he might have the good of the island at heart. But it seems he intends to give Fairhaven away—'

She broke off and her pale face flushed bright red. 'Forgive me, my lady. I was thinking aloud! Excuse me. I will send a maid up with some water...'

And before Beth could say another word, she had turned and fled.

Beth sat down a little heavily on the edge of the big tester bed and pecked half-heartedly at the food on the tray. Now she understood—in part, at least—the hostility of the villagers. Like the McCraes, they had believed that Marcus's arrival on Fairhaven must herald a better time ahead. They had flocked to welcome him, buoyed up by hope and expectation. And almost the first thing that he had done was tell them that he was giving Fairhaven over to her. Worse, her arrival threatened the future of St John and Salome, the only members of the Trevithick family who had ever shown any loyalty to the island and its inhabitants...

The water arrived. Beth stripped off her sodden clothes and washed the sticky salt from her skin. She felt tired and light-headed. The seasickness had gone now, although the floor still showed a disturbing tendency to rock beneath her feet. She donned a fresh petticoat and was about to lie down when she heard the echo of a door closing below and footsteps ascending the stairs.

'All I am saying, my lord, is that the Fairhaven estate is no plaything for a girl—'

The voice was that of Colin McCrae, pitched somewhat louder than his customary soft burr because of the passion with which he spoke. Marcus replied, but Beth could not hear his quieter tones.

'And with the current threat from the sea, it would be the greatest folly—'

'That will be short-lived.' Marcus's voice was clipped. 'We land Marchant's cargo tomorrow night.'

Beth's curiosity was caught. Where previously she had tried not to overhear, now she strained closer. The men had paused on the landing, a little away from her room. They were speaking quietly, but she caught the odd phrase here and there and pressed against the door to try to hear more.

'Will you tell Lady Salome?' Colin McCrae was asking now, his voice amused. 'I can imagine her reaction...'

'Oh, Aunt Sal is up to all the rigs!' Marcus laughed. 'There can be no harm in telling her about the business with Marchant!'

'And Lady Allerton?'

Marcus's voice had sobered. 'No. There is no need

for that. Now, Colin, you were telling me about the need to build a new barn up at Longhouses…'

Their footsteps and their voices blurred as they passed Beth's door and moved on. She expelled a sharp breath and leant against the panels, pushing the door closed. Her head was spinning.

The threat from the sea…Marchant's cargo…and the fact that Marcus did not intend to tell her… Her imagination raced. Could it be—was it possible—that Marcus was using Fairhaven Island for smuggling, as his grandfather had done before him? Certainly the island was perfectly placed for such a venture and she knew that Marcus needed to make money.

Beth lay down on the bed and stared fixedly up at the vast canopy. It all seemed to hang together. She had suspected from the first that Marcus intended to travel to Fairhaven. Her presence had provided the perfect excuse and the perfect camouflage. His ship had been ready and waiting in Bridgwater, so clearly his men must have received their instructions some days before. Lady Salome and all the villagers had been expecting their arrival. There was evidently a plan.

And who knew what cargo the *Marie Louise* had been carrying today. Marchant's cargo, Marcus had said. Perhaps Marchant was the free trader with whom Marcus was in business… Beth turned over restlessly, wondering if she should confront Marcus straight away or wait until she had some evidence. Her instinct was to challenge him at once, to demand an interview now and have it out with him, but she reluctantly decided to wait. It went against her nature but Marcus had been so sparing of the truth up until now that Beth had no doubt he would think of some plausible excuse. Better to keep quiet and watch what happened. And she would not have long to wait, for if Marcus was correct, tomorrow night would reveal the truth.

Dinner the following day was an entertaining meal. Beth had spent much of the day resting and felt quite restored by the time she joined Marcus and his aunt in the castle's impressive dining room. Lady Salome was resplendent in purple satin, orange turban and pearls, and Beth felt supremely dowdy in her practical grey gown. She remained quiet whilst Marcus and his aunt covered all the family gossip, but then Salome moved on to ply her with eager questions about London, the fashions, the scandals and the entertainments, and Beth soon forgot her reserve. They chatted through to dessert, when Lady Salome started on a series of outrageous anecdotes about her own Season some thirty years before, looking from Beth to Marcus with sparkling brown eyes.

'I did not *take*, my dears. The style was for plump girls with fluffy blonde hair—rather like those little dogs that Lady Caroline Lamb is said to favour—so I was utterly unfashionable! I was in despair of ever finding a rich husband and even considered running off with my piano teacher, but he always smelled of mothballs and that was quite quelling to passion!' She popped a sugared plum into her mouth and pushed the dish in Beth's direction. 'Where was I? Oh, yes… Well Papa was a man of little patience and when I had not caught a husband after a few months he decided to despatch me to Fairhaven! St John had lost his housekeeper here—she fell from the cliffs in strange circumstances—and so Papa thought to save some money by sending me in her place!'

Beth smiled. 'Have you lived here ever since, Lady Salome? It is a very long time!'

'Oh, yes, my dear, but then it is my home. Home is where the heart is. Now is that St Mark's Gospel or the Book of Proverbs?'

'Neither, I believe.' Marcus laughed. He stood up. 'Excuse me, ladies. I will take my port and rejoin you in the drawing room shortly.'

'Take your time, dear,' Salome said absently. 'Lady Allerton and I have much to talk about! Ah, the sweetness of a friend!' She looked triumphant. 'Now, *that* is the Book of Proverbs!'

Marcus bowed and went out, a twinkle in his eye, and Beth sighed unconsciously. For all the relaxed atmosphere of the meal and the entertaining company of Lady Salome, she did not delude herself that she was forgiven. Marcus had barely spoken to her directly during the evening, except to ask if her room was comfortable and if she had everything she required, and she felt uncomfortable in his presence. Once or twice she had caught his gaze upon her, expressionless or stern, but when she had looked up at him he had not smiled in return. There was so much that needed to be said between them, yet she did not know where to start. Last night he had been too angry to listen to her. Now she hardly dared approach him, particularly if it were only to stir up more trouble on the matter of smuggling.

'You look sad, my dear,' Lady Salome said comfortingly, when they were ensconced in front of the drawing-room fire and had a big pot of tea between them. 'I suppose you must be tired from your travels and all the excitement of reaching Fairhaven at last! Marcus tells me that it has long been an ambition of yours to regain the island for your family!'

'Yes, I suppose so.' Beth said dolefully. Suddenly, sitting here under Lady Salome's bright gaze, it did not seem such a worthy thing to want to reclaim Fairhaven. 'Ever since I was a little girl I wanted to come here, but…' she looked up, troubled '…I did not think… What will you do, ma'am, if you leave the island?'

'Oh, I shall travel to the fleshpots of Exeter!' Salome said enthusiastically, ladling three spoonfuls of sugar into her tea. 'Or perhaps to London itself— Sodom and Gomorrah rolled into one! You have no idea, my love, how frustrating it is to receive six-month-old copies of the *Ladies' Magazine* and never to have the fashionable clothes to wear when one goes out! And then there is the food—salted, pickled but seldom fresh! Unless one likes turnips, of course, but I never have! Indeed, I am *aux anges* to be thinking of escape!'

Beth smiled, but she was not convinced. She knew that Lady Salome thought of Fairhaven as home and suspected that the redoubtable spinster was just putting a brave face on things. Besides, there was St John to think of as well—how would an elderly cleric cope with a new parish when he had become so attached to his eccentric islanders, and they to him?

'Besides—' Lady Salome leant forward a little arthritically to put another log on the fire and Beth hurried to help her '—you are so rich, my dear! You may give the island all the things it needs!'

'Materially, perhaps,' Beth murmured. She smiled at Lady Salome. 'Surely there are other things more important? The love of money is the root of all evil, after all! The Book of Timothy, I think!'

'Very good!' Lady Salome clapped her hands. 'But, oh, to be the one camel that passes through the eye of the needle! Matthew nineteen, verse twenty-four!' She happily capped Beth's quotation, then fixed her with her perceptive dark gaze. 'Tell me, do you like Marcus, Lady Allerton?'

The abrupt change of subject took Beth aback a little. Normally she would have prevaricated, particularly on so short an acquaintance. Yet there was something about Lady Salome's open friendliness that made her reply truthfully.

'Yes. Yes, I do. I like the Earl of Trevithick a lot, but…' A tiny frown wrinkled her brow.

'But!' Lady Salome said sonorously. 'There is always a but!'

Beth laughed. 'Oh, Lady Salome, there are difficulties. We do not know each other very well—'

'Love conquers all!' Lady Salome said grandly. 'The Book of Kings—'

'Quite,' Beth said, thinking it unlikely. She saw that Marcus had come in and hastily changed the subject. 'Are there many tales of smuggling in these parts, Lady Salome?'

Lady Salome gave her a penetrating look. 'Not since the time of your grandfather, my dear! There's no money in the trade these days and little interest in it!'

Beth could feel Marcus's gaze resting on her thoughtfully. She gave him a dazzling smile. 'I was asking your aunt about smugglers' tales, my lord—'

'I heard you.' Marcus took a cup of tea from Lady Salome and sat back, stretching his long legs out to the fire. 'The profession has almost died out, has it not, Aunt Sal?'

'Along with piracy and wrecking!' Lady Salome agreed. 'Life on Fairhaven is nowhere near as exciting as one might imagine, my dear! Why, even the American War scarce touches us here!'

'That reminds me,' Marcus said. 'McCrae has given me the direction of one of the islanders who knew your grandfather, Lady Allerton. I am sure he will be pleased to talk to you! Jack Cade, I believe his name is, up at Halfway Cottage. Perhaps you may choose to walk up in the morning?'

'Perhaps I shall,' Beth agreed. 'Thank you, my lord.' She was not sure why she did not feel more exhilarated at the news, but for some reason she could summon up little enthusiasm. It was all very odd. She had been wanting to come to Fairhaven for years, with an intensity that had eclipsed all else, yet now she was here it was all falling oddly flat. Beth wondered if she was one of those tiresome people who, once they had achieved something, had no use for it any more. She hoped not.

She stood up and smiled at Lady Salome. 'Pray excuse me, ma'am, Lord Trevithick...' she gave Marcus a distant nod '...I am tired and would like to retire. There is no need to accompany me,' she added sharply, as Marcus rose from his chair with some reluctance, 'I can find my own way. Goodnight!'

As she went up the stairs, Beth reflected that there was nothing more insulting than Marcus's pretence of courtesy towards her, no doubt assumed for Lady Salome's benefit. She hated this coldness between them that threatened to harden into indifference, then plain dislike. Already she felt absurdly distanced from

Marcus, as though their earlier intimacy had never
been. It seemed almost impossible to believe that
Marcus had once held her in his arms, had kissed her,
had evoked a response from her that she had not even
known could exist. Yet all that was in the past. From
now on a slightly bored courtesy was probably all that
she could expect.

Beth sat on the window seat in her bedroom and
looked out at the moonlight skipping across the black
water. The poor weather that had dogged their
crossing the day before had vanished and it was a
clear night with the stars showing bright and hard in
the heavens. Somewhere in the depths of the castle,
a clock struck one. The chimes echoed through the
stone walls and died away. Beth shivered a little. She
had been waiting for four hours and was thoroughly
tired and chilled, but she had been determined not to
miss whatever it was that Marcus and Colin McCrae
were up to that night.

The sound of stone on stone far below cut through
her boredom. Someone had opened the door of the
castle and was even now setting off down the twisting
track to the beach. Beth pressed her nose to the cold
window glass. Her bedroom looked out on a short
stretch of grass that ended abruptly where the track
began its descent of the cliff. She could hear nothing,
but she could just see the dancing flame of a torch as
someone picked their way down towards the harbour.
Beth slid off the window seat, reached for her cloak,
and made for the door.

She drew back the bolt, turned the huge knob and
pushed. The door did not move. Beth pushed again
but it remained shut fast. She stood back, frowning.

The door had not stuck earlier in the evening. Then, it had swung smoothly on oiled hinges. Which meant that now it could only be locked—on the far side. She pushed the door again, sharply. Nothing happened.

Kneeling down, Beth peered through the keyhole. She could see the key still in the lock on the other side of the door. Indignation swelled in her, confirming her suspicions. Marcus had locked her in, and she knew why.

Beth went to her trunk and took out the enamelled box that held her hairpins. Near the window stood an old wooden writing desk and she was almost certain she had seen some thick blotting paper there earlier. She whipped it up and hurried back to the door. There was a gap of at least an inch between the smooth stone step and the bottom of the door and Beth bent down, stealthily inserting the paper into the space. The first hairpin bent when she pushed it into the lock but the second loosened the key and after a little jiggling, it fell to the floor. The blotting paper muffled the sound and all Beth heard was a soft thud.

Holding her breath, she drew the paper towards her. The key caught on the bottom of the door and she bit her lip, trying to manoeuvre the paper through the gap without making any noise. After a few nerve-racking seconds, it slid smoothly into her grasp.

Dusting her skirts down, Beth turned the key and opened the door a crack. The corridor outside was faintly lit by lamplight and was quite empty. She pulled the door closed behind her and tiptoed to the top of the stairs.

It took her several minutes to negotiate Saintonge Castle's dark corridors and stairs, for she was anxious to make no noise and draw no attention. At one point

she was obliged to dodge into the Great Hall when a
servant came out of the kitchens with a pile of clean
crockery, and she had almost reached the front door
when Martha McCrae came hurrying down the nursery stairs, a candle in her hand. By the time that Beth
slipped out into the night, her heart was in her mouth
and she had to stop to rest for a moment in the lee
of the castle wall.

It was a fine night, but there as a strong wind
blowing. Beth quickly realised that it would be the
utmost folly to try to descend the cliff path without
the aid of a light, for even in the daytime the track
was treacherous. It was also the perfect way to walk
directly into the smugglers' path before she had realised it. She had just resigned herself to another long
wait out in the cold dark when she saw the glint of
torchlight below and heard the crunch of footsteps on
shingle. They were already coming back. She dived
for shelter behind the nearest wall.

She was just in time and the sight that met her eyes
was a curious one. A torch-lit procession of men was
coming up the cliff path, but where Beth's imagination had supplied all the trappings of a smuggling
operation—the donkeys, the panniers full of bottles,
the packets of lace—they were carrying two coffins
high on their shoulders. Beth recognised the crew of
the *Marie Louise* and some of the village men she
had seen earlier in the day. Amongst them, Marcus
was carrying the corner of one coffin and Colin
McCrae another. Beth crouched behind the wall and
watched them pass by, and stared after them into the
darkness.

She had not been aware that the *Marie Louise* was
carrying any men home for burial, but then she sup-

posed that Marcus would not necessarily want to distress her with the fact. Perhaps this was what McCrae had been referring to when he had asked Marcus if he would tell her, and Marcus had said that there was no need. Perhaps so, perhaps not. The whole thing was odd in the extreme.

The more Beth thought about it, the odder it became. The men had been smiling and chatting amongst themselves and there had been none of the grim-faced respect that she would have expected on such an occasion. She pulled her cloak about her and tried to huddle more closely into the shelter of the wall. Where did Marcus's reference to 'Marchant's cargo' fit in? Were the coffins the cargo, and if so, were the deaths suspicious? Why not wait until daylight to bring the coffins home to rest? And why lock her in her room to ensure that she knew nothing of the night's activities?

Beth scrambled out onto the track and set off towards the village in the direction that the men had taken. She could just see the flickering of the lanterns up ahead and the moon cast enough light on the track for her to pick her way. All the same it was an uncomfortable walk and she almost slipped and fell several times. She resolved that the road was the first thing that she would spend money improving when once she was the official owner of Fairhaven.

By the time that Beth reached the first cottages, the pallbearers were entering the church, which, Beth thought, was entirely appropriate if they had a couple of dead men for burial. She felt cold, stiff and rather silly to have become so wrapped up in her own imaginings, and she was about to turn back when she heard a crash in the church porch and Marcus's voice carried to her on the wind.

'Careful there! Marchant will not be pleased if the goods are damaged...'

Curiosity aroused once more, Beth picked her way across the graveyard and peeked around the church door. She knew she was taking a big risk, but it was dark and the men were safely inside the church, so it seemed safe to take a look.

Fairhaven's chapel was small and ill lit and though she could just make out the shapes of the coffins laid out before the altar, a huge pillar obscured the rest of her view. The smell of musty cloth and dust hung in the air. Taking care to remain unseen, Beth slipped behind one of the Mostyn family memorials and peered round.

Two lanterns had been placed at either end of the altar and in their flickering light Beth could see the men from the ship busy with the coffin lids. They were showing little respect for the dead now. One man had a crowbar that he was wedging under one corner. There was a creak of protest from the wood and then a splintering noise as the lid came free. Beth smothered a gasp.

'Fine workmanship on these,' she heard one of the sailors say appreciatively as he leant over the coffin.

'Aye...nothing but the best...' One of his colleagues was lifting something from inside. The lantern light glinted on steel. Beth drew back sharply as she saw the rifle in his hands and the pile of guns spilling over the top of the coffin.

Suddenly there was a prickling feeling on the back of her neck, a warning instinct that was as ancient as it was inexplicable. Beth froze, her eyes still on the scene before her. Several of the crew had guns in their hands now and were inspecting them with admiration. Colin McCrae was exchanging a few words with one of the sailors as they fastened the lids back down. But of Marcus there was no sign.

Beth turned slowly. The empty ranks of pews and the rows of memorials stared back at her, cobwebby and dark. There was nobody there. She started to back towards the door, stepping silently, pausing to check every few seconds that she was unobserved. She could see no one at all but the feeling of being watched persisted. And then someone moved.

Beth caught her breath on a gasp that seemed to echo around the chapel's rafters. She saw the sailors put down the guns and look in her direction and then Marcus Trevithick stepped from the porch directly into her path.

'Good evening, Lady Allerton,' he said politely. 'What an unexpected pleasure to find you here!'

For a moment Beth seriously considered trying to push past him and run, but then Marcus put out one hand and took her arm in a grip that was not tight but that she could not have broken without a struggle.

'Do you know,' he said conversationally, 'that you are forever running away from me, Lady Allerton? On this occasion I do beg you to reconsider. I would be put to the trouble of trying to catch you and you would probably go straight over the side of a cliff in the dark!'

They stood staring at each other, then Beth let go of the breath she had been holding. 'Oh! I might have known that you would find me here! Though why you did nothing to prevent me seeing the rifles—' She broke off as she tried to work out what was going on. She saw Marcus grin.

'Why should I prevent you? There is nothing illegal to hide and if you wish to wander about Fairhaven in the middle of the night, that is your choice!'

'Nothing illegal?' Beth's voice had warmed into indignation. 'You smuggle munitions in here, no doubt intending to sell them on—' Once again she stopped, this time as he laughed.

'Is that what you think? My dear Lady Allerton, I am always astounded by your fertile imagination! This is no Gothic romance!' His voice changed, became grimmer. 'I am less flattered by the fact that you always suspect the worst of me!'

Beth felt suddenly ashamed. She freed herself from his grip and stepped back, smoothing her cloak down with a self-conscious gesture.

'Yes, well you must admit that your actions were of the most suspicious! If I have been mistrustful of you it is only because I found myself a prisoner in my own room!'

'Let us discuss this back at the castle,' Marcus suggested. He drew her through the doorway and into the porch, picking up his lantern as they went. The light skipped over the gravestones and illuminated the uneven stone path to the lych-gate. Marcus took Beth's arm again, this time in a gentler grip as he guided her back to the road.

'Stay close to me,' he said abruptly. 'I am amazed that you did not break an ankle creeping about in the dark!'

They walked back to the castle in silence. The moon was high and the combination of that and the torch lit the way well enough, but by now Beth was shaking with cold and reaction. She was glad when they reached the huge oak front door and Marcus ushered her into the hall.

'Please join me in the drawing room, Lady Allerton.'

Beth, who had been nursing a craven desire to run upstairs and hide in her room, realised that this was not an invitation so much as an order. She reluctantly allowed Marcus to take her cloak from her, noting that the once-smart black velvet was now crushed and stained from its travels and would never be the same again. Marcus held the drawing-room door open and Beth went in. She watched as he kicked the embers of the fire into life before moving over to the silver tray on the sideboard.

'A nightcap, Lady Allerton, to accompany our discussions? The brandy will warm you.'

He put what looked like a huge quantity of amber liquid into the glass before passing it to her. Beth risked a taste and felt the spirit burn her stomach. But Marcus was right. It was warming and in a little while she had stopped shivering.

Marcus gestured her to a chair by the fire and sat down opposite her. In the faint light his face looked brooding, severe. He looked up and their eyes met, and Beth's heart skipped a beat. Marcus smiled faintly.

'I see that the small matter of a locked door cannot stand in your way, Lady Allerton! I have seldom met anyone so indomitable!'

Beth shrugged, avoiding his gaze. ''Tis simple to open a locked door, my lord, when the key is still on the other side!'

Marcus laughed, a laugh that turned into a yawn.

He slid down in the chair and stretched his legs towards the fire. 'Excuse me. It has been a long night. I blame Colin McCrae for leaving the key in the lock. I warned him to make sure that all was secure but, unlike me, he underestimated you!' He looked at her and his smile faded. 'Believe me, Lady Allerton, it was for your own good.'

Beth took a mouthful of brandy. 'I do so detest it when people say that,' she confided, 'for generally it is not true at all! From what were you protecting me, my lord? My own curiosity?'

Marcus inclined his head. 'That, and the vivid imagination that has already led you to invent wild stories this night!' He grimaced. 'But your reproof is fair, Lady Allerton. I should not have had you constrained in your room. Indeed, I should have trusted you with the truth and I apologise that I did not.'

Beth took another sip of brandy. The fiery taste was growing on her and the warm feeling it engendered even more so. She could feel the colour coming back into her face, the relaxation stealing through her limbs.

'And the truth is—what, precisely, my lord?'

Marcus shifted in his chair. 'The truth is that there is a certain Dutch privateer by the name of Godard, who has been taking advantage of the hostilities between our nation and America to prey on the ships trading from Bristol.' He leant forward and threw another log on the fire. 'The guns that you saw were entrusted to me by Captain Marchant of his Majesty's navy. Marchant wanted an arsenal for the navy to draw on locally if they find themselves within striking distance of the enemy. There is more to unload from the *Marie Louise* tomorrow.'

He looked across at her and smiled. 'That is the explanation for tonight's activities, Lady Allerton!'

Beth frowned. 'Do you think this privateer is likely to threaten Fairhaven, my lord?' she asked after a moment.

'It is most unlikely.' Marcus stood up to refill her glass. 'Godard would gain little from taking Fairhaven, for then he would have to defend it. It is more likely that he would stage a raid in order to gain fresh supplies, but even that is improbable. I confess that it was that aspect of the case that held me silent, however, for I did not wish to disturb you with the knowledge unless the threat became real.'

Beth drained her glass. 'I see. But Lady Salome has a stout enough constitution to be told the truth?'

Marcus grinned. 'You heard that, did you? McCrae and I should be more careful of speaking behind peoples' backs!' He shrugged. 'The truth is that Aunt Sal, for all her disclaimers, has dealt with everything from smugglers to pirates in her time here on Fairhaven and is quite up to snuff! Whereas you, Lady Allerton...' his smile robbed the words of any sting '...you are young and have led a more sheltered life!'

Beth decided to let this go. It was indisputable; anyway, there were other matters she wanted to pursue.

'Why go to such an elaborate charade with the coffins, my lord?'

'It was all for show.' Marcus laughed. 'It is, in fact, a convenient way of carrying a large quantity of guns and Marchant and I thought it might confuse any spies...'

'Such as myself,' Beth said ruefully. She had begun to realise just how much she had built up on so little.

What was it that Marcus had said—that she always suspected the worst of him? That, and the fact that she was always running away from him. She bit her lip. Perhaps both charges were true and the thought made her feel uncomfortable. She put her empty glass down carefully on the walnut table, suddenly aware that she was feeling rather light-headed from unaccustomed liquor.

'I am sorry, my lord…'

'For what, Lady Allerton?'

Marcus was sitting forward, his own glass held between his two hands. His dark eyes were fixed on her face. 'Are you apologising for suspecting me unjustly, or for running away from me or even for locking me in a cellar?'

Beth looked up at him, then away quickly. There was something in that intent gaze that disturbed her and though his tone was light she had the oddest feeling that he had been hurt by her behaviour.

'For all of those, I suppose, my lord. I did try to apologise to you before about the cellar incident…' Beth groped for words. 'It was…very bad of me and I truly regret it…'

'Do you?' Marcus's face was unyielding. Beth, who had hoped that time would have softened his anger towards her, felt her heart sink. She had not thought him a man who bore grudges, but perhaps she deserved it.

'It is just that I thought I had to do it in order to reach Fairhaven first!' she burst out. 'That had been my intention all along and I did not think I could expect you to help me.'

'You mean you did not think you could trust me to keep my word even though I told you I would give

Fairhaven to you.' Marcus's quiet tones cut through her excuses and silenced her. He looked at her, a hint of amusement coming into his eyes. 'Well, perhaps you had good reason, my lady. I had broken my word to you twice and you have no reason to suppose I would not do it a third time.'

'No, I...' Beth frowned. That seemed all wrong, but she was tired and light-headed and unable to frame her thoughts properly. She knitted her fingers together in her lap and stared fixedly at them.

'I do not think that is fair, my lord.' She spoke very quickly, before her courage deserted her. 'I do trust you and it was very wrong of me to behave as I have and, if I have hurt—offended—you in any way, I am truly sorry.' She looked up swiftly and gave him a watery smile. 'At least we are speaking to each other again!'

Marcus moved so that one of his hands was covering her clenched fingers. 'Did it trouble you that we were at odds?'

Beth stared at him, unable to tear her gaze away. There was warmth and tenderness in his eyes and she felt such a rush of relief that the tears came into her eyes and she almost cried.

'Oh...' She cleared her throat, embarrassed. 'Well, it was decidedly uncomfortable...'

Marcus smiled. He raised his hand and turned one of her curls absent-mindedly about his fingers, but his eyes never left her face. 'I thought so too.'

'Then—' Beth held her breath '—are we to be... friends...again, my lord?'

'Friends?' Marcus's gaze became thoughtful. 'I do not think so, Lady Allerton. Of all the things we are or could be, that is far too tepid a description!

Passionate enemies or equally passionate lovers, per-haps, but nothing less than that!'

His fingers brushed her cheek and he took her chin in his hand. His gaze dropped to her lips. 'Are you sure that you trust me?'

'Yes,' Beth whispered.

Marcus laughed. He bent his head and kissed her, a brief, hard kiss, before allowing his hand to fall to his side.

'What a way you have of taking the wind from a fellow's sails, Lady Allerton!' His tone was rueful as he pulled Beth to her feet and steered her out into the hall. 'If you could see yourself, ever-so-slightly drunk and more than a little tempting...' He shook his head. 'And for the first time, you are looking at me with utter trust in your eyes! Your sense of timing is im-maculate!'

He lit a candle for her and handed it over with a quizzical lift of his brows. 'I hope that you can find your own way to your room? It would be a mistake to trust me to deliver you there safely!'

Beth took the candle and scurried away up the stairs. She was aware that she was indeed more than a little tipsy, although the blame for that could be laid squarely at Marcus's door for giving her so much brandy. She was more concerned, however, about that casual kiss and the promise behind it. For although Marcus had behaved as a perfect gentleman, there had been an assurance in his tone that Beth was certain would be fulfilled. Enemies or lovers; she knew which she would secretly prefer and it was not just the brandy in her blood that was speaking. She closed her bedroom door behind her and locked it carefully.

For now it was enough to know that she and Marcus were reconciled as friends, but for the future... Beth undressed quickly, lay down and blew out her candle flame.

Chapter Eight

It was in fact a little over a week before Beth found the time to visit Jack Cade and ask about her grandfather. Salome Trevithick had seen it as her duty to show Beth the island and had bundled her into the gig every day, taking her to meet the farmers and cottagers, and to view all the places that Salome whimsically referred to as 'the sights'. By the end of the week Beth's head was spinning with names and faces, but her overriding impression was how deeply Salome was involved in the life of the community and how much the islanders loved her. Beth they greeted with a guarded respect that was cold in comparison, but she knew that love and loyalty had to be earned and were not given for nothing. She set about following Salome's lead and spent hours at the school or in the different houses, chatting to the villagers, reading to the children or playing outside with them when the weather was fine. In the rare moments when she was left to her own devices, Beth would wander for hours along the cliff tops, admiring the view or just watching the clouds chase across the sea.

Meanwhile, Beth could not help but notice that

Marcus was setting out to make a particularly good impression on his tenants. Not only did he spend a great deal of time with Colin McCrae, discussing his plans for the farms and the harbour, but he did not scruple to get his hands dirty. A new barn was being built alongside the five-acre field, and Marcus could be seen there every morning, stripped to the waist and lending a hand.

When Salome had stopped the gig by the gate one day and called Marcus over to tease him about his industry, Beth had tried to look away—the sight of Marcus's bare brown torso and firm muscles had been curiously disturbing. But instead of fixing her gaze on a nearby flock of sheep, she had found herself staring, until Marcus had looked at her with raised eyebrows and asked if she was feeling quite the thing. And certainly Beth had *not* been feeling at all well. Her face was flushed and her pulse was racing and she wondered if she had contracted a fever. Salome had taken one look at her, smiled, and said that she thought Beth was suffering from a certain affliction, but had not said which.

Marcus had sought Beth out one evening and explained that he did not wish to leave Fairhaven until he had had the chance to discuss the future with his uncle St John as well as with Salome. This was clearly impossible with St John in Exeter, and Beth, anxious not to appear to be pushing the Trevithicks from their home, made no demur about extending her time on Fairhaven. She sent a letter to Charlotte, explaining what was happening and saying that she intended to be back at Mostyn Hall for Christmas, then, when she finally had a spare morning, she set off to find Jack Cade.

* * *

Jack Cade's cottage sat about a mile away from the
main village, on a small hill that looked out westward
across the harbour to the coast of Devon. Marcus had
said that Cade had been a fisherman all his life, but
that he was too old to go to sea any more and had
retired to live alone. The other villagers considered
him something of an oddity, but as one of the longest-
lived inhabitants of Fairhaven he was given grudging
respect.

Beth trod up the shell-lined path to the cottage
door. A few straggling plants huddled in the shelter
of its white-painted wall and there was a collection
of floats and old rope tumbled amidst the grass of the
headland, with a sheep grazing placidly nearby. Beth
knocked tentatively at the door. Now that the moment
had come for her to meet one of her grandfather's
contemporaries, she was almost sick with nerves.

The door creaked open to reveal a bent old figure
in the aperture. Beth's smile faltered a little.

'Mr Cade? I am Beth Allerton. I heard that you
knew my grandfather, Charles Mostyn, and I wondered if you would be able to tell me about him,
please?'

The old fisherman looked at her. His eyes were as
sharp and bright as a hawk's in a face of old leather.
He smiled, showing the stumps of blackened teeth. 'I
thought you'd be a'coming, my lady. Yes, I knew
Charles Mostyn. I could tell you about him.'

A trickle of anticipation crept down Beth's spine,
making her shiver. She was shaking at the prospect
of being so close to the truth at last and hearing directly what had happened to Lord Mostyn on the
night he had died.

'Take a seat, ma'am,' the old man said courteously,

stepping back to allow her to precede him into the cottage. He swept a pile of floats and nets from the armchair nearest the fire and Beth sat down, looking about her with interest.

There was only the one room but it was snug and wood-lined, with a roaring fire in the grate. Various bits of flotsam and jetsam adorned the walls: a set of antlers, a brown glass bottle, a twisted piece of bleached wood—all the bits and pieces that Cade must have picked up throughout his life at sea.

The old man sat down on the settle opposite Beth, groaning and creaking like the old wood as he found a comfortable position. He pulled a bottle of whisky towards him, knocked his pipe out on the arm of the chair and stuffed it full of fresh tobacco. He did not speak until it was lit and he was puffing away, with several clouds of evil-smelling smoke adding to the alcoholic fug in the room.

'Charles Mostyn…' he said, thoughtfully. 'He was the one before the old Earl. The Evil Earl.' He cackled suddenly. 'Not like this young 'un, for all his London ways. Seems like some good can come out of the old stock after all!'

Beth held her tongue and kept her patience. There was no point in hurrying the old man and she had heard plenty of people sing Marcus's praises over the past week.

'The Old Earl,' Jack Cade said again. 'Aye, he were a bad 'un and no mistake. And Mostyn too—as alike as two brothers, with nothing to choose between them!'

Beth sat up straight in her chair, frowning slightly. This did not sound right. 'Nothing to choose? But, Mr Cade—'

Jack Cade puffed hard on the pipe. 'Trevithick had a violent temper, but Mostyn was cruel hard—cold and vicious where Trevithick was loud and brutal. But Mostyn was clever, see?' His sharp gaze pinned Beth to her chair. 'He brought the trade in here, though we said as we wanted no trouble. But he wouldn't listen. Needed the money, I reckon, and the silly lads with him.'

'The…trade?'

'Smuggling!' Cade said triumphantly. 'Smuggling, m'lady! Big business here in the straits it was in them days. Trevithick and Mostyn at each other's throats, allus a struggle to control the trade along the coast. That's all! No more to it. But Mostyn held Fairhaven, see, so he had the advantage and a hard landlord he was, into the bargain.'

Beth swallowed hard. This was not at all as she had imagined it, nor indeed how the old stories had been spun to her in the nursery at Mostyn Hall all those years ago. She cleared her throat.

'Mr Cade, are you sure? I mean—' she saw his piercing gaze resting on her '—it is simply that I was told a vastly different story.'

'Bound to tell you something different, weren't they!' Cade said simply. 'Little lass wi' no family to speak of! Who'd want to tell the truth? Plenty to hide, that family, plenty to hide!'

Beth took a deep breath. She was shaking so much that she had to lock her fingers together to still them, but it was not with anticipation now. There was a pain lodged somewhere in her chest and another that blocked her throat until she could barely speak. But she had to know the truth now.

'What happened?' She whispered. 'In the end, I mean.'

There was pity in Cade's face. She could see it there and it struck another blow to her heart.

'In the end there was so much rivalry for the trade in these waters that Trevithick and Mostyn came to blows.' The old man coughed. 'Trevithick won and he took the island, and no Mostyn has been here since. 'Til now, my lady.'

'How did Trevithick take Fairhaven?' Beth asked. She stared as the old man took a deep swig from his whisky bottle, wiped his mouth on his sleeve and smacked his lips.

'Ah! The last quarrel. It was all over a load of brandy Mostyn was waiting for, see? The free traders brought it in, but Mostyn was late for the meet and Trevithick got here first. Offered to double the payment for the men if they traded with him, not Mostyn, and helped him take the island into the bargain.' Cade shook his head. 'Didn't need much persuasion. Everyone hated Mostyn. Trevithick was little better, but at least he was paying well. So when Mostyn came they ambushed him and cut him to pieces— saving your presence, my lady.'

'But I thought—' Beth stopped, swallowed hard, and started again. 'I had heard that he was ambushed by the Earl of Trevithick's men, and the Earl stole the family silver.'

Cade cackled with laughter. 'Weren't no silver, m'lady. Mostyn was too mean to pay his dues! There was just the sword and the ring.' He got to his feet and hobbled over to an old sea chest in the corner, rummaging about inside. 'I've never worn this. Didn't seem right, somehow, after Trevithick had cut it from his finger! Best for you to have it now, perhaps, seeing as he was your grandfather!'

Beth held out her hand automatically and Cade dropped the signet ring into it. Through the blur of her tears, she saw the arms of Mostyn cut deep into the gold, the motto that was barely legible after all these years: *Remember*. She closed her fist tightly about it.

'What happened to the Sword of Saintonge?' she asked, marvelling at the steadiness of her own voice. 'Did Trevithick take that too?'

Cade was shaking his head. 'The sword broke in the fight, my lady. I have the stump of it here, but it's nothing but rust now—'

Beth was suddenly, devastatingly aware that she was about to cry and she had absolutely no wish to do so in Cade's cottage. She stood up abruptly.

'Excuse me. You have been more than kind, Mr Cade, but I fear I must go.'

The old man patted her arm clumsily. 'Forgive me, my lady. I did not know what to do for the best, but his lordship said that it was important I tell you the truth.'

Beth paused, her tears suddenly forgotten. A ray of sunlight struck across her eyes from the open door and she moved impatiently into the shade. 'His lordship said so? Lord Trevithick? When?'

Cade shifted awkwardly. 'When he came to see me, ma'am. Said you were looking for someone who knew your grandfather and that I was to tell you everything, honestly. Imperative, he said it was—'

Beth wheeled round and ran out of the cottage door, scaring the sheep that had been calmly grazing by the gate. She plunged down the village street, conscious that people were looking at her curiously, and practically crashed into the farm gate where she had last seen Marcus helping to stack some hay. He was still there. The last of the bales had been moved into the barn and he was standing nearby, talking to Colin McCrae.

'Lord Trevithick!' Beth had intended to sound imperious, but her voice came out with a desperate wobble in it. She tried to steel herself. 'Lord Trevithick, I require to speak with you! At once!'

Marcus exchanged a few quick words with Colin McCrae, then came across to her, vaulting over the gate and taking her arm. His gaze was searching.

'You have seen Cade, then, Lady Allerton? Are you all right?'

'No, I am not all right!' Beth said stormily. Two bright spots of angry colour shone in her cheeks. Despite the chill of the day, she felt feverishly hot. 'How dare you, Lord Trevithick!' Her voice rose. 'How dare you let me go to speak to that old man when you knew the truth about my grandfather and could have told me yourself and spared me the pain!'

'Not here,' Marcus said. His grip tightened on her arm. He was looking over her shoulder at the crowd of farmworkers and villagers who were now providing an embarrassed but none the less interested audience. Beth shook herself free. At that moment she would not have cared if the entire island had gathered for the entertainment.

'Let go of me!' she hissed. 'I detest your behaviour, sir.'

There was the flash of something elemental and angry in Marcus's eyes. This time his grip bruised her skin. 'And would you have believed me if I had told you that your grandfather was nothing but a common free trader, Lady Allerton? I think not! Your trust in me has been notable for its absence up until now! You had to hear the truth from someone else!'

Beth stared into his angry eyes for what seemed like hours. Behind her the crowd shifted and murmured and even through her preoccupation she heard one buxom lady saying to another: 'Cade has told her all about Charles Mostyn... They'd told her he was a good man, poor lamb...'

It was the pity that broke Beth. She could see it on the faces of all those about her as they witnessed her terrible distress. It was the same sympathy that had been reflected in Jack Cade's eyes at the end. Probably they had all known the truth about Charles Mostyn, but no one had wanted to mention it to her. At first they might even have imagined her to be a chip off the Mostyn block, come to take them back to the bad times. She and Marcus both. Trevithick and Mostyn, at each other's throats, dragging their people down with them when they should have been defending them.

There was no sympathy on Marcus's face. He looked at her and his expression was carved from stone. With a cry, Beth tore herself from his grip and turned her back on all of them, running down the hill towards the castle until her legs were going so fast that she was almost falling over herself. The wind roared in her ears and her hair whipped about her face, blinding her. She slammed the castle gate open and raced across the greensward to the cliff edge.

'Beth! For God's sake! Stop before you fall!'

Marcus caught her from behind, knocking all the breath from her body as he pulled her to the ground.

She was crying now, struggling and pummelling him in her efforts to get away from him, gasping for breath until he had quite simply to lean the whole of his weight on her to subdue her. Beth lay still, trying to calm her sobs, feeling the cold grass beneath her cheek and the warm tears that ran down her face and splashed onto the springy turf.

'Oh, Beth...'

There was a world of pity in Marcus's voice now and she did not resist him when he pulled her into his arms, half-cradling her as she cried as though her heart was breaking.

For what seemed like endless hours she wept into his jacket and felt his hands stroking her and his voice murmuring words that made no sense but sounded inexpressibly comforting. And at length she sat up a little, wiped her hand across her wet cheeks and said, in a small voice, 'I never cry!'

Marcus smiled, brushing the hair back from her face. 'No, indeed. I had noticed.' He got to his feet, pulling her with him. 'Come, we must get you inside. Sitting on the damp grass will not make you feel any better...'

Beth clung to him. 'Marcus...'

'I know.' For a moment Marcus's arms tightened about her in a hug before he slid one arm about her waist and guided her back towards the castle. Lady Salome met them at the door, her gardening trug over her arm, a look of distress on her face.

'I heard,' she said, patting Beth's shoulder consolingly. 'My poor girl, to have all your memories dashed in such a cruel way! Oh, the betrayal of innocent blood! Matthew twenty-six, verse twenty-seven!'

Beth hiccuped a little and smothered a giggle. 'Oh, Lady Salome, you are a very present help in trouble!'

'A glass of madeira and a hot brick are what we need!' Lady Salome said bracingly. 'Come upstairs, my dear, and I will give you rest!'

'Exodus thirty-three, verse sixteen,' Marcus said, with a sigh.

'Matthew eleven, verse twenty-eight!' Lady Salome called, over her shoulder. 'Marcus, pray ask Mrs McCrae to bring some hot soup and some physick—'

'I am not ill!' Beth objected, borne irresistibly upwards on Lady Salome's arm.

'Nonsense! You have sustained a shock and require food, drink and rest,' Lady Salome said decisively. She opened the bedroom door and pushed Beth inside. 'You mark my words—within half an hour you will be asleep!'

The sound of the sea was in Beth's ears and it was very soothing. She opened her eyes reluctantly. The room was bathed in candlelight and the long curtains were drawn. Martha McCrae was sitting beside the bed, reading a book. She looked up as Beth opened her eyes and her face broke into a smile.

'Oh, my lady! How are you feeling now?'

Beth frowned slightly. 'Have I been asleep, Martha? Good gracious! Lady Salome gave me a glass of ratafia and the next thing I remember... Why, I do believe I feel hungry!'

Martha jumped up. 'There is some fresh broth made this afternoon, my lady, the very thing! I will go and fetch some for you—'

'Stay a moment, please!' Beth put out her hand and

caught the girl's sleeve. 'Martha, will you answer something for me?'

'If I can, my lady.' Martha looked apprehensive.

'Does everyone on the island know the truth of my grandfather's dishonour?'

Martha fidgeted, avoiding Beth's gaze. 'Oh, my lady! Everyone knows the old stories, of course, though it was only Jack Cade and one or two others actually remember...' She twisted her hands together. 'I'm sorry, my lady. We thought you knew, you see, until his lordship told Colin that you had been told quite a different tale! Then we were afraid, for we knew you would find out...' Her unhappy brown eyes met Beth's and there was apology in their depths. 'It has all been so difficult, my lady, what with thinking his lordship was showing an interest in the place, then hearing that you would be taking Fairhaven over, and worrying for Lady Salome, and not knowing what was really going on.'

Beth nodded. 'I understand. But Lord Trevithick *has* shown a genuine interest in Fairhaven and has done so much for the island—'

Martha smiled and it was like the sun breaking through clouds. 'Oh, my lady! Now we don't know what to think! We know you care about Fairhaven, but Lord Trevithick is a good man and has already helped us so much! If only you could both keep Fairhaven—' She broke off, getting to her feet. 'Excuse me, my lady. I will go to fetch that soup.'

Beth turned her head against the pillow. Now she fully understood the hostility of the villagers when first she had come to Fairhaven. They had either remembered the bad old days of the Mostyns or remembered hearing stories of that time. Her grandfa-

ther's legacy had gone deep and in ways that she had
not even imagined. Beth sat up, reached for her wrap
and propped herself up on her pillows. She had seldom had a day's illness in her life, but just for now
it felt pleasantly indulgent to stay in bed and let
Martha wait on her. She no longer felt tearful, but she
did feel tired.

'Entirely respectable, alas!' The voice from the
doorway made her jump and she turned to see Marcus
strolling forward into the room. He grinned at her in
the old way that she remembered and gestured to the
edge of the bed.

'May I?'

'Well…' Beth frowned. 'You should not be here,
my lord! Whatever would Lady Salome say?'

'I know!' Marcus looked unabashed. 'But Martha
left the door open and I was anxious to see if you
were really better!'

Beth dropped her gaze. She felt curiously shy,
aware of the thinness of her nightgown and wrap,
even if Marcus seemed oblivious to it. Which was in
itself rather disappointing… Annoyed at the direction
of her thoughts, she forced herself to meet his gaze.

'Please, my lord, before you say anything else I
must apologise—'

Marcus touched her hand. He shook his head.
'Beth, do not. You had sustained a huge shock and
anything you said was entirely understandable.'

Beth gave him a slight smile. 'Thank you.' She
hesitated. 'I do understand why you did not tell me.
I had to hear it from someone who had been there,
someone who had seen with their own eyes—'

'Believe me—' Marcus voice was a little rough '—if
I had thought that there could be any other way…'

Beth felt her face grow warm. She was glad that there was no light but the glow of the fire. She felt a constraint between them, a tension that was due to all the emotions that were present but unspoken.

'I confess I feel rather foolish,' she said, after a moment. 'For so long, the history of the Mostyns has been like…' she hesitated '…almost like a talisman to me, I suppose. The romantic history, the feud, good vanquished by evil, or so I thought, when really…' Her voice trailed away.

'When really there were two warring families, neither of whom deserved your good opinion,' Marcus finished drily.

Beth sighed. 'The whole quest for Fairhaven was based on a false dream. I can scarce believe it! Ever since I was a child I have longed for it!'

Marcus let go of her hand and stood up a little abruptly. She could not read his expression but his voice was once more his own. 'It is not surprising. Children are most tenacious of dreams, after all, and you were orphaned young and needed something on which to hang your hopes.' He smiled down at her. 'Now I must go. Martha will be back soon with the soup and would be scandalised to find me here!'

He went out, leaving Beth staring blindly into the fire. Something in Marcus's tone had pierced her, stripping away the remaining illusions from before her eyes. Somewhere in the past few weeks she had become so intent on gaining Fairhaven and achieving her dream that she had been prepared to sacrifice anything to win it. That feeling had possessed her when she had met Marcus in London, it had prompted her to start the chase down to Devon, it had even driven her to lock him in Theo March's wine cellar just so that she could get ahead. The obsession with Fairhaven had always been slumbering, but once the island had seemed almost within her grasp, it had taken over.

Beth slid down under the blankets. It seemed extraordinary now, for she no longer felt that way. She could see clearly for the first time in years, and what she saw was that her quest had exacted a higher price than any wild goose chase. There was Charlotte, who had loyally accompanied her from London on what she had surely known was a fool's errand, only to be abandoned at Theo's vicarage for her pains. Beth had regretted her behaviour to her cousin before, but now she saw its full magnitude.

And there was Marcus… Weeks ago—it seemed like years to Beth now—she had realised that she was in danger of falling in love with Marcus too quickly, too soon. She had distracted herself by the race for Fairhaven, pretending that they were in opposition when, in fact, their conflict had only masked the growing attraction between them. An attraction that Beth now realised, with a dreadful sinking feeling, had developed on her part at least into a hopelessly deep love…

With a groan, Beth rolled over and buried her face in the pillow.

'My lady, are you feeling poorly again?'

Beth raised her head to see Martha McCrae standing by the bed with a steaming pot of soup on a tray. 'Oh, Martha! I did not see you there! No, I am very well…'

After she had finished the chicken broth, she slipped out of bed and trod across the room. Her cloak was still hanging over a chair before the fire. Beth

put a hand in the pocket. Her grandfather's signet ring
was still in there. She took it out and held it up to
the firelight, reading the inscription once more. *Remember*. There had been too much of that. Beth
opened the casement window and a flurry of snow
blew in on the cutting edge of the wind. Beth gave
her grandfather's ring one last glance and flung it out
into the darkness.

'You look very beautiful, my lady,' Martha
McCrae said with a smile, twisting the last lock of
hair into Beth's chignon.

Beth looked at her reflection and smiled. 'Certainly
no one would know that you had fashioned my dress
out of some old curtains, Martha! You have done a
splendid job!'

Martha giggled. 'But they were the best drawing-
room curtains, ma'am, and you have the figure to
carry anything off!' She gave Beth a sly look. 'I'll
wager his lordship will think so too!'

Beth could feel herself colouring up. Now that she
was so aware of her feelings for Marcus she was
hopelessly self-conscious. She had done everything
she could to avoid him over the past week and had
been practically tongue-tied in his presence, feeling
like a green girl scarcely out of the schoolroom.
Fortunately Marcus did not seem to have noticed, for
he was so involved in various projects of Colin's devising that Bath barely saw him. He had gone about
the estate and she had helped out in Lady Salome's
garden and another week had slipped by, bringing
them to the date of the annual Fairhaven dance.

'I imagine that there will be plenty of young ladies

vying for Lord Trevithick's attention tonight,' Beth said lightly. 'I shall not expect to monopolise him!'

Martha looked disappointed. It had amused Beth that the villagers, who had started by assuming that she was Marcus's mistress, had swiftly learned of their error and had actually seemed disappointed that she and Marcus were not in fact lovers. Beth had wondered if this was because they wanted a neat solution to the future ownership of the island. It would certainly solve the problem if she and Marcus were to share ownership of Fairhaven, but she knew this was not to be. For several days, watching him about the estate, she had felt a growing conviction that it would be wrong to take Fairhaven away from Marcus. Soon she would have to tell him so.

Beth saw that Martha was still watching her and gave her a quick smile. 'Besides, I shall want at least one dance with your Colin tonight, Martha! Now, should you not run along and get ready yourself? You have spent so much time helping me that it is almost time to go down!'

After Martha had hurried away to her own toilette, Beth picked up her reticule and stood up to admire the clinging cherry-red velvet dress. With her black hair and silver eyes it did indeed look striking and appropriately festive since this was the island's annual dance. Beth sighed unconsciously. She felt as gauche as a debutante and hoped that the young ladies of Fairhaven would distract Marcus's attention. With his strong physique and dark good looks she knew that he was much admired, for she had seen the village girls watching him and giggling together in corners. But perhaps the good people of Fairhaven had had enough of a lord with a wandering eye. The stories of the Evil Earl's philandering had been enough to shock even Beth's strong constitution.

She realised that she could hear music playing below, the pluck of the violins and the thump of drums. That meant that the musicians had already arrived and with them, no doubt, most of the other villagers. It was time to go down and she just hoped that Marcus would be too occupied to notice her.

That vain hope died as she went slowly down the stairs. Marcus was standing in the hall, dressed in evening clothes that had certainly not been fashioned from some cast-off furnishings. He was talking to Lady Salome, who looked glorious in a dress of yellow satin with an overskirt of green sewn with lots of tiny diamonds. Her hair was dressed with pheasant and seagull feathers. Beth hoped that the birds of Fairhaven had not died in vain.

Marcus looked up as Beth came down the final flight and watched her all the way, with a disconcertingly direct gaze that made her feel totally flustered. As she reached the hall, he took her hand and raised it to his lips.

'You look very beautiful, Lady Allerton. I particularly like your necklace! It matches your eyes!'

Beth laughed, fingering the beads a little self-consciously. She had brought no jewellery with her on her journey, but the low-cut dress had cried out for something and Martha had tentatively pressed on her a necklace made of tiny grey pebbles from the beach. Beth had thought it quite as beautiful as the expensive pearls and diamonds she had locked away in London and had been touched by Martha's gesture.

'Sheba dressed to greet Solomon!' Lady Salome said expansively, enveloping Beth in a scented hug.

'I hear that the dancing has started. Excuse me, my dears, I am off to tread a measure!'

Marcus offered Beth his arm and they followed slowly. A lively country dance was striking up as they came into the Great Hall. 'It is remarkable that there are so many musicians on the island, my lord,' Beth observed, looking at the motley orchestra, 'especially with the ruinous effect of the sea air in warping their instruments!'

Marcus laughed. 'A resourceful lot, our islanders! If one asks why there are so many young children on the island or why there are so many musicians, one receives the same answer—that there is nothing else to do during the long winter!'

'My lord!' Beth laughed in spite of herself.

'Come and dance with me,' Marcus said persuasively, smiling down at her. 'I have been saving the first dance for you!'

'In the face of much temptation from other young ladies, no doubt,' Beth said, arching her brows.

Marcus gave her an expressive look. 'There is only one lady who throws temptation in my path, Lady Allerton, and sooner or later I will fall!'

Beth had always considered the Great Hall to be a cold and bare room, but tonight it looked as she imagined it might have done for some masque centuries before. A huge fire roared in the grate and the light from a score of torches reflected off the polished shields and swords on the walls. The tapestries glowed with rich colour and between them were draped boughs of evergreen as a reminder of the approaching Christmas season. It seemed that all eighty-six inhabitants of Fairhaven were present, resplendent in their best party clothes.

As all the servants had been invited to the dance, the food and drink was very much a matter of helping oneself. A large table almost bowed under the weight of Christmas pies made of minced beef and spices and everyone was dipping into a large cauldron that held a brew that Marcus informed Beth was called Puffin Punch.

'The bird does not form the chief ingredient, however,' he added, when Beth drew back, wrinkling her nose up. 'I believe you will find it quite appetising.'

He was right. The mixture of wine, spices, oranges and lemon was thoroughly delicious and put Beth in mind of the soothing mulled wine that Marcus had sent up for her and Charlotte that night at the inn in Marlborough. The memory brought a strange lump to her throat, for it seemed that so much had happened since that night and not all of it as she had planned. Marcus was watching her, his eyes narrowed on her face.

'What is it, Beth? You look as though you've seen a ghost!'

Beth raised her eyebrows haughtily. 'My name, my lord?'

Marcus laughed. 'You think me inappropriate? After all that we have…been through together? You have called me by name before!'

'You are certainly inappropriate to remind me, my lord,' Beth said pertly, looking at him over the rim of her drinking cup.

'Yet on such an evening as this we could dispense with formality, perhaps?'

Beth finished her punch. 'Very well then, Marcus. But we must not let Lady Salome hear us, for I am sure she is a stickler for formality—' She broke off as Lady Salome whirled past them clasped in the arms of one of the sheep farmers. His face was flushed with drink and excitement and Lady Salome was roaring with laughter at whatever tale he was telling her.

'Well, perhaps not!' Beth finished.

'I hope that the Fairhaven festivities will not shock you, Beth,' Marcus said, grinning. 'They are rumoured to be quite outrageous!'

Beth tried to look cool and unshakable but it was difficult under Marcus's mocking gaze. She looked down the table, seeking distraction.

'Good gracious, what is that?' She pointed to an orange studded with cloves and decorated with a sprig of holly that stood in the centre of the table on a little tripod of twigs.

'The Calennig,' Marcus said indulgently. 'I believe it is a Welsh tradition, for here the customs of Wales and England merge sometimes. It is a symbol to bring a fertile harvest.'

Beth looked around. 'And are there any other traditional decorations here tonight?'

'There is the mistletoe,' Marcus said, a wicked gleam suddenly in his eye. He pointed to the beams above her head. 'If you would care to glance up, my lady…'

Beth evaded the snare deftly. 'Hmm. I think not, my lord. I would prefer to dance!'

The country dance was ending and the impromptu orchestra swung straight into the next tune. Beth clapped her hands.

'Oh! The Furry Dance! I have not danced this since I was a child!'

The dancing was fast and furious, and bore little resemblance to the sedate entertainment of a London ballroom. Beth managed one country dance with Marcus before he was snatched away from her and she was whirled into a jig by one of the village lads. They had no shyness in approaching her and she barely had any rest during the evening as the old folk dances of her childhood and familiar country airs intermingled. The dancing became progressively less decorous as the evening went on and finally she was swept into the lilting rhythm of something called the Brawl, and ended up face to face with Marcus, as she had begun. Dark eyes blazing, he swept her into his arms.

'A kiss under the mistletoe!' one of the village lads shouted, energetically setting the example with his own partner.

Beth saw Marcus grin. 'It is customary,' he murmured, and before she could reply he bent his head and kissed her. His lips were gentle at first, but Beth could not conceal her instinctive response and he crushed her to him, unleashing a passion in both of them that could not be denied. When he let her go and steadied her with a hand on her arm, Beth felt dizzy and confused, aware of the curiosity and approval on the faces all about her.

Marcus kept a protective arm about her as he steered her towards the refreshments and someone pressed another glass of Puffin Punch into her hands.

'This is probably a mistake,' Beth said hopelessly, aware that she was already more than a little inebriated. 'If you do not wish me to be drunk, my lord—'

'Marcus, remember?' Marcus was smiling down at her in a way that made Beth feel distinctly unsteady. 'My dear Beth, I should be delighted to see you a little foxed if it makes you more receptive to my advances! Would you care to see the castle gardens by moonlight?'

'Marcus, it has been snowing these five days past!' Beth said severely. 'If it is your wish that we catch our deaths—'

'Then perhaps we could watch the snow falling from Lady Salome's orangery?' Marcus suggested, a glint of amusement in his eyes. 'That would be most romantic and so very pretty…'

'Lady Salome would scarce approve!' Beth said lightly. The idea held much appeal but she was no green girl to fall for such a suggestion. She knew exactly what would happen once the orangery doors were closed behind them.

'Marcus, why do you not take Beth to see the view from the orangery?' Lady Salome said, appearing beside them with a huge glass of Puffin Punch clasped in her hands. 'It would be so very pretty with all the snow!'

'Exactly what I have been saying, ma'am!' Marcus agreed, whilst Beth smothered her giggles. 'Come now, Lady Allerton, surely you cannot resist such a recommendation!'

'She is matchmaking,' Beth said, as Marcus tucked her arm through his and steered her firmly out of the hall and along the corridor to the orangery. 'Or making an alliance to save Fairhaven, perhaps!'

'I imagine all the villagers are behind her!' Marcus agreed. He held open the orangery doors. 'There…and is that not as pretty as I promised it would be?'

Beth moved forward to the big windows, feeling the cold coming from the glass in contrast to the warmth of the room behind. The bare branches of the orange and lemon trees struck spiky shadows across the floor. The snow brushed softly against the windows, melting as it ran down the glass. Outside, nothing could be seen but the soft darkness and the falling flakes.

Beth turned. Marcus was standing just inside the door, his face shadowed, but a faint smile on his lips. She felt puzzled. She had been certain that he would kiss her as soon as they were alone and she had been ready, waiting even. Such sweet pleasure could not be denied even if she was uncertain where it was leading. Yet now he made no move towards her and she felt confused—and more than a little disappointed.

'It is very pretty, my lord.' Her tone was cool as she struggled to master her feelings. 'However, I think I should retire now, if you will excuse me—'

'I will escort you to your room,' Marcus murmured.

Beth looked him in the eye. 'I am not likely to become lost, my lord.'

'No, but you are a little intoxicated—'

'I am not foxed!' Beth said indignantly, clutching the nearest orange tree for support and belying her words. 'I may be a little merry—'

'More than a little,' Marcus said, lips twitching.

'But it is a most pleasant feeling…'

'Not to be recommended on a daily basis, however.'

'Dear me…' Beth wavered a little '…you have become most censorious, my lord!' She had reached the orangery door and looked up into his face. 'Yet it seems to me that, for all your severity, you are not above taking advantage!'

'It is well-nigh impossible,' Marcus said solemnly, 'and I swear you are deliberately tempting me...'

He took a step forward and drew her into his arms. His lips touched her cheek. 'Dear Lady Allerton, have I told you how much I esteem and admire you?'

'No,' Beth said, determined to be prosaic despite the excitement racing through her blood, 'you have not.'

'Well, I do.' Marcus's mouth grazed the corner of hers. Beth stood quite still repressing the urge to press closer to him. He took her chin in his hand and brushed his thumb across her lower lip. Beth felt a shudder go straight through her. Desire swept over her in a crashing wave, leaving her thoroughly shaken.

'My lord—'

'Marcus, remember...' Marcus's voice was husky. He kissed her lightly, slowly, his lips just touching hers. Beth made a small, inarticulate sound deep in her throat and melted against him.

'Marcus...'

'Mmm...no.' Marcus drew back slightly. 'Beth, there is something I must ask you. Will you marry me?'

For a moment Beth clung to him, her senses still adrift, then her mind focused on what he had said.

'Marry you? I don't think... What...? Why...?'

She lost the thread as Marcus took her earlobe between his teeth and bit gently. 'I want to marry you, Beth. I want you very much.'

Beth's eyes, a cloudy silver grey, searched his face. 'Marcus, I cannot think properly if you keep kissing me.'

'Fortunately, there is no necessity to think. Will you marry me? Here on Fairhaven? Say yes.'

'Because of Fairhaven?'

'Devil take Fairhaven! I want you, not the island!'

Marcus was kissing her again fiercely, robbing her of breath. Beth realised that he had abandoned the idea of a gentle approach, abandoned restraint. Her whole body shook with the force of his passion—and of her own, for she was wrapping her arms round his neck to pull him to her with an urgent need that matched his own. Her body was besieged by heat and desire, desperate to be closer to his.

There was an insistent tapping on the orangery window behind them. Beth spun round.

'Marcus!' Lady Salome was peering at them through the glass. 'How much longer do you need? We are all waiting for an announcement!'

Beth laughed shakily. 'My guardian angel!'

'With the devil's own timing,' Marcus said ruefully. 'Very well, Aunt Salome. We will be with you shortly.' He took both of Beth's hands in his. In the pale, white light of the snowbound conservatory, Beth saw him smile faintly.

'So what do you think, my love? If you do not like the idea you need only say!'

Beth smiled shyly. 'I do quite like the idea—' she confessed, and got no further as Marcus swept her back into his arms again.

Chapter Nine

'I fear I must be leaving you for a trip to the mainland,' Lady Salome said dolefully to Beth, leaning on her hoe and tucking the ends of her orange and purple scarf more firmly inside her green velvet coat. They were standing in the castle garden, where Lady Salome had been using the hoe to break the ice on the fishpond, so that the golden carp could breathe. Beth could see the faint flash of a fin deep in the gloom at the bottom of the pond. She hoped that the carp were warmer than she was, or at least more able to withstand the cold.

'Drat this frost!' Lady Salome proclaimed. 'We cannot be doing with a hard winter! Not when there is so much to do about the island!'

'Why are you leaving, Lady Salome?' Beth asked, as they crunched across the fresh snow to the castle door.

'A letter from St John!' Lady Salome said. 'He has been delayed in Exeter and asks that I join him. He is worried that we may be away for Christmas and what our poor, benighted islanders will do for pastoral care in the meantime is not to be imagined! I suspect that there will be any number of christenings to attend to next autumn!'

Beth giggled. 'Surely the Bishop will send a curate to take care of your flock here?'

Lady Salome humphed. 'Very likely, but it will not be the same! And indeed, my dear—' she fixed Beth with a stern gaze '—I cannot like leaving you alone here with Marcus, for all that you are betrothed! It is most irregular!'

Beth blushed and made a little business of wiping all the snow from her boots before she followed Lady Salome into the warmth of the hall.

'You know that we intend to leave Fairhaven in a few weeks, Lady Salome!' she said. 'I have promised to join my cousins at Mostyn for Christmas and Marcus is going to Trevithick, and the wedding will probably be in the spring—'

'It is what happens in the next week that concerns me,' Lady Salome said darkly. 'It is easy to stray from the path of righteousness! And without me here to act as chaperon—well, the descent into hell is easy, but there is no turning back!'

Beth tried not to smile. To her mind, being seduced by Marcus would be heaven rather than hell, but she could scarcely express such inappropriate remarks to Lady Salome.

'I really do not think that you need to worry, Lady Salome!' she said wistfully. 'Marcus has been a very pattern of propriety these last three days since the dance!'

Lady Salome looked unconvinced. 'You mark my words, child—once a rake! Still…' her face softened '…I do believe that Marcus truly loves you! It is a blessing to see it!'

Beth was not so convinced. Although she did not think that Marcus had proposed merely to reach a compromise over Fairhaven, she was not certain that he loved her. She was even beginning to doubt that he desired her for, although he had been ardent in his pursuit of her before their betrothal, since the dance he had been positively distant. Beth knew that Marcus was deeply engrossed in the plans for the estate, even more so now that he knew there would be her money to back his projects. Even so, she thought he might have been a little more attentive as they were so newly engaged.

The week following Lady Salome's departure did nothing to change this view. Marcus either worked in his study with Colin McCrae or was out and about the island. He and Beth dined together in the evenings, took a pot of tea like any old married couple and sat chatting, reading or playing cards. When it was time for Beth to retire, Marcus would escort her to the bottom of the stairs, light her candle for her and give her a chaste peck on the cheek. It was becoming so frustrating that Beth swore to herself that she would cast herself into Marcus's arms the next night just to see how he reacted. She was tolerably certain that he would simply disentangle himself and ask her if she was feeling unwell. It was as though the passion that had flared between them had never existed at all.

Now that Lady Salome had gone to the mainland, Beth found herself taking over many of that redoubtable spinster's responsibilities towards the islanders. She would visit the sick or call in at the school and she kept a keen eye on Lady Salome's garden, knowing that her future aunt-in-law would never forgive her if the orange trees died or the fish perished. On days when the weather was crisp and fine she would sometimes walk along the shore or over the hills, delighting in the beauty of the island and the freedom of the open air. Once, when she had returned to her room at the castle after a scramble over a rocky beach, Beth had looked at her reflection in the mirror and wondered what on earth Charlotte would say if only she could see her now; her hair was all tumbled and windblown and her cheeks flushed from the cold air. There was a long rent in her skirt where it had snagged on the rocks and her petticoat was stained equally with mud and seawater. Decidedly she did not look like a lady, or at least not the sort of lady who flourished on the rarefied air of a London drawing room. Charlotte would despair of her.

November slid into December. It was a full two weeks since Lady Salome had left for Exeter and still they had had no word of whether she and St John would be returning for Christmas or whether a curate would be sent in their place. Beth knew that Marcus was delaying his departure from Fairhaven until he had word, but she had reluctantly started to think that she needed to make her own plans to rejoin Charlotte at Mostyn. She was thinking about it as she walked along the seashore that afternoon, idly tossing pebbles into the water. Martha McCrae was also on the beach; she had brought Annie, baby Jamie and some of the village children down to the shore to see if they could find any driftwood to fashion into decorations for Christmas. Martha had explained that there were so few trees on the island that had to improvise with

other ideas and a fine, imaginative time they had of
it.

The tide was coming in. The water sucked at the
pebbles about Beth's feet, splashing on to the hem of
her dress. Beth turned and looked back down the
beach. Martha and the children had walked a long
way now and were examining some shells that one
of the girls had picked up from the sand. The children's cries mingled with the call of the seabirds,
tossed on the wind. There was another cry too, thin
and faint, but closer at hand. Beth stared. Martha had
put the reed basket with the baby in it on the rocks
some twenty yards away, but with the incoming tide
it had slid into the water and was bobbing about in
the waves, already several yards from the shore.
Martha, engrossed in keeping her flock together, had
not yet noticed.

Beth started to run. The wind was cold on her
cheeks and the pebbles slid from beneath her shoes,
hampering her. By the time she reached the rocks
where Martha had left Jamie she could hardly see the
reed basket in the dips between the waves.

Beth waded out to the rocks, feeling the tug of the
tide seize her. Even here, so close to the shore, there
was a strong tidal race out to sea. A rowing boat was
tied up there, dipping on the rising waves. Beth was
already up to her waist and her soaking skirts wrapped
about her legs so that she almost fell. The basket was
bobbing further away all the time and she knew she
could not swim out to it, knew that the tide race was
pulling too fast for her to catch up. She heard Jamie
wail again as a wave splashed over the side of the
basket and it threatened to tip over. In desperation she
grabbed the rowing boat and tumbled over the side.

The rope burned her palms as she pulled it free of its mooring, then she had grabbed the oars clumsily and turned it out to sea.

Beth had never rowed a boat before and whilst she soon realised that the tide was carrying her in the right direction, she had no skill to direct her course. Out of the corner of her eye she saw the shoreline receding with frightening speed. The children had realised now that something was wrong; one of them had grabbed Martha's skirts and started to cry. Several were screaming whilst one little girl, more resourceful than the rest, was running in the direction of the harbour and help, as fast as her small legs could carry her.

Beth was within a few feet of the basket. She could see Jamie's crumpled little face and hear his screams above the splash of the waves. She leant out, almost overturning the boat in her desperation. A wave hit her in the face and she gasped, shaking the blinding water from her eyes. Then her fingers grazed the edge of the wicker and she clung on and pulled, regardless of the cold that numbed her hands and the force of the waves that threatened to pull her arms from their sockets.

When she finally heaved the basket aboard, Jamie was soaking and screaming and Beth was exhausted and her clothes stiff and face sore with salt spray. She had paid no attention to the shore for several minutes and was horrified to discover that they were now at least a hundred yards out, with the strong tide pulling them towards Rat Island. One of her oars was gone and she had not even noticed. The prospects for both herself and Jamie were looking increasingly bleak.

'Hold on!'

The shout came from behind her and she squirmed around, collapsing back in the boat with relief as she saw another small craft drawing close. Colin McCrae was in the bows, his face a tight mask of tension as the men behind him rowed like the devil to reach her side. The two boats bumped together and Colin grabbed the bulwark, pulling them alongside. Beth reached for Jamie and thrust the screaming bundle into his father's arms.

Strong hands grasped her and half-lifted, half-pulled her into the other boat. She felt Marcus's arms close around her—she knew it was Marcus even though her eyes were closed—and she turned her face into his neck, breathing in the warm and reassuring scent of his skin. Then she burst into tears. She could feel Marcus's mouth pressed against the salty coldness of her cheek and heard him say, 'Oh, Beth,' as he held on to her as though he would never let her go. The feeling soothed her and she lay still, paying no more attention to their rescue.

Things became even more confused when they reached the jetty. Quite a crowd had gathered, with other people coming running as word went around about the accident. Colin jumped ashore and handed Jamie to Martha. She was crying as well and squeezed the baby to her so tightly that he promptly started to scream again.

'Nothing wrong with his lungs,' Colin commented with a grin, giving his wife a hug. 'I think he has survived the ordeal with no harm done!'

Beth had stopped crying, but when she tried to step ashore her legs buckled beneath her and Marcus was obliged to pick her up into his arms. A ragged cheer went up as the crowd saw her and started to push forward to shake her hand and pat her on the back. Beth, who wanted nothing more than a hot bath and peace and quiet to recover from the shock, found it unnerving. Martha pushed close, trying to thank her, and she could see the tears in Colin's eyes now as he started to relate the details of the rescue to the eager crowd.

In the end Marcus was obliged to force his way through them all to reach the horse and cart, and she, Martha, Jamie, Colin and Marcus piled aboard. Marcus held her firmly cradled on his knee, regardless of propriety. He did not speak, however, and stealing a look at his face, Beth saw that it was set and grim, his previous tenderness replaced by what looked like anger. Her heart sank. She did not feel she could bear him to ring a peal over her just now.

'Mustard baths, steaming gruel and physic,' Martha was saying, having recovered her self-possession now that she was certain baby Jamie was safe. 'Oh, Lady Allerton, how can we ever thank you? You were unconscionably brave!'

'Unconscionably foolish!' Marcus said shortly, earning himself an indignant exclamation from Martha before she fell silent under her husband's meaningful glare.

Marcus put Beth down at last when they reached the castle entrance. She was feeling much recovered, although the wind had flattened her wet clothes against her body in a manner that was unpleasantly clinging. She could feel the water dripping from her hair and splashing on the stone floor. Martha started to fuss about her, but Beth interrupted.

'Martha, why do you not go to the nursery and tend

to Jamie? All I need is a hot bath and some rest. I have taken no hurt—'

'Which is less than you deserve!' Marcus snapped. 'I shall see you to your room, Lady Allerton, lest you fall into some foolish scrape on the way!'

Beth heard both Colin and Martha gasp at his tone. At the back of her mind she knew that his short temper was probably only the product of relief, but indignation flooded through her and with it an anger that was warming.

'You shall not escort me, Lord Trevithick!' she said smartly, striding away towards the stair. 'I have no need of your further censure! I did what I thought was right—'

'Almost drowning yourself in the process!' Marcus finished curtly. 'When will you learn, Lady Allerton, that such impulsive actions lead only to trouble? There were plenty of men there eminently more capable than you of handling a rowing boat—'

'My lord—' Colin McCrae objected, only to fall back under Marcus's withering glare.

'Do not mistake me, Colin,' he said, more gently, 'I am more than glad that Jamie is safe and would have done anything to see him so.' He swung back to look at Beth, who was dripping quietly onto the stairs. 'What I object to is those who are not qualified wilfully rushing towards danger and causing more difficulties for themselves and other people—'

Beth did not wait to hear any more. She stalked off up the stairs, aware that she was making an undignified squelching noise and that there was a wet footprint on every step.

She felt cold and unpleasantly damp, and wanted nothing more than to strip off her clothes and rub herself dry. She devoutly hoped that Marcus would leave her alone, for she was in no mood to endure his condemnation. She was still shaking from a combination of shock and reaction. She slammed her bedroom door behind her. How dared Marcus! How dared he condemn her when she had been doing her best to save Jamie. Perhaps he was right in that there had been others more capable, but she could not stand by and simply watch the basket float out to sea!

She peeled off her soaking clothes, dropping them on the floor and hurrying into the closet to find a towel. Once she was dry she felt much better, although her hair had been blown into a hopeless tangle by the wind and would take hours to comb out. Beth wrapped herself in her brocade robe, picked up her comb and hurried back to the fire. She had just sat down and started to tease the tangles from her silky black hair, when there was a knock at the door.

'Come in!' Beth called. She had expected to see one of the maids there and her eyes widened in shock as Marcus strode into the room. He had evidently had time to change, for although his hair looked damp, his clothes were dry. Beth looked at him dubiously.

'Oh! Lord Trevithick! I did not think… You should not be here—'

'I wanted to talk to you,' Marcus said abruptly, closing the door behind him.

Beth fired up. 'Well, I do not want to hear any more! Ringing a peal over me when all I was trying to do was help—'

'I am aware of that,' Marcus said tightly. Beth saw that his hands were clenched at his side. 'What you do not seem to understand, Beth, is that the sea is treacherous around here and that you could so easily have been drowned yourself! Sometimes I think that you have no more sense than a child!'

Beth's eyes filled with easy tears. She had had a nasty shock and now she felt decidedly humiliated. 'Well, if I am lacking in sense, you are surely lacking in sensibility, my lord!' She made a wild gesture with the hand that held the comb. 'It is the cruellest thing to censure me when I am so upset—' She broke off as she saw that Marcus's attention had shifted from her white face to somewhere considerably lower. The brocade robe had loosened at her dramatic wave of the hand and was now falling open. Suddenly Beth was devastatingly aware that she was naked beneath its slippery folds. She gathered the material closely at her neck with a defensive gesture and fell silent. Her throat was dry and she could only watch as Marcus, eyebrows slightly raised, allowed his gaze to travel up again to rest thoughtfully on her now flushed face.

'You are correct, Beth.' His voice was husky now as he took a step towards her. 'It is quite wrong of me to reproach you. My anger arose only from a desire to protect you, for it seems to me that you plunge headlong towards danger without any thought of self-preservation…'

It seemed to Beth that she was racing towards danger at that very moment. The warmth of the fire could not account for the sudden heat that suffused her skin from her bare toes to the top of her head. The soft material of the robe seemed unbearably stimulating against her naked flesh. She cleared her throat, intending to ask Marcus to leave, but some inexplicable impulse kept her silent. Instead she just watched as he took the final step towards her. His eyes were very dark, reflecting his desire for her, but overlaid with

an expression of tenderness that held her still. He took
hold of her upper arms and drew her very gently towards him, and as his own arms closed about her, his
mouth came down on hers.

An involuntary shudder went through Beth's body
as her lips parted under his. His skin smelled clean
and fresh, and without conscious thought her hands
unclenched their hold on her gown so that she could
tangle her fingers in the thick darkness of his hair.
Marcus deepened the kiss and Beth moved closer into
his arms with a tiny moan. She blinked dizzily as he
lifted his mouth from hers and touched her lips with
the tip of his tongue. Conventional behaviour, the dic-
tates of society, had ceased to exist for her as soon
as Marcus had started to kiss her; all Beth knew was
that her pent-up fear and anger had fused into something exquisitely tender and sweet.

Her head fell back against Marcus's supporting
arm, allowing his mouth to drift down the taut line
of her throat to the hollow at its base. She felt his
tongue flick over her skin, tasting her, and shivered
beneath the caress. Her legs were trembling so much
that she was afraid that she might fall, and Marcus
evidently thought the same, for he picked her up and
placed her gently on the big bed. Beth felt the cold
air against her legs and realised with a faint shock
that the brocade robe was almost completely undone;
as soon as it came to her the knowledge seemed almost irrelevant, for Marcus was beside her and the
warmth of his body kept out the cold.

She felt his fingers at her waist, loosening the robe
so that it fell back completely. A moment later,
Marcus's palm brushed the slope of her breast and his
mouth closed over the tight peak of her nipple, the

gentle caress becoming firmer and stronger as Beth gave a soft moan of satisfaction. She was adrift with pleasure, unaware of anything except her need for him. She reached out to him blindly, digging her fingers into his back, tugging at his shirt so that she could run her hands over the hard, bare skin beneath.

It felt cold as soon as Marcus left her side. Beth rolled over, the brocade robe crushed beneath her, and opened her eyes. There was the most extraordinary ache inside her and she had never experienced anything like it, nor the violent desire for that ache to be satisfied.

'Marcus…' She realised that he had only left her in order to remove his clothes and smiled a little. She was still smiling when he came back to her side a moment later.

'Beth…' There was a fierce desire in his face, but she could see that he was frowning. 'Beth, if you do not wish for this, you must say so—now…'

Beth opened her eyes very wide. 'I wish it more than anything…'

There was a moment of stillness and then Marcus smiled too and lay down to take her in his arms again. He kissed her gently, but not so gently that the effect did not vibrate all the way through Beth's body. He was stroking her back, a soft sweep of a caress from her shoulder to the curve of her buttocks, with a touch so sensual that Beth was almost melting. She rolled over helplessly on to her back, then squirmed with renewed pleasure as Marcus's mouth closed over her breast again.

'Oh, please…'

She felt his hand dip between her trembling thighs, parting her legs. He was still kissing her when he entered her and Beth was engulfed immediately in a violent surge of pleasure that made her cry out against his mouth. A second later Marcus followed and he gasped her name, pressing his face to her throat until the pleasure died away.

Beth lay quite still, her body quiescent, her mind floating. She could not even begin to think, nor did she feel that there was any immediate necessity to do so, for Marcus had pulled the covers over them and had drawn her close to his side. She turned her head against his shoulder and drifted into sleep.

When Beth woke again it was almost dark outside. Marcus was lying beside her, deeply asleep. She looked at him, marvelling at the black sweep of his eyelashes against his cheek, the faint shadow of the stubble that darkened his chin, the hard lines of his face that were soft in sleep. She wanted to touch them all. A piercing stab of love washed over her, so intense and poignant that it almost hurt. Smiling a little sadly, she picked up her robe and went over to the window embrasure, curling up so that she could look out at the pewter sea.

Charlotte had always said that she was too impulsive, but her impulses had never led her to such a point before. She and Marcus were lovers now and the whole castle, the whole island, must surely know it, for he had been alone with her in her room for hours. Beth frowned. She did not feel like a fallen woman, for her mind was so full of love for Marcus that it seemed to transcend everything else.

Beth supposed that she was now only one of a great number of rich widows who had taken a lover, yet that seemed too shabby, too unemotional a description for what had happened between herself and Marcus. She knew that society's rules, whilst allowing no latitude for unmarried girls, were far more understanding of ladies in her position. Widows and married women were given a certain freedom, one might even say laxity, to behave as they pleased. And after all, she and Marcus were already betrothed. So, provided that they were discreet... Beth frowned again. She knew she had never been very good at being discreet. Her temperament was too open and now she wanted to shout from the rooftops that she loved Marcus to distraction.

Beth drew her knees up to her chin. She felt warm and happy and satisfied in a way that she had never felt with Frank Allerton. He had shown her none of the physical pleasure or the tenderness that Marcus had. She smiled wryly, remembering that she had previously thought herself physically cold. She had started to discover her mistake when she had first encountered Marcus in London and the explosive nature of their attraction had made her realise there was a whole side of her character that she had not known existed. Now she realised that to the full.

'Beth?' Marcus had stirred and was leaning on one elbow, watching her. Her heart swelled with love for him. She went across to the bed and sat on the edge, looking at him. A faint smile touched his mouth.

'Are you quite well, my love?'

Beth dropped her gaze. It was very nice to be called that and perhaps it might even be taken to imply that he loved her... She waited, hoping he would say so, but he did not.

'I am well,' she said, a little shyly.

'What were you thinking?' Marcus asked. His dark gaze was very direct. Beth plucked at the bedcovers.

'I was thinking that…oh, that Lady Salome and Charlotte and everyone else would not approve, and that I am indeed a shameless creature…'

She saw Marcus smile, but his gaze remained grave. 'So you regret what has happened?'

'No,' Beth said, hampered by her honesty. 'I cannot. But Marcus—do you…I mean, do you think me—?'

Marcus raised a hand and touched her cheek. 'I think that you are lovely, Beth. We are to be married and I do not think the opinions of others matter.'

A strange feeling took Beth, part triumphant and part forlorn. Whilst reassured that Marcus thought no less of her, she could not help feeling that he could afford to be hardy about the opinions of others whereas she was more vulnerable. She watched as he sat up and wrapped the sheet about him. He was still watching her, but with a speculation now that made her skin prickle with excitement.

'I wondered if you would care to take a bath,' Marcus said. 'After your ordeal in the sea it would perhaps be efficacious for your health…'

Beth looked at him. There was a spark of teasing in his eye, a hint of mischief and something more. The prickle of excitement turned into a tingle of un-mistakable anticipation.

'Well, if you think I should—'

'I am certain.' Marcus swung his legs over the side of the bed and reached for his shirt. 'But only if you share it with me.'

Beth's eyes opened to their widest extent. 'Oh! But…could we?'

Marcus grinned. 'I do not see why not!'

He wandered over to the fireplace and rang the bell. Beth gave a squeak. 'Marcus, the servants—'

Marcus only grinned at her again. He sauntered back to her side and slipped his arms about her, dropping a light kiss on her lips. 'So shy, my love? I fear it is a little late for that…'

Beth knew this was true but, all the same, it seemed sensible for Marcus to go to his own rooms and for her to wait discreetly alone whilst the water was drawn.

It was Martha McCrae who delivered it herself, in company with two maids, and their faces were so blank that Beth almost had a fit of the giggles. Tellingly Martha did not enquire after Beth's health, but her gaze did rest for a moment on the tumbled bedsheets and Beth thought that she almost smiled.

'Martha,' she said quickly, as they were leaving, 'how does baby Jamie? I hope that he is fully recovered?'

Martha did smile then, and a wicked dimple appeared in her cheek. 'Yes, thank you, milady.' She dropped a curtsey. 'He has taken no hurt, as indeed I hope you have not…'

Beth blushed, flustered. Martha gave her an innocent smile and closed the door softly.

Beth went through to the bathroom. The water had been scented with lavender and smelled delicious. She slipped out of her robe and into the hot water, closing her eyes with a sigh.

A moment later she opened them wide with a little shriek as Marcus slid into the bath behind her. She felt the press of his body against hers and almost squeaked again when he pulled her back against him.

The water rose dangerously, threatening to slop over the sides of the bath on to the floor.

'Stop wriggling,' Marcus instructed, laughing softly. 'Just keep still, or you will drown us both! We are fortunate that there is so much room in here…'

Beth complied, holding her breath as she felt his hands start to massage her shoulders gently. It felt delicious. The scent of the water, the hot, rising steam, the smell of lavender and the soapy slipperiness of Marcus's hands against her skin provoked the most delightful sensations within her. When he bent his head to kiss the side of her neck, where the damp black curls stuck to her skin, she leant back against his chest and closed her eyes. When his hands slipped lower to caress her breasts, she was certain she was about to dissolve with sheer pleasure.

So rapt was she in the desire he was invoking that Beth barely noticed when Marcus scooped her out of the bath and swept her up into his arms. He wrapped her in a huge towel and carried her through to the bedroom. They tumbled down on to the big bed together, Marcus pulling her under him. His mouth took the place of his hands at her breast and the exquisite surge of pleasure almost pushed Beth over the edge. She reached for him, gasping his name. Then all thought was lost as her mind was swamped in pure delight.

'You have been very quiet tonight, my dear,' Marcus observed, as he and Beth sat over the chessboard the following evening. 'Are you too tired to play? Do you wish to go to bed?'

They had taken dinner together and had now retired to the green drawing room, as had become their habit during the past two weeks. Although they usually played cards or talked, tonight Beth had chosen to play chess instead and had promptly lost the first game. She had been totally preoccupied because she had been wondering what was going to happen between herself and Marcus that night.

Marcus had stayed the previous night with her but when she had woken that morning he had been gone and she had not seen him for the whole of the day. The servants had told her that he was out with Colin McCrae on estate business, which was only natural, but Beth had been unable to settle all day. She had gone on a long walk to Admiral's Point, had done some unnecessary gardening and probably killed some of Lady Salome's wintering bulbs, and had undertaken any number of tasks to distract her thoughts from the night before. She wondered if their love-making had perhaps been an aberration, a night borne out of the indisputable tension that had built up between herself and Marcus. Perhaps neither of them would ever speak of it again and pretend that it had never happened, and she was not sure how she would feel if that was the case. Her emotions felt too raw and new for too much soul-searching.

Beth's pulse jumped as she saw Marcus's dark gaze resting on her, wickedly assessing, and she suddenly thought that perhaps the previous night had not been an aberration after all. Her face warmed as she thought about it. The room was intimately dark, shadowed and fire lit, with only one additional branch of candles.

Beth realised that Marcus was still awaiting her reply. She looked up, met his eyes and smiled demurely. 'No, I am not tired. Perhaps I do not have the right kind of calculating mind for chess.'

'But you always respond to a challenge,' Marcus murmured. 'How if we were to make the stakes higher? If you lose a pawn…' he paused, his gaze considering her '…then you also lose…a garment?'

Beth almost choked on her tea. 'Marcus! No, really! Surely you are in jest?'

'What, too afraid to take the challenge?' Marcus laughed, leaning back in his chair. 'That is not like you, my love, and this way the game is so much more enjoyable…'

Beth bit her lip. It was difficult to decide, to think clearly, for her mind was dizzy with anticipation and remembered desire. She admitted to herself that the challenge was well nigh irresistible and that she might as well be hung for a sheep as a lamb…

Marcus was still watching her with speculative amusement. She met his gaze directly. 'What if I should win, my lord? Once before I won a wager against you.'

'That's true…' Marcus started to set up the chessboard again. 'Well, sweetheart, we shall see!'

Beth stared at the checkerboard squares, concentrating hard. Frank had taught her chess, but he had never made it as interesting as this. On the other hand, he had taught her a sound strategy and she was determined to use it. The trouble was that Marcus was a very good player and she found she could not concentrate for long…

Even so, it was several minutes before she lost her first pawn. She paused, considering, then removed her spencer and folded it neatly over the arm of the chair. She did not dare look at Marcus for she knew that he would be watching her and that would put her off even more. The room was warm and from that point of view she scarcely noticed the loss of the spencer, and a quick mental inventory of her remaining clothes reassured her that there were plenty left. All the same, there were seven pawns left on the board...

Marcus lost two pawns in quick succession and shrugged out of his jacket and untied his stock. Beth glanced at him and looked quickly away. He was still wearing his blue embroidered waistcoat and beneath that, his linen shirt, but he already looked slightly dishevelled. His shirt was now open, revealing the strong brown column of his neck and the sight of the bronze sheen of his skin was wholly disturbing to Beth's senses. It certainly would not help her concentration to keep looking at him. She gazed fixedly at the chessboard and moved her castle, a little tentatively. A moment later she realised that she had made a mistake. A bad one.

She saw Marcus move a pawn and his hand close over the castle to take it off the board. He was watching her with a look of amusement.

'That counts as three items of clothing, I fear, my love. I forgot to tell you that there was a...sliding scale.'

Beth sighed. 'My slippers? That must be two items...'

Marcus sat back in his chair. 'I rather think that they should count as only one.'

Beth frowned at him. 'It seems to me that you are making up the rules as you go along, my lord!'

'Perhaps so.' Marcus smiled. 'That is part of the fun.'

Beth kicked off her slippers under the table, then

after a moment, put a hand up to unpin her lace cap.
She was very conscious of Marcus watching her every
move, his dark eyes never leaving her face. She tossed
the cap aside. Now she had something of a dilemma.
Unless she chose to unroll her stockings, it had to be
her dress.

'You will have to help me, my lord...' Her voice
was husky. She stood up and turned around. Marcus
came round the table and a moment later she felt his
fingers on the buttons of her gown, moving method-
ically downwards. Then his hands skimmed her bare
shoulders, sliding the dress down.

Beth discovered that the potent effect of his touch
on her skin, so explosive the previous night, had not
lessened. With a little sigh, she let the dress fall to
the ground. Anticipation was hammering through her
body with each beat of her pulse, its dizzy stroke
making her feel utterly light-headed. And she still had
a game to complete. She had thought that the wager
at the Cyprians' Ball had been perilous enough. Now
she had an entirely new sense of danger. Danger and
excitement, inextricably linked. She slid from under
Marcus's hands and resumed her seat, focusing on the
board.

When she captured his bishop she looked at him
triumphantly. 'If the castle counts for three items of
clothing, my lord, surely the bishop is two? Can you
deny it?'

Marcus grinned. 'Absolutely right, sweetheart!
What would you like me to remove?'

Beth swallowed hard. Her throat was suddenly dry.
'Your waistcoat and...your shirt?'

Marcus smiled with devilish pleasure. 'Certainly...'
The rustle of starched linen filled Beth's ears. She

was not yet accustomed to seeing Marcus naked and knew perfectly well that the sight of his bare brown torso would destroy any remaining chance she had of concentrating. When Marcus sat down again she deliberately averted her gaze from him, despite the almost overwhelming temptation to stare. But it was already too late. Her attention had been fatally distracted and her next move was disastrous.

Marcus moved a pawn across the board and captured her queen. 'Check,' he said contentedly.

'Is that the end?' Beth whispered.

'Not yet,' Marcus said thoughtfully. 'That is, you need not necessarily lose the chess game, but I suspect you have insufficient clothing left to cover your debt—amongst other things…'

When Beth looked at him she saw that the devilish light in his eyes had deepened and he was watching her with undisguised desire. He got up and came round the table again, taking her hand and drawing her to her feet. Beth shivered a little, suddenly aware that she was already wearing little more than her chemise.

'I protest,' she said huskily, 'that you have changed the rules shamelessly, my lord—'

'I always play by my own rules,' Marcus pointed out.

He bent his head and kissed her. His mouth was soft and seductive, spinning a snare of delight. His fingers moved to unpin her hair.

Beth's mind cleared briefly. 'Marcus, we are in the drawing room! The servants—'

'—will not come in. They are too discreet.'

He kissed her again, moulding her yielding body against the hard lines of his. Beth ran her hands over the hard muscles of his chest and felt herself tremble, faint with the taste, touch and smell of him. She felt his hands move, deft and warm. Something gave, and she realised that her stays were gone, discarded. Marcus pulled her down with him on the rug in front of the fire.

The light was pale, bathing them both in its gentle glow. The fire felt warm through the thinness of Beth's chemise. Marcus pulled the tapes and undid the bodice, exposing her breasts. She saw desire distilled in his face as he bent his head to take one rosy tip in his mouth. Beth squirmed then, shivers of pleasure coursing through her. She could not believe that this was happening, not here, not now. She opened dazed grey eyes as she felt Marcus move to kneel between her thighs.

'Marcus…you still have your clothes on—'

'Barely.' She heard the laughter in his voice. She knew he still had his boots on and his pantaloons, and he was now undoing the fastening in a feverish hurry. There was something inexpressibly exciting in the urgency of the need that ran between them.

Marcus's hands slid under the hem of the chemise, pulled it up to her hips and lingered on the bare flesh at the tops of her silk stockings. She heard him give a rough groan against her throat.

'Oh, Beth, my love…'

She felt him shudder convulsively as soon as he came into her and she dug her fingernails into his back, exulting in the power she had over him. But it was too soon to feel triumphant, for the same conflagration swept over her, leaving her breathless and shaking. They lay still in the warm glow of the fire, then Marcus rolled away from her and for a moment

Beth felt cold and bereft. Then he propped himself on one elbow and leant over to kiss her, tiny, teasing kisses that were very sweet.

'Such haste is not always a good thing, however...'

Beth felt his hand brush her thigh, moving intimately to part her flesh again, and groaned aloud.

'Marcus, I do not think I can—'

'Yes, you can.' His breath was soft against her face. His fingers caressed her. 'I have won this wager, remember...'

This time he took his time, spinning out the pleasure for both of them. Beth was so lost in her feelings that she did not even realise that she cried aloud as her body shook again in exquisite torment. When she finally opened her eyes, it was to see Marcus pushing the tumbled hair away from her brow as he bent to kiss her once more.

'Checkmate,' he said.

Marcus pushed the pile of papers away from him with an exclamation of disgust and rose to his feet, stretching vigorously in an attempt to shake off some of the lethargy that seemed to possess him every time he tried to study the maps. McCrae had explained it all to him several times and yet he appeared to be utterly incapable of concentrating on the plans for the new harbour. On one sheet were the scale drawings of the building work required and on the other were neat columns of costs, timings and the manpower needed. Yet more pages gave a detailed plan of how the project would be managed and supplied. McCrae was nothing if not thorough.

Marcus poured himself a glass of whisky and wandered moodily over to the window. He knew the reason for his preoccupation, of course—Beth. All the time that he was trying to concentrate on the business of the estate, she seemed to insinuate herself into his thoughts, easily clouding out every other consideration. It was not simply her physical attributes that obsessed him, although he had to admit that he had spent as much time thinking about them as any infatuated boy. Marcus laughed with self-deprecation. It was a new experience for him to be so besotted, but not an unpleasant one. He knew that Beth was revelling in her newly found sensuality and so was he. There was no likelihood that she would consider herself physically cold ever again.

However, he had to acknowledge that there was far more to his feelings than that. He loved Beth. He loved her for her openness and her lack of artifice and pretence. He loved the innocence of character that made her give so generously of herself. He had watched her with the servants and villagers, seen her genuine interest in their lives and their concerns, and it had made him want to crush her to him and never let her go.

Marcus wandered back to his desk and picked up the letter that lay a little apart from the rest of the papers. It had come that day from Lady Salome, and related that she and St John would not be returning to Fairhaven until the spring. Church business was keeping St John occupied, Lady Salome explained, and in the meantime she was visiting old friends and making the most of a sojourn on the mainland. She finished off with many expressions of affection for him and especially for Beth, and had included a paragraph about expecting him to behave with honour, which she had underlined several times.

Marcus frowned, tossing the letter down onto the table. He had been desperately hoping that St John and Salome would be back imminently, bringing a special licence from the Bishop with them. It had always been his intention to ask his cousin to marry him to Beth on Fairhaven and he had been severely disappointed to find St John away when they had arrived. Now his final hope had been dashed with the news that St John would not return before Christmas.

Marcus took a mouthful of whisky and sat back in his chair, considering his options. Suddenly it all seemed damnably difficult and he felt a keen pang of guilt at ever getting into the situation. Lady Salome's letter, with its underlined paragraph, reproached him. He had compromised Beth and now he could not put the matter right as he had intended. The only thing that he could do was marry her as soon as possible once they had returned to the mainland, and such a hasty match seemed furtive and not good enough for her when he had intended matters to be so different. The best compromise that he could think of was that they might marry at Mostyn just after Christmas, which would give time for the banns to be read and would also be an appropriate place. Beth would probably like that but he could not be sure. After all, her first marriage had taken place there.

With a groan, he pushed the glass away before he was tempted to top it up and turned back to the map of the harbour with a mixture of irritation and grim determination. McCrae would be back to ask him for his decision within the hour and he did not want his estate manager to think he had been wasting his time. And once he had dealt with business he would turn to the pressing and more important matter of his marriage. He wanted it resolved.

Beth stood by her bed, folding her clothes and tucking them neatly into her trunk in preparation for her journey to the mainland. She had considered taking the ball gown made from the drawing-room curtains because it had special sentimental value since she had been wearing it when Marcus proposed. However, she did not have enough room, so she had hung the gown up in the closet, hoping she would return to Fairhaven before too long and wear it once again.

The previous week had passed in a whirl. During the day, Marcus was still spending some of his time out and about on the estate or talking to Colin McCrae about his plans for the island. It pleased Beth to see just how involved Marcus had become in the future of Fairhaven and how much he cared that the farm would prosper and succeed. Sometimes she rode with him about the island, exploring the rocky crags and the secluded bays with their stretches of pure white sand. Once she had been tempted to paddle in the winter sea, charmed into thinking it would not be too cold because the sun was shining and the water gleamed blue in the light. She had been frozen within a few seconds, and Marcus had laughed and pulled her to him and kissed her, and she could taste the salt on his lips and would almost have sworn that it was love that she saw reflected in his eyes. Perhaps it had only been a reflection of her own feelings, for she loved Marcus and her love for him seemed to deepen every day.

She sighed. It was that love that led her to be free and unguarded, with her feelings as well as her body.

And that was another story... Beth shifted a little as she thought about it. The foolish pretence that she was nothing more than a friend to Marcus had been thoroughly disproved on the very first afternoon that he had spent in bed with her, and since then there had been several others. What the servants thought when they disappeared after lunch was anyone's guess and at first Beth had been appalled. It had never occurred to her that people might make love during the day rather than wait for the night, nor had she realised the infinite variations that might apply. Marcus had seemed amused at her naïveté and quite evidently delighted to extend her education. And there was no doubt that she had been an apt pupil.

Now, however, all that might change. Being on Fairhaven had been unreal in some ways, a paradise cut off from the rest of the world where society's rules need not apply and she and Marcus had been protected from censure. Now they were to return to the mainland, to marry and to resume their place in society. There would be their estates to visit and the London Season and the Dowager Countess of Trevithick to contend with... Beth sighed. No, matters could not be the same.

In bed in the following dawn, Beth awoke and lay still, watching the grey light filter from behind the curtains and hearing the faint rhythmic roar of the sea on the rocks far below. She knew that it would be the last time she would wake like this and she was imprinting it on her memory. When she moved a little, Marcus pulled her into his arms, his mouth against her hair.

'Why are you not asleep, sweetheart?'

'I was thinking,' Beth said. She rolled on to her stomach and lay looking down into his face.

'Marcus, I was thinking that my dreams of Fairhaven were not real at all…'

She saw that he was wide awake and watching her. A tender smile was curving his lips. 'Oh, Beth. Was it so hard to find out the truth about your grandfather?'

'Yes,' Beth said softly. She bent her head. 'At the time it was hard. But now it is not so bad after all. But, Marcus, I am afraid that everything will change once we leave here—'

Marcus pulled her into the crook of his arm. 'Do not be afraid, sweetheart. This is just the start.' He paused. His fingers were tracing the path of her spine and it was most distracting.

'We are to be married straight after Christmas— and at Mostyn. What could be better than that?'

Beth smiled. 'I know. It will be lovely.' Despite her words, a tiny qualm of disquiet remained and she did not understand it. She wriggled a little as Marcus's fingers drifted lower and his caresses became more insistent. Her melancholy thoughts faded. The urgent touch of Marcus's hands on her body was enough to send all other thoughts spinning out of her head. He made love to her slowly, with a tender intensity that left them both trembling. And when it was over he wrapped her in his arms and pulled her close to him. Beth was just drifting off to sleep again when she heard him whisper:

'Beth, I love you.'

Beth's whole body felt soft and satisfied. A little smile curled her lips. Yet at the back of her mind the doubt returned, faint but disturbing. She tried to push it away but it would not go, not completely. With a sigh she fell asleep again, but her worries pursued her, nameless and threatening, through her dreams.

When she woke in the morning, Marcus had already gone. That was not unusual in itself. At the start of their affair he had always been sure to be back in his own rooms before the other inhabitants of the castle started to stir, then Beth had pointed out to him what an unnecessary fiction this was and he had gladly stayed by her side. This morning, however, his absence left her feeling somewhat lonely and she was at a loss to explain why.

She had barely finished dressing when there was a knock at the door and Martha McCrae stuck her head round.

'Oh, my lady, I am sorry to disturb you but an urgent letter has come from London! His lordship is about to depart—'

Beth's eyebrows shot up. 'Good God, whatever can be so pressing—?'

Marcus and Colin McCrae were in the study when she hurried down. Marcus was already dressed for travelling, booted and cloaked, and when he saw Beth his face lightened for a moment before a frown returned. Colin glanced from one to the other and withdrew softly.

'Beth.' Marcus came across and took both her hands in his. 'I am so sorry. I have to leave for London at once. A letter has come—' He gestured to the desk behind him. 'Well, you may read for yourself. My mother is in despair. She writes that my sister Eleanor has been seduced and abandoned, and begs me to return to help her.'

Beth stared up at him, shocked. 'Good God, how

dreadful! But who can possibly—?' She was not sure
whether her own heart provided the answer or
whether she read it in Marcus's face. She drew her
hands away.

'Oh, no, not Kit…'

'It seems so.' Marcus's face was grim. 'I cannot be
sure of the precise situation, for the letter is somewhat
incoherent. But I must go, Beth. You must see…'

'Yes, of course…' Beth stared at the sheets of paper on the desk. She knew that Kit had had a *tendre*
for Eleanor Trevithick. She had observed it herself
and had even teased him about it, but to ruin the girl
was another matter…

'I cannot believe it!' she burst out. 'Kit would
never behave so! It cannot be true!'

Marcus's face was set. 'Well, I shall find out. I am
sorry, Beth, but I must go.' He came back to her side.
'Go back to Mostyn Hall—'

'I shall not!' Beth screwed up her face, trying to
think straight. 'If you are for London, I shall go too!
Charlotte will be distressed and all alone—'

Marcus was controlling his impatience with difficulty. 'There is no time to talk now. I have to catch
the tide. Beth, you must see that this changes all our
plans! I fear our wedding cannot go ahead as we had
intended, but if you go to Mostyn—'

'No!' Beth said again. 'I cannot stay quiet in the
country whilst this is happening!'

Marcus pulled on his gloves. 'Then contact me as
soon as you reach London. And take great care on
the journey.' He took her hands in an urgent grip.
'Promise me!'

'I promise,' Beth said.

'This was not how I wanted it to be for us,' Marcus

said, in a hard, angry voice. 'To have everything spoiled—' He broke off, gave her a fierce kiss and straightened up. For a moment, Beth thought that he was about to say something else, then he turned on his heel and she heard his footsteps fading away across the hall.

Beth picked the Dowager Viscountess's letter from the desk and sat down in the armchair. Five minutes later, when she had perused the contents twice, she let the letter fall to her lap and stared into the fire.

The letter had been written a week before and it was evident that its author had been in a tearing hurry as well as great distress. Amidst the invective against the Mostyn family was the core of the tale: how Kit Mostyn had tricked and seduced Eleanor, then promptly abandoned her and disappeared.

Beth frowned. She knew Kit had a rake's reputation, but he had never stooped to seducing innocent young girls. He had never needed or wanted to. Besides, Beth was certain that his feelings for Eleanor had been sincere and he would never act dishonourably. Nevertheless, the facts appeared damning. She would have to go to London herself and find out.

She crossed to the window and looked out. It was a beautiful sunny morning and she could already see the speck that was Marcus's boat, growing smaller all the time, as it tacked across the strait to Bideford. Her heart felt heavy. She knew Marcus had not had the time to wait for her and that if the two of them had travelled together it would have slowed his journey down. Nevertheless, she felt an irrational disappointment that he had not suggested it. It felt as though he did not want her with him.

Standing there, she went over the conversation that

she had just had with Marcus. Of course their wedding would have to be postponed, but... She felt suddenly chill. What was it that he had said? *You must see that this changes all our plans! I fear our wedding cannot go ahead...*

But she had not seen what he was trying to say, not immediately. She had assumed that he meant only to delay rather than to call it off. It was only now, as she watched him leave without her, that the true implication of his words hit her.

This was not how I wanted it to be for us. To have everything spoiled...

She had thought that he had been going to say something else—something more final, but at the last moment he had not. Had that, perhaps, been when he was about to end everything between them, but had decided to spare her feelings until he had time to soften the blow—when they met in London, perhaps?

Beth watched the boat until the sun on the water made her eyes ache, then she turned back to the room. It seemed darker now, depressing. She hurried out into the hall and up the stairs, determined to press on with her own departure. It was the only way to keep her fears at bay. And deepest and most unacknowledged was the growing fear that Kit's actions had ruined them all and damned forever the relationship between her and Marcus. Their engagement had not been officially announced and now, surely, the marriage would not take place. For how could Marcus wish to associate with her after her cousin had apparently brought such dishonour on the Trevithick family by ruining his sister? His parting words had confirmed as much. Kit had caused the most immense scandal and all relations between the Mostyns and Trevithicks must, by necessity, be severed once again.

Chapter Ten

'You are looking very sickly, my love,' Charlotte said, holding her cousin at arm's length and looking her over critically. 'It is all this worry over Kit and Miss Trevithick, I suppose! And travelling in winter, of course. That is never to be recommended.'

There was a certain strange hush about the house in Upper Grosvenor Street, a gloominess that mirrored Beth's own feelings most accurately. She had been travelling for four long weeks in the most dreadful conditions and had finally reached London ten days after Christmas. The capital was shuttered and silent, for everyone had left Town to celebrate the twelve days of Christmas in the country. The streets were empty and cold, the skies a dull grey and the joyful Christmas spirit most noticeably lacking, particularly in their townhouse where everyone looked pinched and fearful, waiting for information about Kit and yet dreading that it might be bad. Charlotte had been relieved to see her, but the first piece of news that she had imparted was that Kit had not reappeared and there had been no progress in finding him.

'I am sorry that you had to chase all the way to

Mostyn Hall only to find that I had come up to London,' Charlotte said, leading Beth into the drawing room. 'My letter must have passed you on the road. How was everyone at home?'

'Well enough.' Beth gave her cousin a watery smile. She stripped off her gloves and cloak, and hurried gratefully over to the fire. 'They are all very worried, of course, but there is no news from Mostyn either. Kit certainly did not go there after he disappeared.'

Charlotte wrinkled up her face. 'It was the first place that I thought he might go to if there was trouble—' She broke off. 'I am sorry! You are barely through the door and here I am regaling you with nothing but bad news! Let us at least wait until the tea is served!'

Beth laughed. 'Or let us speak of more pleasant matters! Despite our troubles you look radiant, Charlotte! I believe you must have some good news for me!'

Charlotte's worried expression immediately dissolved into a glowing smile. 'Oh, Beth, it seems all wrong to be so happy when Kit has caused so much trouble, but…yes, that is…Mr Trevithick and I are betrothed!'

Although the news was not unexpected, Beth had to fight hard to crush down an unworthy feeling of jealousy. She gave Charlotte a tight hug that left her cousin breathless. 'Charlotte, I am so happy for you! You see, travelling in the winter *can* be beneficial!'

Charlotte blushed. 'Indeed, it was all settled by the time that Justin—Mr Trevithick—had escorted me back to Mostyn Hall…'

'Just as I had thought it would!'

'And we are to be married in the spring!' Charlotte hugged her back hard. 'Oh, Beth, how can I be so fortunate when Kit…'

'You deserve your good fortune,' Beth said staunchly, 'if that is what it is! Personally, I feel that Mr Trevithick is the lucky one!'

Charlotte blushed and disclaimed, 'Of course, I was concerned that this dreadful behaviour of Kit's might put an end to our engagement, but Justin—' she blushed harder '—assured me that it did not weigh with him. He has no position to uphold within the family, of course. If it had been his cousin the Earl it would have been a different matter—' She broke off. 'All the same, it is decidedly awkward!'

Beth nodded sadly. Charlotte's words had only confirmed her own conviction that Marcus could not possibly have anything to do with her in the future. Once again his parting words came back into her mind. But perhaps it was for the best. Their relationship on Fairhaven had been decidedly irregular. Beth shuddered to think what would be said in the *ton* if it all came out—the callous seduction and abandonment of Eleanor was bad enough and the scandalous affair between herself and Marcus could only be grist to the gossips' mill. She had had plenty of time to think about it on her journey up from Devon—and plenty of time to tell herself that she had to try to learn to live without Marcus. Her heart was not listening to her head; she had missed him dreadfully and her love had not weakened but her hope had, with each hour that passed.

She sat down a little heavily.

'Let us have tea at once,' Charlotte said, ringing the bell. 'Indeed, dearest Beth, you look worn to a thread! Tell me what has happened to you! I have been so selfishly full of my good news—'

'Nonsense!' Beth said. She was finding it very difficult to remain bright when she found that all she wanted to do was to cry. 'Besides, I have nothing to tell you! I have agreed that Fairhaven Island should remain the property of the Earl of Trevithick and that is the end of the tale!'

Charlotte looked startled. 'But, Beth… After you were so anxious to claim the place—'

'I know!' Beth clasped her hands together. 'Well, now I have been there I realise how different from my imaginings was the reality! I will tell you about it all some time, Charlotte, but not now if you will forgive me. I am a little tired.'

'Of course.' Charlotte frowned a little as she watched Beth's face. 'But, Beth, I thought that Lord Trevithick was intending to ask you—'

'Let us not speak of that now,' Beth said hastily. She had no desire to explain the complexities of her stay on Fairhaven to Charlotte. 'The matter of Kit and Eleanor is surely more pressing…'

The tea arrived at that moment and Beth was relieved when Charlotte appeared distracted, although sorry to bring the frown back to her cousin's face with thoughts of Kit's disappearance. Charlotte pressed her hands together distressfully.

'Oh, Beth, is it not terrible? I came up from Mostyn Hall as soon as Gough informed me, although I do not know what good I can do here! How could Kit ruin and abandon the poor child? I can scarcely believe it of him!'

'But is it certain?' Beth enquired, accepting the cup of tea Charlotte handed her. She was glad to be speaking of someone else's affairs rather than her own, even if they were so bleak. 'I simply cannot believe that Kit would seduce and desert an innocent girl!'

Charlotte looked dubious. 'Oh, but it is worse than that apparently! Eleanor claims that they are married!'

'Is that worse?' Beth asked, a little bitterly. She saw Charlotte give her a curious look and said hastily, 'At least Miss Trevithick does not have the shame of being ruined—'

'No, but such a scandalous marriage!' Charlotte looked as though she was about to cry. 'And then to desert her and disappear only a day later! I cannot believe he could be so dishonourable!'

Beth put down her teacup and came across to take Charlotte's cold hands in hers. 'He is not! Something must have happened to him that we do not yet know—'

'That could be even worse!' Charlotte clutched Beth's hands. 'Needless to say, I have had Gough look everywhere, but to no avail! Oh, Beth!'

Beth sat down beside her. 'You had best tell me the whole story,' she said. 'I may not be able to think of anything new, but at least I can try!'

The tea had gone cold and a fresh pot had been delivered before Charlotte had finished the tale. Much of it was third-hand from Justin, who had apparently heard the whole from Marcus, who had in turn spoken to his sister. It seemed that six weeks before, Eleanor Trevithick had taken exception to the man that her mother had indicated she should marry and had fool-ishly fled to Kit for help. According to Eleanor, they had been married by special licence and Kit had aban-doned her the very next day. Since then there had been no word from him and Eleanor had returned to Trevithick House, heartbroken and disgraced.

'The Viscountess has been most intemperate in her condemnation,' Charlotte said, with a little sniff. Her tragic blue eyes met Beth's. 'I cannot believe that she has helped her daughter's cause by speaking as she has done! Why, the entire *ton* is aware of all the intimate details, even down to why there can be no annulment!'

Beth raised her eyebrows expressively. 'Oh, dear, poor Eleanor! I suppose we must be grateful that most people are out of town now, and the scandal must surely die down through lack of interest!'

Charlotte smoothed her dress with nervous fingers. 'Justin feels that matters will improve now that the Earl has returned, for he and his sister are close. But if we cannot find Kit I cannot see what else can be done—' Her voice broke on a sob. Beth pressed her hands.

'Oh, Charlotte, do not! All will be well, I am convinced of it!'

She was not, but she knew that it would do her cousin no good to sink into a fit of the dismals.

'Excuse me, my lady.' Carrick was in the doorway. 'Mr Justin Trevithick has called.'

Beth jumped, terror coursing through her. On no account could she face seeing Justin, for he would undoubtedly bring news of Marcus and just at the moment Beth did not feel strong enough to hear it. She saw Charlotte's face brighten immediately and knew her own had lost what little colour it had. She got to her feet.

'Oh, excuse me, Charlotte! I have not yet washed

the journey off and am in sore need of a rest! Please give Mr Trevithick my best wishes.'

She saw Charlotte's look of amazement as she sped from the room with just a whisper of time to spare before Justin came in. Once in her bedroom, she collapsed on the bed and tried to still her trembling. It was going to be decidedly difficult if Justin persisted in calling on Charlotte every day, as her cousin had intimated he did. Even now he would be aware that she had returned from Fairhaven and he would certainly tell Marcus.

Beth lay back against her pillows. On the journey up from Devon she had decided that she must not see Marcus again. There were a hundred good reasons that said that this was the best course of action. Firstly there was Kit's behaviour, which had destroyed even the remote possibility of an alliance between the two families. Unlike Justin, Marcus *did* have a position to uphold within the Trevithick family and that made any link he might have with the Mostyns quite untenable. Once Beth had accepted the truth of this, any remaining hope she had harboured of marrying Marcus had died a swift death. She had only to remind herself of what he had said that last morning on Fairhaven, to know that there was no hope. Yet the irony was that there was now a reason why marriage might be even more desirable…

Beth closed her eyes. She loved Marcus too much to torture herself with seeing him when she could not have him. The thought of meeting him, talking to him and agreeing that they must part was exquisitely painful to her. She had already decided that once she had done the best she could to help with the search for Kit, and had given Charlotte the moral support she needed, she would return to Mostyn Hall. It would be a strange and lonely January without either of her cousins, but at least Charlotte had Justin to look after her now… Beth impatiently dashed away a tear that persisted in squeezing from under her eyelids. She had never felt sorry for herself in all her life and she did not intend to start now.

The following morning, rather than feeling an improvement from having a good night's rest, Beth felt so sick that she could scarcely raise her head from the pillow. Charlotte came to see her, most concerned, and Beth felt quite angry with herself for adding to her cousin's troubles.

'It is nothing serious,' she croaked, in answer to Charlotte's anxious enquiry. 'I shall rest here today and be as right as rain by the evening!'

Charlotte was wearing a smart walking dress and confessed shyly that she had started to venture out a little with Justin as her escort. London was quiet and the crowds were small and not too frightening. Beth watched her go with pleasure and not a little envy, then turned over and fell asleep immediately.

She awoke in the middle of the afternoon, uncertain just what had disturbed her, until she heard a familiar voice down in the hall.

'I understand that Lady Allerton has returned to town?'

Marcus! Beth struggled to sit up, then changed her mind and lay very still, as though her immobility might actually convince him that she was not in the house at all. She knew Marcus was perfectly capable of walking right into her bedroom—he had done so often enough, after all, albeit in Fairhaven, not London. She held her breath as the butler replied.

'Lady Allerton is resting after her journey and has asked not to be disturbed, my lord. I will tell her that you called.'

'Please do so.' Beth could read a wealth of displeasure in Marcus's tone. 'Pray tell her that I will call on her tomorrow.'

She did not relax until the door had closed behind him, when she slid supine beneath the covers and lay trembling. So Marcus had come to find her, as she might have imagined he would do. Beth knew Marcus was not the sort of man to ignore a difficult situation and hope it would just go away. He was far too honourable for that. He would deem it his duty to see her and tell her that their betrothal must end. It was a private matter between the two of them, for the engagement had never been officially announced, or at least only on Fairhaven. She could leave the island in Marcus's care, could write to Lady Salome explaining that family circumstances prevented the marriage, and could then return to Mostyn Hall and forget the whole thing. Except that she could not. For in addition to her feelings for Marcus, which would not simply go away, there would soon be a very real reminder of what had happened between them...

Beth groaned and rolled over in the bed. In her heart she knew it was going to be hopeless to try to avoid Marcus but just at the moment she did not feel she had the strength to face him, and certainly not to keep secrets from him.

In the evening Beth managed to struggle from her bed but as soon as she joined Charlotte for dinner she realised that she could not bear to eat a mouthful and promptly retired to the drawing room. Charlotte reported that Gough had no further news of Kit's whereabouts; he had sent word to all the ports but to no avail and none of Kit's friends claimed to have seen him for well over two months. It appeared that he had vanished into thin air.

'Justin says that his cousin the Earl is most anxious to see you, Beth,' Charlotte said, when they had fruitlessly discussed Kit's disappearance for half an hour. 'Apparently Lord Trevithick called here earlier—'

'I heard him,' Beth said hurriedly. 'Unfortunately, I did not feel well enough to receive visitors.'

Charlotte was looking at her thoughtfully. 'Well, perhaps tomorrow? It may help in the hunt for Kit if we share our information.'

Beth shook her head stubbornly. 'I do not wish to see Lord Trevithick, Charlotte. I will not be at home.'

A frown furrowed Charlotte's brow. 'But, Beth, why—?'

'Please...' To her horror, Beth felt the weak tears rise in her throat. 'I do not wish to speak of Lord Trevithick!' And once again she hurried from the room before Charlotte could remonstrate with her.

On the next day she was as good as her word. When Marcus called she refused to see him and had the satisfaction if hearing him storm from the house, slamming the door behind him. Beth knew she was being cowardly in avoiding him, and when Charlotte returned from her walk with Justin, she told Beth so in no uncertain terms.

'As though things were not difficult enough as they

are,' Charlotte scolded. 'Really, Beth, have you quar-relled with Trevithick again? Because, if so—'

'Please!' Beth said quickly. 'Charlotte, please do not!'

In desperation she put on her coat, hat and gloves and called the carriage to take her to Gough's cham-bers in Holborn. The man of business had nothing new to impart, but at least Beth felt that she was doing something useful and it took her away from Charlotte's too-perceptive questioning.

It was as she was leaving the building that she saw the Earl of Trevithick across the street, with Eleanor by his side. Beth's heart began to race. Just seeing him again was dreadful. He looked tired and worn and Beth wanted to rush across the street and fling herself into his arms.

They were taking a farewell of a gentleman whom Beth took to be the Earl's man of business, Gower. She had forgotten that he and Gough had rooms so close to one another and cursed herself for not think-ing of it. Even as she made to turn away, Marcus saw her, exchanged a quick word with Eleanor and then set off across the street towards her. Quick as a flash, Beth jumped into her coach, without even pausing to thank Gough for his help. She was aware of similar looks of astonishment on the faces of both Gough and Marcus, though Marcus's look was decidedly more threatening. Before she could give the order to drive off, he had swung open the carriage door.

'Lady Allerton!'

Beth adopted her most haughty tone. It was the only way she could keep her voice from shaking.

'Lord Trevithick?'

Marcus was looking puzzled and annoyed. It made Beth want to cry.

'Will you step down and speak with me, ma'am?'

'No!' Beth snapped. 'I do not wish to, my lord!'

She saw Marcus flinch and it gave her a pain inside. He still looked more bewildered than angry, which only made Beth feel worse about the way she was treating him.

'Is this because of what has happened, ma'am?' he asked with constraint. 'Your cousin's behaviour—'

'It has nothing to do with that!' Beth said stonily. She wished that he would not persevere in questioning her, for she was sure that she would burst into tears in a moment.

'Then it must be the change in our own circumstances,' Marcus persisted, running a hand through his tumbled dark hair. He looked cross and confused. 'You have every right to be angry at the changes this has necessitated, Beth, but at the least let us discuss the matter.'

Although it was only what Beth had expected, the confirmation hit her like a blow. She tried to tell herself that it was no surprise, that she had known since Fairhaven that Marcus no longer wished them to marry, but she could not be reasonable about it. She felt herself shake with the shock and misery.

'I do not believe that we can speak with each other again, Lord Trevithick,' she said, as firmly as she could. She avoided Marcus's eye. 'It would not be appropriate!'

She saw his gaze narrow furiously on her. 'Inappropriate, ma'am? I never heard such nonsense! Shall I remind you just how inappropriate your behaviour has been with me?'

Beth shrank back. 'I would be obliged if you would leave me alone, sir! We have nothing more to say to each other!'

For what seemed like an age Marcus's gaze searched her face, then he stood back abruptly. 'Very well! You always were very attached to the idea of the feud between our families, were you not? If you are determined to pursue it, then I shall not oppose you! Good day to you, ma'am!'

The door swung closed. Beth leant back against the cushions and closed her eyes, but the tears slid out from beneath her lids. She had burned her boats now and, although she knew there was no alternative, she felt more desolate than she had ever done before.

Beth was down early for breakfast the next day, for she was intending to tell Charlotte of her plan to return to Mostyn Hall. It was the second week of January and seemed an appropriate enough time for a new start, except that it was not always possible to leave the past behind entirely. Beth needed no reminder that she would be taking a substantial keepsake of the past few months with her.

Her cousin was already at the table, looking fresh and pretty in a yellow and white striped dress, her hair confined in a matching bandeau. Her face was radiant and Beth felt decidedly wan in comparison. She slid into the seat opposite.

'Charlotte,' she began, 'I have decided to go back to Mostyn tomorrow—' She broke off as Charlotte lifted the lid off one if the serving dishes and placed it carefully on the sideboard behind. Beth stared at the devilled kidneys with fascinated repulsion.

'It always was Kit's favourite,' Charlotte was saying despondently, 'and I had no heart to tell Cook that I could not eat it. I believe that the servants are as upset as we are over Kit's unaccountable disappearance—'

Feeling an uprush of nausea, Beth pressed a hand over her mouth and got hastily to her feet. 'Excuse me, Charlotte!'

She only just managed to gain the shelter of her room in time; after she had been sick, she washed her face and peered dispiritedly at her reflection in the mirror. She looked dreadful, her face as pasty as parchment and her hair hanging damp and lifeless about her face. She still felt sick and dizzy, and went over to the bed to lie down.

There was a knock at the door.

'Beth?'

Beth closed her eyes in despair. She felt too wretched to curse the kind nature that prompted Charlotte to check up on her, but she would have given anything for her cousin not to see her just now. But it was too late. Charlotte had opened the bedroom door and was advancing towards the bed with a determined expression. She sat down next to Beth with a soft hush of silk skirts.

'Beth, how long have you been sick like this?'

Beth looked at her cousin and swiftly away. There was a knowledge in Charlotte's eyes that meant that she needed no explanations. With a sinking heart Beth acknowledged that she would never lie to her anyway, not to Charlotte, her dearest friend.

'Only a few days,' Beth said weakly. 'I feel wretched.' A tear squeezed from the corner of each eye and slid down her cheeks. Charlotte took her hand.

'You will feel better soon,' Charlotte said, in a practical voice. 'After twelve weeks the sickness generally improves—'

'Charlotte—'

Charlotte shook her head slightly. 'Oh, Beth, I may not have had any children of my own yet, but I saw many born on campaign! I know about all sorts of things, from how to deliver a baby to the best cures for the morning sickness—'

'Not just the morning!' Beth said dolefully.

Charlotte smiled. 'No, well, it takes some people that way, unfortunately! But there are remedies.' She leant forward and gave her cousin a gentle hug. 'Thank you for not trying to pretend that you had travel sickness, or had eaten something disagreeable…'

Beth burst into tears. 'Oh, Charlotte…'

'I know.' Her cousin gentled her.

'I'm so unhappy and confused! I cry all the time and I hate it!'

Charlotte laughed a little shakily. 'Yes, it is so unlike you! It was one of the first things that alerted me—that and your persistent refusal to speak of Lord Trevithick! Beth…' she put her cousin away from her a little '…what happened?'

Beth sniffed, reaching for a handkerchief. 'I would have thought that that was obvious, Charlotte!'

'Yes, well…I mean…' Charlotte hesitated. 'But how…?'

Beth sighed. 'I am sorry, Charlotte. I did not mean to be flippant! Marcus did not seduce me, if that is what you mean.' A shade of colour came into her pale face. 'It just happened. I became his mistress… I chose to do so, there was no coercion! Quite the reverse...'

Charlotte frowned. 'But I thought—we all thought—that Lord Trevithick intended marriage! Justin was quite certain of it.'

Beth winced. 'Well, we are betrothed, or at least we were—' She stopped and started again. 'Marcus always intended that we should be married on Fairhaven, but then his cousin the vicar was absent, so it could not be. So then we planned to marry at Mostyn after Christmas—' she swallowed a sob '—but now this business with Kit and Eleanor has ruined our plans and we are not to marry after all and I certainly did not intend—' She gestured vaguely.

'Your planning does not seem very good all round!' Charlotte said drily. 'And I would venture that you have not even told Trevithick that you are increasing! *That* is why you keep avoiding him.'

Beth clutched at the bedspread. 'You will not tell him—'

'No,' Charlotte said, sounding sterner than Beth had heard her in a long time. 'You will tell him yourself!'

Beth shook her head. Her eyes sought Charlotte's. 'Oh, Lottie, I cannot. Not because I am afraid—' she spoke quickly as she saw Charlotte was about to interrupt '—but because I know he will insist on marrying me! He is too honourable to do otherwise!'

'So I should hope—'

'No, please!' Beth twitched the material between her fingers. 'I could not bear to be married to Marcus simply because of the baby! I love him so much and I would always be thinking that he had only proposed to save my reputation!'

Charlotte frowned. 'Beth, you are not thinking straight! Marcus has already proposed to you—why, you were betrothed on Fairhaven! Of course he wants to marry you! There is no difficulty—'

Beth shook her head. 'Yes, there is! The matter of Kit's dishonour—'

'Oh, fie!' Charlotte was starting to look really cross now. 'Are you to martyr yourself because of my foolish brother? I know it is the most monstrous scandal, but it is not your fault!'

Beth turned her face away. 'You said yourself that someone in Trevithick's position, with the honour of his family to uphold, could not possibly even speak with us any more, let alone consider a marriage alliance!'

'I...' Charlotte hesitated. 'I know that I said that before, but this puts a different complexion on the matter...' She fell silent.

Beth turned her head tiredly on the pillow. 'No, you were correct, Charlotte. Before he left Fairhaven, Marcus told me that the marriage could not go ahead. There is no more to be said!'

Charlotte put her hands on her hips. 'Have you discussed this properly with him, Beth? I thought that you had not even done the Earl the courtesy of seeing him!'

'I have told Marcus that I do not want to see him ever again—' Beth's voice broke on the words. 'It is better this way! I cannot see him again, for I would not be able to keep the secret of my condition from him!'

Charlotte looked stubborn, but she did not argue. 'So what will you do?' she asked quietly, after a moment.

Beth looked at her defiantly. 'I shall go back to Devon just as soon as I can manage it. Tomorrow, perhaps, if I am well enough to travel! There is nothing I can do to help find Kit, and should Marcus discover my situation...'

'Beth, he find out soon enough! You cannot hope to give birth to Marcus Trevithick's child without the most immense scandal!'

Beth looked mulish. 'I shall deal with that as and when it happens!'

Charlotte got to her feet. 'Well, we shall see. For myself, I think you are speaking a deal of nonsense, but we shall not quarrel now! I will go to fetch you some dry toast. It may sound odd, but it will make you feel better!'

Charlotte had been down to the kitchen, fetched the toast and was about to knock on the door of Beth's room again when she heard a sound from within. She paused. It sounded as though Beth was crying again, and in an intense, heartbreaking way that suggested that to disturb her would be too cruel. With a heavy heart, Charlotte retraced her steps and went to sit in the drawing room whilst she tried to think.

She sat down in an armchair with a heavy sigh. She did not doubt that Beth loved Marcus deeply, for her cousin had never shown any interest in casual love affairs. Charlotte had always thought Beth too impulsive, too unguarded, and had wanted to protect her cousin. Now she could see that Beth had given her heart and herself where she loved, and was set to be dreadfully hurt because she believed that her marriage to Marcus could not go ahead.

Charlotte sighed again. She was utterly convinced

that her cousin would do exactly as she had said, and would run away to Devon without seeing the Earl of Trevithick again. Obstinate, headstrong and in this situation just plain wrong… Charlotte smiled sadly. She loved Beth for all her faults and she was determined not to allow her to make so terrible a mistake. The issue of Kit's dishonour was a powerful one, but surely not enough to keep Marcus from Beth's side once he knew the truth.

Charlotte frowned as she thought it over. Beth's obstinacy was clear, but what was Marcus's view? Surely if he had become concerned to sever all connections between the Mostyns and Trevithicks, Justin would have told her. Yet not only was Justin as ardent in his attentions as ever, but he had also brought messages from his cousin, the Earl, showing that Marcus was anxious to see Beth as soon as possible. To Charlotte's mind, that was not the behaviour of a man who wished to break his engagement.

She drummed her fingers on the arm of the chair. Beth had said that Marcus had told her the wedding would not take place, but Charlotte wondered if Beth had misunderstood. In the rush and distress of their parting it would have been all too easy to misconstrue his words, and after that they had never discussed the matter properly. And now Beth had told Marcus some cock-and-bull story about not wishing to see him again and his pride had no doubt prevented him from persisting. They were apart and unhappy. Charlotte tutted to herself. Really, they deserved each other! But she could not let them suffer…

She got up and went to fetch her cloak, bonnet and gloves. Her conscience was troubling her a little. It was really Beth's place to tell Marcus that she was in a delicate condition and strictly none of her business at all, but she knew that Beth was too stubborn to be persuaded. That being the case, she was acting in Beth's best interests...

Charlotte had never been out on her own in London, for her agoraphobia had made her shy away from the busy streets and crush of passers-by. When she had had Justin by her side she was reassured, but now she was alone. She almost gave up on the steps and went back into the house, but the memory of Beth's white face and desperate sobs was enough to drive her on. Even so, she was shaking by the time she reached Trevithick House and could barely tell the impassive butler that she wished to see the Earl of Trevithick. It was inevitable that she should be told that the Earl was not at home.

Charlotte was trembling like a leaf. Tears of fear and abject misery were not far away, but she drew herself up and said:

'Indeed? Tell Lord Trevithick that Mrs Cavendish wishes to speak to him on a matter of the highest importance—'

One of the doors to the entrance hall opened and Marcus Trevithick came out, deep in conversation with another man. Charlotte noticed that there was a deep frown on his forehead and he looked as though he was in an exceptionally bad mood. Her heart sank.

'We have tried the Port of London and sent runners to Southampton—' The other man was saying. Both of them broke off when they saw Charlotte and after a moment, to her inexpressible relief, Charlotte saw Trevithick's expression lighten.

'Mrs Cavendish! Pray forgive me for not receiving you sooner, ma'am! Gower...' he turned courteously to the other man '...excuse me. We will talk again later and I thank you for your help.'

Charlotte came forward a little shakily as Marcus held the door of the study open for her. 'Let me send for a glass of wine for you, Mrs Cavendish,' he said solicitously. 'You look somewhat done up! What can have put you to so much trouble as to come here in person? Has there been some news of your brother?'

Charlotte smiled a little shakily. 'No, sir, I am afraid not. This is far more important. This is to do with my cousin...with Beth—Lady Allerton.'

She saw Marcus's expression harden, felt him withdraw from her, and put a pleading hand out.

'Please...'

She was not sure what was showing in her face but, whatever it was, Marcus's own expression softened and he took her arm and guided her to a chair. 'I am sorry, ma'am. Pray do not be distressed. Now, what is it that you wished to tell me?'

Some ten minutes later, Justin Trevithick called at Trevithick House and was astounded to hear from the butler that a Mrs Cavendish was with his cousin the Earl. Another moment, and the door of the study was flung open and Marcus strode out across the hall, his face set and intent. He checked on seeing his cousin.

'Justin! The very man! Mrs Cavendish is here and I fear I must desert both of you! Pressing business! If you could escort the lady home I should be most grateful, old fellow, but pray leave it for at least a half-hour! I rely upon you to think of a way to pass the time!' And, without another word, he was gone.

On gaining the study, Justin found his betrothed sitting calmly sipping a glass of madeira and looking quite pleased with herself. There was a twinkle in her eye as she gave her hand to him.

'Good morning, Mr Trevithick! How do you do?'

'I should be considerably better if someone could explain to me just what the devil is going on!' Justin said feelingly. 'How comes it that you are here, Charlotte, and what have you said to Trevithick, to send him off in such a confounded hurry?'

He thought that Charlotte looked positively mischievous as she replied. 'I have struck a light,' she said contentedly, 'and I am certain it is about to explode into flames!'

Beth had found the plate of dry toast waiting outside the door and was astonished to discover that it had indeed made her feel better—so much restored, in fact, that she decided there was no point in delaying her preparations to remove to Mostyn. Happily, her trunk was still out since she had not bothered to unpack it from her last journey. She did not think of Charlotte's reaction to her hasty departure, nor of Kit's mysterious disappearance, and especially not of Marcus Trevithick. She knew that she would only become odiously miserable if she dwelled on any of them and she was running for home out of simple instinct.

At first she did not hear the fuss in the entrance hall and then assumed that Gough had called to see Charlotte. After a moment, however, she heard an unmistakable male voice.

'Don't be so bloody foolish, man! Of course Lady Allerton is at home!'

Then there was a step on the stair, and the door was thrown open.

'Running away again, my dear?' the Earl of Trevithick said with silky politeness. 'It is become quite a habit!'

To Beth's eyes he looked both devastatingly handsome and frighteningly unyielding. With her hands full of underwear and the half-open trunk giving her away, she decided to hold her ground. Her heart was beating uncomfortably fast, but she raised her chin defiantly to stare him out.

'Good day, Lord Trevithick! I fear that you find me on the point of departing for Devon—'

'Again?' Marcus lounged in the doorway, making it quite clear that she was unable to go anywhere. 'You rocket about the countryside like a dangerously loose cannon, my dear!' He came forward into the room. 'I fear I cannot allow it. Not in your condition!'

Beth lowered her hands slowly. She could feel what little colour she had fading from her face.

'You know!' she whispered.

'I know,' Marcus confirmed grimly. 'Your cousin had the grace to tell me, Lady Allerton, where you did not.'

'She had no right,' Beth said stiffly.

Marcus strode over to the window. There was so much suppressed violence in his movements that Beth shrank away. 'Maybe not,' he said evenly, 'but when were you going to tell me, Lady Allerton? Ever? Or was I to hear about my own child from some gossip at a *ton* party?'

Beth's eyes filled with the infuriating tears that beset her all the time. 'Oh, do not! I did not intend...I just thought that you would insist on marrying me.'

Marcus raised his eyebrows. He took a deep, impatient breath. 'Beth, I have been wanting to marry you this past age—'

Beth's tears overflowed. 'You said that we could not be married!' she contradicted him crossly. 'You know it is impossible because of Kit's behaviour to Eleanor! You have only changed your mind because of the baby—' She broke off, crying too hard to carry on.

Marcus sat down on the bed and pulled her on to his knee. He took a clean handkerchief out of his pocket and carefully wiped her face, kissing her gently when he was done.

'This is foolish. I *never* said that we could not be married—'

'Yes, you did!' Beth burst out. 'When you were leaving Fairhaven you said that all our plans were changed and our wedding could not go ahead! You said that everything was spoiled for us...' She gave a huge gulp and fell silent.

Marcus was frowning. 'I remember. We did not really have time to talk properly, did we? I only meant that our Christmas wedding could not take place, but I had every intention of rearranging it as soon as I could! I never meant for the engagement to end!'

Beth gave a doleful sniff. Another tear slid down her cheek. 'But—'

Marcus gave her a little shake. 'Listen to me, my darling. I have had a special licence for the past four weeks—you may check the date if you wish!—and all because I wanted to marry you so much that I obtained one as soon as I arrived in London!' His arm tightened about her. 'I did that before all else— before seeing Eleanor, or enquiring into your cousin's whereabouts, or discussing matters with Gower. It was always the most important thing to me and the fact that your cousin has ruined my sister is irrelevant to our marriage! I do not intend to let him ruin my happiness as well as Eleanor's!'

Beth was so astounded that she stopped crying altogether. She borrowed the handkerchief and blew her nose hard. 'But I thought—Marcus, it is impossible for you to associate with the Mostyn family, with me—'

Marcus started to laugh. 'I have already associated with you and I intend to continue to do so at every available opportunity! I love you, Beth! You know that I always wanted to marry you—I was in a fever of impatience for St John to return to Fairhaven, and it was not because I simply wished to see him! When he did not return in time to marry us, and then all my plans were dashed again, I was frustrated and most disappointed!'

Beth looked at him. Marcus was smiling at her with a gentleness that somehow made her feel quite weak inside. She squashed the treacherous warmth and frowned at him.

'Promise me that this is not simply because I am increasing…'

Marcus pulled her into his arms again. 'Oh, Beth, do you doubt me still? I blame myself more than you could know, my darling, for damaging your reputation and exposing you to gossip through what happened on Fairhaven…' He hesitated. 'I wanted to marry you almost from the first time we met, when you challenged me to that ridiculous wager.' He brushed his mouth against her hair. 'Beth, I am more happy than I can say about the child, but I wanted to marry you long before I knew. I love you...'

Later, when she had stopped kissing him long enough to draw breath, Beth said a little diffidently, 'I thought perhaps that you would not wish to marry me because I was not suitable...'

Marcus kissed her again. 'It seems to me that you have imagined every possible or impossible reason to keep us apart! How could you not be suitable?'

Beth fidgeted. 'Well, because I...because we—did things together that were not at all respectable—'

Marcus started to laugh. 'Oh, Beth, I can see I need to change your view of how married people behave! And you must never think I believe you unsuitable. I love you for your openness and your lack of artifice!'

This seemed to warrant another kiss. Then Beth drew back again.

'I have been so miserable without you, Marcus! It has been the most unhappy Christmas—'

'We shall make up for it, I promise you!' Marcus kissed her again.

'But what are we to do about this dreadful situation of Kit and Eleanor?' Beth frowned. 'I could not blame you if you damned the name of Mostyn forever!'

Marcus's face hardened. 'My love, I wish your cousin to the devil for what he has done but, as I told you, I refuse to let it ruin my happiness! Justin is in the right of it—we shall end the Mostyn and Trevithick feud and damn the gossips!'

'Passionate enemies and passionate lovers?' Beth asked mischievously and smiled as Marcus started to kiss her again. She freed herself for a moment. 'My lord, you mentioned the wager and, strictly speaking, I have still won Fairhaven—'

Marcus pulled her back firmly into his arms. 'Wager be damned!' he said.

*   *   *   *   *

NICOLA CORNICK

is passionate about many things: her country cottage and its garden, her two small cats, her husband and her writing, though not necessarily in that order! She has always been fascinated by history, both as her chosen subject at university and subsequently as an engrossing hobby. She works as a university administrator and finds her writing the perfect antidote to the demands of life in a busy office.

COMING NEXT MONTH FROM

HARLEQUIN HISTORICALS®

BEAUTY AND THE BARON
by **Deborah Hale**, author of LADY LYTE'S LITTLE SECRET
Lucius, Lord Daventry retreated from society after being disfigured
in the war. But in order to satisfy his grandfather's dying wish,
Lucius proposes a temporary engagement to Angela Lacewood, with
the understanding that she'll break it once his grandfather dies. When
the old man rallies, will their engagement become a reality?
HH #655 ISBN# 29255-4 $5.25 U.S./$6.25 CAN.

• **SCOUNDREL'S DAUGHTER**
by **Margo Maguire**, author of NORWYCK'S LADY
When prim and proper Dorothea Bright comes home to reconcile
with her estranged father, he is nowhere to be found. Instead, she
encounters Jack Temple, a handsome archaeologist who is intent on
dragging her along for the adventure—and love—of her life!
HH #656 ISBN# 29256-2 $5.25 U.S./$6.25 CAN.

• **WYOMING WIDOW**
by **Elizabeth Lane**, author of NAVAJO SUNRISE
Desperate, widowed Cassandra Riley Logan claims that the missing
son of a wealthy Wyoming rancher is the father of her unborn child.
His family takes her in, and Cassandra finds herself drawn to Mor-
gan, the missing man's brother. But when her secret threatens to tear
them apart, will their love be strong enough to overcome Cassandra's reluctant deception?
HH #657 ISBN# 29257-0 $5.25 U.S./$6.25 CAN.

• **THE OTHER BRIDE**
by **Lisa Bingham**, Harlequin Historical debut
Though Lady Louisa Haversham is married by proxy to a wealthy
American, she isn't ready to settle down. Instead, she convinces her
maid, Phoebe Gray, to trade places with her. As Phoebe, Louisa must
now masquerade as a mail-order bride. Gabe Cutter, the trail boss
escorting several mail-order brides to their grooms, proves to be a
thorn in her side—and a constant temptation!
HH #658 ISBN# 29258-9 $5.25 U.S./$6.25 CAN.

KEEP AN EYE OUT FOR ALL FOUR
OF THESE TERRIFIC NEW TITLES